Mutual Combat

Mutual Respect

By Clarence L. Lewis III

ISBN
1-933177-15-2 (10 digit)
978-1-933177-15-1 (13 digit)

Library of Congress Control Number: 2009925402

First Edition

Printed in the United States of America

What They're Saying About Mutual Combat/Mutual Respect

Congratulations! Your book is quite wonderful. It rings with street cred and authenticity that is almost too raw to digest. It paints a vivid portrait of the desperate lives that so many inner city families can't seem to escape – from neighborhood conflict to county jail to the funerals of people that no one intended to kill. When the laws of the State fail, the only law that matters is a homegrown code of respect. Best wishes.

Michael Hennessey, Sheriff
San Francisco Sheriff's Department

Mutual Combat/Mutual Respect is an outstanding novel. Audiences of all ages, race, economical status and educational background will be astonished at the contents of this book. The historical events mentioned will knock your socks off. Reading it actually took me down memory lane. Churches, public school, private schools, universities, etc. will benefit by having MC/MR on their shelves.

Dr. Reginna L. Criswell, Ed.D.
High School Principal

Clarence Lewis the III writes a rare and wonderful book that is both easy and painful to read but ultimately you become a better person as a result of his compassionate sense of life. You will cry, rejoice, and become part of the solution to enhance our civilization. This is a must read for people living in urban, suburban and rural America.

Sunny Schwartz, Esq.
Author of "Dreams From The Monster Factory"
SF Sheriff's Department, Program Administrator

In my 20 years of experience working in the Criminal Justice System, this book addresses the ramification of the young men & women being incarcerated at high rates, yet without the underlining dynamics that have a causative effect. Great dialog for public examination.

George Jurand, CADC, RPS.

In the many years I worked with Clarence Lewis, he buffered my cynicism and reminded me of why I entered this business in the first place. As a deputy sheriff in our jails and as a pastor in our community, Clarence refuses to write off those who have given up on themselves and who are written off by most of us. He believes that to hold young offenders accountable we must also hold ourselves accountable, and that to offer them hope and dignity is to dignify ourselves. This book is a painful, powerful and authentic portrait of the needless, shameful destruction of our most precious resource: our own children. Clarence Lewis' faith reveals, simply, it does not have to be this way; it must not be this way. Listen to him. I do.

Michael J. Marcum, Assistant Sheriff (ret.)
City and County of San Francisco

In my 28 years of law enforcement experience, I have seen second and third generations come through our county jails in the criminal justice system. *Mutual Combat/Mutual Respect* ventures in areas where most refuse to go into: the effects of drugs, crime, incarceration, and the cost of it to families and communities. From his position within the Sheriff's Department, Clarence Lewis hasn't just written about it, he has experienced it. Even more so, because of his calling, he won't stop until there is change.

Albert B. Waters II, Chief Deputy
San Francisco Sheriff Department

I found *Mutual Combat/Mutual Respect* to be powerful, insightful and realistic. If used seriously, it can move many people from a viewpoint of feeling hopeless and helpless toward responsibly examining and actively, choosing values that will guide their lives toward being self-respecting and helpful human beings.

Ramona Massey BA, Lead Program Coordinator
San Francisco Sheriff's Department

I applaud the author, Clarence Lewis for debuting *Mutual Combat/Mutual Respect*. A must-read for all ages, and particularly beneficial to students and young adults residing in both urban and rural areas. The book shares the life, soul, and experiences of its characters in great depth, and portrays how survival and love is possible to those faced with the most difficult obstacles. In Community,

Yolanda McGary-Beitia, M.P.A., Executive Director
'N' The Classroom: Restoring the Community

Mr. Clarence L. Lewis III, with great skill and insight, paints a vivid, powerful picture of the cycle of violence, hopelessness and despair that can transform an "Emmanuel Charles Harris" into a "Little Mack." He not only demonstrates the insidious nature of life growing up as a black male in Urban America, but also how the mindless adherence to destructive values can lead to the perpetuation of meaningless hostility and destruction in our communities. However…Mr. Lewis also presents recipes for hope and redemption. It reinforces our knowledge that we can make a difference, one "Little Mack" at a time. This book is a "must read" and is enthusiastically endorsed.

Floyd D. Johnson M.S
Lead Program Coordinator, County Jail #5

Thank you for sharing your story with me. The book is great. I wish nothing but success as it relates to this project. This will touch the lives of many individuals.

Silvester Henderson, Professor of Music,
Los Medanos College, University of California-Berkeley

Table of Contents

Introduction and Acknowledgements

This project started in 1993 with an opportunity from Sheriff Michael Hennessey to work at the San Francisco Youth Guidance Center. I thought, I'm going up here to impact troubled young people and rescue them from lives of crime and disobedience. They are all going to be angels when I'm done. The hero I am, I was there to change the whole thing.

Wow. It changed me.

I watched grandmothers come through the front doors over and over again, trying to keep up with *their* children's children, most of whom had no boundaries or limits on their little life's speedometers. Mothers switching in with their daughters like mirrored "best friends," both being beaten by their boyfriends. Mammoth young boys with old daddies who thought they were smarter than the booty call somewhere across town. Those sugar daddies' money was fast enough to catch the young mommas, but when the young boys needed fathers to run and catch a ball, daddies were either too busy, trying to keep them a secret, or too tired, old, and slow. Now, their giant babies had no respect for them. The front desk was the greatest position for peering into the future of many lives. I knew it was bad when the Hindu mothers in historical headdress and gown would be following their turned-out daughters up the walkway. The young girl's earphones blasting, a halter-top with no deodorant, and eating fast food, which made her jeans skin tight. To top it off, "Dis is Ray-Ray's" was tattooed on her uncovered belly with an arrow pointing downward. The mother left her homeland to come ten thousand miles to find freedom, only having to pay for it with her child. Let the wrong one get a hold of your son or daughter? It may take generations to

1

correct.

But even in this, I saw hope. So I got an eight and a half by fourteen inch yellow writing pad, thus Mutual Combat/Mutual Respect began to pour out. Then my big brother Freddie Carter came up strong for my first run at putting this in print. He brought me his company's 1981 IBM personal computer with the five-inch floppy disk and digital green screen monitor. I wasn't high tech.

I took those first initial handwritten pages through almost fifteen years of evolution. I learned that only time and years on this planet could be the component that would begin to give this story a body to live in. I stopped about two years ago, till my dear friend Yolanda McGary-Beitia jacked me up! "No-no brother, Um-um-no, we don't stop writing. I don't care where. On the BART, in the morning before the kids wake up, but we finish what we write." That blew me back out of the water and on to complete this course. Your boy is forever grateful.

There are so many people to thank for their support and encouragement that it would take a book itself. But if I don't mention your name this first go round, just know I truly thank you. To Susan Malone of Malone Editorial Services, Ennis, Texas, thank you for all your professional 'nuts and bolts work' and continued support. "Show me, don't tell me." That blew my mind and will live with me forever. To my Balboa High School fellow Buccaneer, Class of 1981, Sculptor Agelio Batle and nephew Jonathan Batle of Batle Studio San Francisco (www.ASBworkshop.com) for reaching into my imagination and etching life into the cover design.

To my true proofing queens, Romunda Craft, Carla Duke, Karla Guillory, Tara Cooper, Imelda Johnson, and Crystal Strickland. You women pressed me into my best and cut my stuff up till it made some sense. Thank you. Canisha Smith and Jazzmine Duke (from young women's perspectives), thanks for having eyes for the futures and wanting to see the outcome of the book. A special blessing for two focus groups that helped me determined if flesh and blood was really on my manuscript. To Floyd Johnson, Unit Manager, County Jail No. 5 Program Director, and an inspirational group of men who opened their hearts to the work. Lloyd Glover, Floyd H. Johnson, Abner 'N9ne'Dighero, Michael E. Wright, Prentiss Mayo III, Donte 'Stunna' Lewis, and Marlon Bishop. Our time together was simply powerful. We got past the surface and the costumes we wear to survive. We got down to the spirit. Stay on course to let the real man be released and fulfill the purposes of why you are here on earth. To Ms. Ramona Massey and Power PREP Crew, David Ball, Charles Hammons, Jae Sohn, Beth Ingram, Dwight Young, and Carmelia Hamilton. Thank you for letting me know that the manuscript touched "the *real* of life."

To my entire family, I thank you all, even if I don't mention you name by name.

To Momma, my mother Vivian Lewis, the one who cooked for us every day.

(Fast-food; what was that? I can count the times we had fast-food for dinner on one hand growing up.) We had a hot meal every day and enough sense to eat it too. Now at seventy years old, you worry about your grandchildren. (She has more influence in their lives than the parents; they call her for everything!) You came out of retirement to teach your great-grandchildren. Literally, Momma, what can I say? You've been "Grandma" to thousands of students over your thirty-five years of work in the San Francisco Unified School District. Your son is totally indebted to you.

And Daddy, my father Clarence L. Lewis Jr., the man who worked sixteen hours a day *for years* for me and my sisters. Before I was born, Momma said you were glad to bring home an overtime check for twenty-two dollars. In 1970, you sent all of us with Momma to Alabama on our first airplane trip and couldn't afford a ticket for yourself, so you stayed at home. Now that's my hero. I got the chance recently to sit down with a couple of my aunts and heard them talk about the respect they have for their big brother. And at seventy-four years old, you're still a man not to be played with. They love you. I love you and respect you.

To the best mother-and father-in-law in the world, John A. and Barbara Knox. I am utterly grateful. You did a good job with Kellye. Special hugs to Doris (you are Momma too) and I will never forget the life, smile, and charisma of Jimmy Hall. To my sisters, Francena, Stephanie, and Cynthia, if you think I was talking about you all in here, I really wasn't. Just somebody who looked like y'all. Ha-ha! Don't kill me, remember I'm the baby. To our committed friend Sonya Reddick, you make our family complete. My covenant brothers Freddie Carter and Eric Claybon, my safety nets. Who would have thought that God would "say" and "send" us to the Nations?

My children, Tyelah, Clarence IV, and Jessica. Dad's trying to leave you what God says I should leave you; an inheritance. Not all money either, but more of Him. Vanesse, Dad loves you, too. My granddaughters Bryeah and Noelle, "Paw-Paw and Gammy love you both like none other." Thanks to Sheriff Michael Hennessy and the San Francisco Sheriff's Department Command Staff for your support and confidence in me to do my job. I am truly grateful. To the entire San Francisco Sheriff Department personal, sworn and civilian staff, my appreciation of service for twenty years with you. Don't worry; I'm not going anywhere soon. And my partner in the Community Relation/Eviction Assistance Unit, Joe Crittle, "Hey, where we gonna eat!" To a great teacher and mentor in law-enforcement relations to the communities, and helping people in crisis, a gracious-hearted man, Retired Lieutenant Frank Hutchins. There is none better. Hey Sunny Schwartz, thank you for even the thought and open heart of letting your people see my work. Karen Levin, a great person with whom I had the opportunity to begin the STEPS Program. Girl, getting that baby off the ground was something, but for those willing, it keeps them from living on the streets. All my love to the entire Perazim Church family for letting me be me. (And that can be a hand full on any given Sunday.) Remember always, Christ is our life and all I want do is point you to Him alone, who can do His good pleasure in you.

Finally, to my brothers whom I have been joined to from all over the world that meet at Hothorpe Hall, Theddingworth, Leicestershire, United Kingdom. We are New Creations, so Create Your Future!

And Father, thank You, for You do all things well. My words are futile to bless You, so I will let my life do that.

Dedications

To My wife, Kellye Jarene Lewis, we've got twenty-one years in and seventy-nine more to go. It's good to know what it means to be "safe" in a marriage. We have learned that wedding vows can bring life; all of them.

This dream is about the strength of my matriarchs and patriarchs. Though they are gone, they have been the greatest inspiration for this work, so they live. Willie Mae Brice "Ganny," Stella Wagner "Grandmamma," Clarence L. Lewis Sr. "Grandpa," and Robert Wagner "Granddaddy." My grandmother's pictures sit on my office desk. I can close my eyes and hear their voices. Ganny singing, "Jesus Can Work It Out" and Grandmamma stirring up an old Southern Negro hymn, "Children There's A Dark Cloud Arising, Let's Go Home." I see Grandpa's smile, being proud of his family. And Granddaddy, there you are on the tractor, plowing your fields, and then pulling the rope to ring the church bell. It would lift you off the ground.

It's a true saying that you never miss what you have, till it's gone. And for me, it doesn't mean money; it's them, the richness of their lives.

Thank you for letting me know what kind of tree I'm from.
Now, I know what kind of fruit I should and must bear.

Your grandson, Dunieboy

Forward

Thoughts about the book....

Mutual Combat/Mutual Respect is a rare glimpse into the inner dimensions of the urban black youth experience and the complexities of becoming a black man in America. While Clarence Lewis makes it read like a novel, Mutual Combat/Mutual Respect relives the best of times and worst of times for San Francisco. The story is rich in the historical context of the 70's and 80's. It paints a picture of fractured families, and a society that juxtaposes technological leaps made during the period, with the slow crawl of recovery communities experienced trying to regain a sense of purpose and direction at the height of the crack epidemic. More importantly, it shows how the power of God works for good, even when we don't know it.

My work with the San Francisco Sheriff's Department only recently brought me into contact with Senior Deputy Clarence Lewis. As I have gotten to know him I am in awe of his dedication to people, especially young black men. His "people" skills are recognized as an asset within the Department and he has worked in many capacities where there is a need to interface with people of color in the community. He serves with distinction and provides a level of experience and calm that allows you to immediately know that he is working in your best interest. In addition, he is the pastor of a growing church and also a devoted husband and father. After reading this novel, God only knows where on earth he found the time to write it!

Mutual Combat/Mutual Respect has an important and credible message that should be mandatory reading for all young people. While this story may not be a biography, it could only have been written by someone who has walked the walk and come out on the other side.

Marsha Pendergrass
Principal Consultant for the NoVA Project
Pendergrass Smith Consulting

Prologue

The question *again* is "why?"

In such a privileged society, why are so many young people in this generation mad? Just imagine, right up the street in one household, there's a young person who's striving for success. It seems built in; achievement for them is normal. And just within fifty feet, to the right or to the left, you'll find another front door. There you find another young person with the same great potential, but this one is determined to fail.

They destroy themselves, and in today's view of "always hating to see somebody else come up," brothers act like the "Kingdom of Crabs" in the water tank at the corner Chinese-food restaurant, attempting to clip anyone else who looks like they're even *trying* to climb out. In our neighborhoods, you and I may feel free to hang out, kick it, or run amok, but other people are too scared to stop at the mailbox because of how we do each other. With crime cameras overhead, perched like news reporters, and unskilled, undisciplined minds below, many stand posted, being taped without hope. Valuable lives move around like blown litter with the mentality of,

"If I don't care about me, you know I don't care about you."

My precious and priceless young brothers fill the street corners like cardboard targets. There is a cost to all of us for that. Now, you know how we do it, "Aaa, Aaa, Aaa!" The street soldiers, standing like Iraqi affiliates, yell to each other on the corners. Remember who the Iraqis are? They are the ones we were told with, "Weapons of Mass Destruction." Yet, unlike those brothers, you really don't want to blow yourself up for the cause, but you defend your right to stand there on the corners, waiting for the next drive-by ignited war.

It's like you know something bad is coming; yet you're

willing to stand in the very place marked with the last life-choked-out event. Many will stand there for more than your average eight-hour job, and with what as a reminder? Some balloons, some teddy bears and pictures taped to a street light or telephone pole, old funeral flowers, a few cheap candles somebody got last Christmas for which they had no use, E'N'J bottles, and to close it out, a gumbo of vomit? Hey, pour me somebody's last glass! Today, these are *our babies'* horrific memorials. And you know what? Some still wouldn't move if Hell and the devil himself showed up, and lo and behold, he does!

I could make light of the fact that we don't live in Vietnam, Afghanistan, or Iraq. But the religion of greed, which is "got to have mines," and self-mutilation of, "I'll get killed trying to take yours," takes many forms when none of it is ours.

I heard the promise, "We shall overcome," but now, it's muffled by loud beats and microphones, clanging gold chains, slamming jail cells, or the quiet closure of coffins. These days to the breaking of my heart, I see my young sisters out there now. Yeah, I was out there too, but that was in years past. But as I have matured and look at it now, I see it differently. Is this really honoring your dead homeboy or homegirl? Or are you protecting the next place for death on the concrete?

Oh, my apologies first. Let me introduce myself. My name is Emmanuel Charles Harris. I'm in my early thirties and someone you may possibly call, half and half. I could be "half-real" in how I come out of almost impossible circumstances. Or I could also be "half-a-nightmare," as someone you know, may come to know, or one who grips your heart, standing in your darkest hour of helplessness. The plight of my life for most people is no longer interesting public information.

You might see the early portions of my life as *de`ja vu* on the 6 o'clock news as you bite into a piece of chicken. Others glanced over my statistics through their bifocals, after digesting the *Wall Street Journal*. And a few see it as a blur, while they

10

run to the bathroom like my youngest daughter, who holds her pee to the last minute. I hope there's some toilet paper in there?

If possible, let's look back through the lenses of my early days and yet even deeper, my inception. Not just my conception with Mack's sperm and Michelle's egg, but the making of my mindset through the files of my DNA. This will help you keep up with my life's journey, as I broke away from the path of un-positive directions.

Now by grace, I am able to stand, after my brains had been so long on its knees, surrendering to the local craziness I grew up in. My thoughts bowed and served the lives around me. The big money, fast talk, super bad songs, and mind-blowing experiences. These were trying to lead me, to destroy me. In my mind, nickel bag weed storm clouds like mating tornadoes, and evil funky Knights of the Round Table with wild damsels danced, and swirled above me. At the same time, my great big neighborhood world, hustlers and runners with "hubbas" (one early name for crack cocaine), attempted to carve me into what it desired me to be.

But! And thank God for "But!" because that meant the future for me (and you) was not over yet. Some heard and believed the hope of a better life, whispered by my ancestor in the great days past, which have become my today. I am on a carefully beaten, prophetic path, to what I am supposed to be. That's just a creative way of saying, "Thank God, I'm free, from me."

The anger in me started way before my folks met. Matter of fact, I was *almost* a product of their failure to take responsibility for their actions, failure to remember how hard our people had struggled to get as far as they have, and failure to teach how to press into purpose, and destiny for the future. *Almost.*

Please, forgive my personal confusion. It wasn't my fault my life started this way. And for many of you it's not your fault how it started, but it's your responsibility how it ends. Put

11

that on somebody else if you want to, but truly, it's on you.

So let's just take this journey, and stay with me through the whole voyage. If you walk through these pages of my life, you may find you. Others of you may see paintings of my decisions on the walls of your heart that identify with a little something in me. You will see the bitter, the sweet, the loved, and even the love of toying with pain, because until you know better, it's all fun. You'll meet the afflicted, the inflicted, those who succumb and perish, and more so, those who are victorious.

And yet, with all these platters of "*D*-rama" splattered on the canvases of my life, I can see they were there to help me, become me. Here's the catch: I'm convinced with all of our successes and failures, the ultimate Creator shall complete His will in all of us, who believe.

Believe it or not?

Don't worry, the love's mutual.

Mutual Combat/Mutual Respect

Interlude:

They hated each other and didn't know why.

It was just in their blood; a disease, keenly aware of itself.

At visual contact, it erupted in them like a volcano.

Both of them knew it had to be put out. But how?

Reason; because of its long-term effects. It breeds.

One man gets a proposition. "When I give you what you need to cure this disease, you must give it to the one you've hated the most."

Chapter 1
From My Father's Loins:
Wow! I'm His Seed?

It's the early 1970s in San Francisco.

A twelve-inch, black and white Zenith TV sat on the kitchen table with channels two, four, five, seven, and nine. If you were lucky and lived close to Sutro Tower standing with its legs wide open, channels thirty-six and forty-four came in real clear, but that's it. Rowan and Martin's Laugh-In, The Flip Wilson Show, and Good Times were our good clean humor. Yet, Archie Bunker and All in the Family presented much of the cynicism of America's perception, which many were able to stomach from a safe distance between us, and the screen.

The fogbanks lowered like patched sheep's wool over Diamond Heights, with the grace of a new white tablecloth catching a living room breeze draped for Thanksgiving dinner. Then massively, it slowed in Indian regimen under Geronimo's hand signal, dropping its edge over the Western Addition. Its breath blew dew on every pair of eyeglasses, standing a good distance back from the curb, waiting for the evening MUNI 22 Fillmore bus line. That bus would run you over, and had changed its colors from military green, to the 49er's Red and Gold. As the street lamp pecked on and off, it tried to gain strength to provide a spotlight for the crazy nightlife. Coldness turned the corner. Something's up?

Michelle (my mother) paced the floor waiting for a knock on the door. She was a young fine little momma, big banging chest, and with her cheap bra not ashamed to show those sisters off! The girl got backs, or a yum-yum butt (depending on which set and part of the country you're from), and yes, stupid at this time of her life. Society and the medical profession say

14

that girls mature faster than boys. Um, I don't know? Maybe with those big butts and breasts, but not all of them got good sense. Don't matter what color either, they all crazy when they young.

At a certain age, and now in your days of looking at booty videos all night, their hormones be racing just like ours. Right now, she's hooked up with somebody like Mack (my father), yeah, she real stupid.

She called him over an hour ago, and he still as usual hadn't shown up. He had a hot gold Rolex from somebody who owed him some money. It was too big for his wrist. He never got it to tell time, and was too scared to take it to the pawnshop for a new battery. It might get traced to the actual owner, and he was still late. Most people had enough sense to be inside early since the Zodiac was killing young white folks, and was still on the loose. He had everybody scared. Heck, we were scared and he wasn't even looking for no black folks. Please, don't get me wrong. I love my folks. Without them I would not be here, and no matter what your momma or daddy was, neither would you. But Mack, he was a "WOW!" I really don't think it was entirely his fault. His daddy left his momma with a bunch of kids, and that was a lot for one woman to handle in them days. Now, a bunch of kids without a father is not all the time a bad situation, but this kid needed the choke-collar of a father. Hey, if for nothing else but to slap somebody upside the head, and keep the madness down to a dull roar. Some daddies do more harm than good, if they expose their family to just unnecessary madness.

In an interview, a guy who worked in the jails spoke about a father who was just like that. He and his three sons were in custody, all at the same time. The father was walking around bragging that one of his sons beat a guy up. "You see my boy; you-you see my boy?" His big whale mouth open, stuttering, with spit drops jumping from his lips for their lives. All twenty-seven of his remaining rotting teeth scattered through his mouth like a busted fence, cased in infected gums.

Mack's family fit that American mold. Mack was wild as all get out and loved craziness. You know how we want everybody to be our cousin? Mack may be a distant cousin of Idi Amin who was running wild and loose in Uganda then. As my dad got older and grew to a size where as the old folks said, "He started smelling his-self," his momma couldn't handle him. And if you really knew him, or if you'd see someone who even looked like him, your chest muscles would grip around your heart, your lips would shift to the left corner of your mouth going numb, making you light headed. You'd have to catch yourself and take a deep breath. A loose cannon, he could go off at anytime. The old people say, "He was the kind of kid you take way out in the woods with something wrapped in an old croaker sack, and never bring back." Now, you fill in the blanks on that one.

So with all that intro of a brotha, you would almost wonder about the mindset of any young woman caught with him? My question for Michelle would be with all that bright-red-fire and burning-brimstone-sea-horses-from-Hell's-fire circling around this cat, how on earth didn't you see him coming?

The phone rang. Mack was at the phone booth down the street with his hand covering the receiver, and breathing hard. "Hurry up and open up the door, I got to get in quick!" he said.

Michelle's heart beat hard as she went to the door, waiting to see him in the distance. This had become as common a fright drama as the three o'clock soap opera Dark Shadows.

Out of the darkness, from under a streetlight, Mack came running at full speed. His windbreaker up around his neck like a cape and those karate shoes with white socks floated across the concrete. He hit the small cement porch through the open rear gate and slid through the slightly opened glass door. The door almost knocked Michelle down.

Mack slammed the door and jumped away from it, then

moved ever so carefully toward the window. "Got them cats tripping again." He stood there peeking out. Then he walked toward Michelle and winked.

Moments later, a car sped down the street and skidded to a stop.

A voice screamed out, "Mack, we see you, boy! Tomb town, baby! Don't miss yo reservations, you sucka!"

The tire spun in place. Smoke lifted like oil hitting a hot grill. The car blasted around the corner, tires screeching sounding like a pig being skinned alive. They drove them big cars and burned rubber like that in Oakland, too. Police said in our neighborhoods, they couldn't do anything about it. Yeah, they better not had done that in Pacific Heights, white folk's area; SFPD would fix that problem quick!

My grandma (Mrs. Harris) came out of her bedroom startled. "Baby, is everything okay?" Her eyes slightly weak like stressed pearls on an antique necklace; she held her blouse collar as she caught her breath. She knew everything and Mack's "foolishness" as she called it.

"Yes, Momma," Michelle answered, looking down so not to have to look Grandma in the eyes.

Grandma had this way of seeing through everything, especially when something was wrong. She always kept reminding Michelle, "I can see further in the dark, than you can see in the light."

At times Michelle would go to the front door and look out. "What is she talking about? I know I can see way farther than she can," with her lips twisted and nose up as if she smelled some fart.

This was a valuable, but slowly vanishing breed of what they call, "wisdom talking." Grandma meant, "I've been where you think you are going, and I've done what you're thinking about doing. Girl, you can't fool me." Grandma said her mother would tell her that when she was young, so she used it on my mom.

"Hello, Mrs. Harris," Mack said. He always tried to put on his so-called gentlemen act, when she was around. But when he was out in the public, he'd act like he didn't have no home training.

Grandma answered, "How are you, Mack, and how's your mother?"

"She's okay, at prayer meeting, like always." Mack bowed his head, and let his neck roll. His eyes were as red as cherries. His clothes and underwear smelled like cherry pickers who hadn't changed in ten days.

"Correct me? Did I hear you say, 'Like always,' Mack? Boy, if you only knew." Grandma cut her eyes at him. Mack's head popped up with his eyes as wide as headlights. But he didn't dare try that stare-down stuff with Grandma as he did with Michelle. She said a many times to Michelle concerning Mack, "I'll cut his throat." Found out years later looking through her things, she had a straight razor.

"Michelle, I'm getting ready for work," Grandma said. "Make sure you lock the door tonight, and Mack, please don't let me catch you here after I'm gone. I'll shoot you myself."

"Ah, Mrs. Harris, you don't ever have to worry about me being on yo hit list."

He wore that old chicken-snatching guilty grin. Always thought the charm was the thing, but Grandma wasn't gray headed for nothing. Grandma went back in her room, and closed the door. Michelle and Mack sat on the couch. She turned, making no eye contact and sucking her lips inward.

"I'm pregnant again," said Michelle.

Wow! What kind of introduction of me was that! I started out as an 'again?'

Mack smiled and leaned over to kiss Michelle, but she pushed him away.

"What's up with you?" he snapped.

"What do you mean, what's up with me? Joe Young and his boys are out to get you, and boy, they are driving down by my momma's house now. You don't even care where you bring that mess. Every time I hear a gun shot, I'm afraid to hear the phone ring. I think somebody will be calling me, telling me to come and identify you at the funeral home. That's why I didn't keep the first one, remember?"

"They cut you up first, then they send you to the dead man's disco," Mack said dancing with himself in the mirror. Michelle stared at him with no emotion.

Mack looked at Michelle with his mouth hanging open. "What's the matter with you? You hav'n my baby, girl! A little Mack pack. You know how many other babes would line up to take your place? We have got something that's ours. Yeah, what's up?"

"Mack, it's going to take more than what you call love to raise a baby! Where am I going to get money, food, somewhere to live?"

"Live? You got a place to stay."

"Yeah, I got a place to stay maybe, maybe not? Do me, and this baby have a place to stay? No. And wrong – me, you, and this baby don't have a place to stay together. You know my momma." Michelle bit her fingernails. "Not even to think about the whipping I might get when she finds out."

"Yo momma ain't gonna whip you!" Mack's bottom lip leaned out with a pound of saliva on the tip.

"Okay, be here, boy, when I tell her and she'll whip yo behind too!"

"Yeah, you right. Yo momma don't play."

Michelle walked toward the window looking out for a future that was not there. "Mack, what's my baby going to do with a daddy on the run or dead?" The bottom dropped out of her voice. "The only reason Joe Young had any respect for me is because of Leah."

"Ah, that old b–"

"Don't you say it, Mack, because if you do, I'll slap the taste out yo' mouth!" She waved those hands in the air, spit flying everywhere.

"Just because you two fools are fighting for what reason I don't know, don't try to mess with me and Leah. We were together before you all, and will be together after you all. Shame we got to sneak to see each other because of you two fools."

Mack's head turned quickly with his mouth wide open. "You saw the baby?"

Michelle shook her head. "Yes, with those big ears and that little nose. Face all scrunched up like he's mad all the time, just like his stupid daddy. Leah said it was like he got something in him before he came out, but thank God he's got a grandmother praying for him, and me too."

"What you mean, you too!" Anger shot through his blood like too sweetened Orange Kool-Aid turning his shiny light complexion into a Bloody Mary. You remember some of you sisters in those early days? Michelle was one of them babes who had to have a light-skinned one, too. She had to find out the hard way that a man is more in content, than texture.

"You got me!" said Mack.

"Yeah, and what is that saying?" Her fingers turned into a Chinese calculator. "I've got you, yo half good looks, yo chemical dripping hair, yo think-you-buffed body, yo broke-joke car, yo no-working broke-butt behind, and all the craziness that comes with you."

Grandma came out of her bedroom on her way to work. A nurse at the twenty-four hour emergency clinic, she told Michelle about two of Mack's friends who were in the hospital two weeks ago. One fella had been shot twice and the other, almost insane because he wasn't. Grandma said that nut almost died of a heart attack, freaking himself out. A few weeks later, the dude who was shot was back out on the street, doing the same thing.

"Michelle, lock the door. And lock Mack out too. I can see in the dark, so don't let me catch you here," Grandma said as she opened the door.

"Um," Mack said slowly, "Mrssss... Harris, can we talk to you? Michelle's pregnant."

Grandma gripped the door handle and stood there. The room submitted to the power of silence. Then she closed the door, ever so gently. "Are you trying to tell me something I already know, Mack?" She turned and made direct eye contact with him.

Mack dropped his head. Michelle turned away, her eyes pressed closed. She slammed her mouth so tight that she bit her lip, yet even in pain she dared not make a sound. Gasping for breath, she coughed. A little blood parachuted out to safety from the corner of her mouth.

Grandma walked over from the door and took a seat, placing her hand on her cheek. Michelle thought she knew what was coming next, but Grandma changed up on her. Grandma sat there in silence. No tears, no emotion, no outburst of anger. She moved her mouth as if she were talking, but nothing came out. She was asking God, what was best to say. She slid one hand down on the inside of the couch as if reaching for something under the pillow, then slowly pulled her hand out. When I was old enough, I asked her why she did that. She said she just wanted Mack to think she had a gun; wanted to watch that fool sweat for a minute. It worked because the brother's Right Guard was gone, and he was funky.

Michelle, still anticipating an atom bomb, felt nauseated. If she had to and it came up, she'd swallow it this time.

The three of us, Mack, Michelle, and me inside, (four weeks old) sat there waiting for Grandma to speak.

Grandma picked up the phone and dialed. "Hey Barbara, it's me, Nurse Harris, I won't be in tonight; thank you, baby. Bye-bye."

Mack's knee shook with the unstableness of an overloaded washing machine.

Grandma in a calm voice began giving orders, "Mack,

21

before you pee on my couch, please go use the bathroom." Mack ran to the bathroom. Grandma echoed out, "And Mack, this would be the wrong time to leave yellow evidence you've been in there."

With the clarity of someone thankful to be saved from drowning, Mack answered, "If I have to, Mrs. Harris, I'll use my shirt to clean it!"

Mack rushed back and sat down, but not too close to Michelle.

"Baby?" Grandma's voice caught Michelle's attention. As Michelle turned, Grandma saw her red flushed watery eyes. They had that rabbit look, ready to hop at any moment. Her jaws bloated with pressure, full of yesterday's slimy back up from her constantly upset reservoir, just above my new incubator.

"Go spit that out, girl!"

Michelle ran to the bathroom but lost her balance. She kissed the floor, so did the back up.

Mack moved as if to get up and help her.

"Don't move! There are a lot of things she'll have to go through because of you, without you, Mack. So she'd better learn how to start now."

"Yes, Mrs. Harris"

A few minutes later, Michelle returned. Her shirt partly wet where she had washed off the vomit. Her hands still tingled from the Ajax cleaner, which burned like little chemical men cleaning between her fingers. Her lips cracked and parched, from dinner bursting over them like hot lava. The scent of Listerine hovered in the afterglow around her. She sat down at Grandma's feet.

The light from the end table lamp draped Grandma's shoulder. It painted her silhouette against the window as if a stranger were looking in. The night wind howled under the unsettled window frame, chilling the atmosphere for a lesson in the unexpected.

"You two don't really know what you've got yourselves into?" Grandma waved one hand real slow. "Not just having a baby, but you two got a lot of people who haven't asked for, nor expect this, involved. Mack...you on the run, and you, girl... you only have a piece of a job. Now you two got this child coming? My God! This baby can't wait or care whether you two have something together, and with all you two can do, which right now is noth'n, you might as well say me and Mack's mother must do."

Grandma was getting hot as a furnace. She leaned forward, thrusting her finger in Michelle's face. "Michelle, we are not no welfare family, and heaven forbid, you ain't gonna start one now! Your father didn't work hard all his life for the government system to care for his next generations! Matter a fact, if he had been here now, this would have probably killed him on the job getting this news. You know, he was working hard the same day you should have had your behind in school but were with this fool trying to make the first one!"

Michelle turned and cried. You could hear Mack's throat, "gulp" across the street.

"Lord, forgive me, Charles." Grandma gazed through the ceiling.

My grandfather died two years before I was born. I never knew him, but my grandma said I would have learned a lot from him.

Mack's curiosity got the best of him in a good way this time. "Mrs. Harris, could you tell me about Mr. Harris?"

"I'm so glad you asked, son," she answered.

Grandma leaned forward with a smile because she was about to tear into Mack. This was familiar territory for her. She was once young and mature enough now to appreciate it, old enough to enjoy and bask in it. Love and life, set in motion during hard times that made her who she was, yet protected and comforted by a man yet gone but ever so present. It was her glory days revisited in the arms of her best friend. The priceless memories had come again, to hold her safely in his world.

Then she started preaching.

"Mr. Charles Francis Harris was a good man, who came from a good man. His life was good ground, so he gave me a good seed. Oh yes!" She popped her finger. "He loved him some Momma. And Michelle came from good people. That's what I mean when I say good seed. His father owned his own land, his own cattle. And nobody! I mean nobody, do you hear me! Called him out of his name, like that slave word nigga, what you and your buddies refer to each other as. Don't even know what you're saying. Y'all have taken the slang from slave traders and put it on your own foreheads. Y'all so silly. But Mr. Harris learned hard work by example."

Her eyes swelled, reflecting the sun-skilled artwork of beveled glass in her smile. She was riding on the bus of his history.

"When he wanted to go to school in the South like other children, he had to work in the fields. So when he got the opportunity to get there, he learned. His father showed him how to work hard and his mother taught him to read. He always told me, 'Baby, there isn't anything you can't do as well as nobody else.' Her emotions shifted and she sat back shaking her head. A smile took hold of her face, big as piece of sweet cut watermelon. Her eyes lifted through the gray sky and caught something higher than Mack or Michelle could see.

She laughed. "I remember when he told me about the time he was in high school, and they went swimming down at Ghost Pond." Michelle and Mack grinned at each other. "You all don't know noth'n about that. He told me the white sheriff said that they were trespassing on somebody's land. So he took your father and his friends to jail. Now, they didn't have a phone in those days, but news traveled fast.

"When old sheriff looked down the road, here comes Charles' father, and all the other black fathers. Shotguns on their shoulders, and they ain't saying a word."

Mack's eyes popped open like a hoot owl. He put his hand over his mouth so tight he almost choked himself.

"When those men reached that police station, they still didn't say a word. They just stood there. See, a black man named Mr. Dillard owned the property and told them they could swim there. But some white folks for the sake of being hateful said they saw Charles and his friends sneak in. Mr. Dillard wasn't there at the time to speak for them, so they went to jail. But by the time the fathers got to the jail, the sheriff was standing outside, his hands up, waving, saying, 'Boys, ah...I means, fellas...Der's been a miss...unnerstanding? You all's chillin's can goes home...They's free to go.'

"So he let them out and guess what, those black men still didn't say a word. They just walked back down the road into the darkness with them shotguns still on they shoulders. See, there can be a whole lot of talking in silence when it comes to someone's child. And his children knew that he was not the type of man to be played with. Charles said his father didn't whip him or any of his brothers. He'd just called them out to the back of the house, and he didn't have to do that but one time. Mr. Harris didn't come from no bad seed. He came from a respectable and a proud people, Mack. A people who loved God and respected whatever pieces of God's Word they got. Whether from their preacher or from those who could understand what they read, his people's life was to go to church every Sunday and worshipped God for all His goodness. Not just living like one day was like any other day." I think she was referring to Mack and some of his folks he lived with, drinking and eating barbeque seven days a week.

"His mother was a woman who knew how to pray. She taught him how to pray. Mack, Charles was a good man and my child is a good seed. Now this baby has to come into the world with a mother still late to school, barely work, and a father running for his life. Michelle still burning grits and half wash dishes! And Mack, you don't have no grits, or no dishes!

25

Now there are three of you. This is not a mistake we are dealing with here? This is life, understand! This is life!"

Her gaze reached for strength, grappling at the wind outside the window. The wind was strong, but silent this time.

"Mack, go home and tell your mother to call me as soon as you get in the house."

Mack answered, "Yes Mama," and leaned over to kiss Michelle.

Grandma cut the smooch cord as she looked out the window. "Isn't that what got you both in trouble in the first place? Keep ya lips to ya self."

Mack and Michelle smiled. He kissed Grandma on the cheek then crept toward the door. Just as he reached for the knob, he stepped back and took a deep breath.

"It's clear, Mack" Grandma said, gaze still fixed outside, "but you better run fast."

Mack's steps turned to lightening bolts through the open gate, blasting down the stairs, till his figure disappeared in the darkness.

Michelle locked the door. She stood, hands glued to the doorknob. Tears like Jordan's river streamed down, breaking at the crest of her swollen nose and tapping a sad rhapsody onto the hardwood floor.

Michelle sat down at Grandma's feet wrapping both arms around her legs. Grandma just sat silent and listened to her.

"Momma, I'm sorry. I'm so sorry. Momma, I'm scared of what going on inside of me. Not just this baby, because it's more to it than that. I mean, Momma, you talked about seed and how Daddy was good seed. He worked hard for us and gave us the best he could."

Her face twisted with the pressure of uncontrolled emotion. Her tears ran like canals as she talks about her father.

"He died working hard for me, even when I was messing up and everything. Daddy was always good to me, even when he had to whip me." Michelle giggled as Grandma handed her a tissue to blow her nose. "He'd hit the pillow three times and hit me once, and I'd be hollering like I was dying, calling for you. And you wouldn't even come in because you knew he'd never really get me the way I needed to be got. He always said, 'You're my good girl. Momma's my girl, but you're my good girl.' Even when I was twelve, I could still get rocked to sleep."

Michelle's voice changed from soft sweet violet to a chain of Velcro around her throat, with very little give. "But Momma, what kind of seed is in me? I'm still careless, and Mack doesn't care, I half work, and Mack don't work. Most of the time I move like an ant and Mack got half cheetah in his blood. How's my baby going to be? I don't know whether it will come out crawling, or running, and Mack with all this crazy stuff, fight'n and shoot'n? I can't even say whether he's been faithful to me or not. Is this stuff going to be in my baby?"

The wind continued to thrust in, refusing to care that it was uninvited. Antique trinket animals on the lamp stand, sheltered in dust, struck poses of interest, but remained lifeless. The night had come, bearing life, death, hope, and hopelessness, in the same breeze.

Chapter 2
Birth Of Fire:
The Unexplainable War

The room stayed hot. Michelle kept the wall heater up full blast as if we were passing through a summer in hell. Tight pants, up and down, in the house, out of the house, Michelle's pregnancy was no easy ride for me. Everything she felt, I felt. Everything she would dream, I dreamt. Ate, drank, and over ate, I'd get it in my water world. And when she couldn't sleep, I had to hear it; T.V. and radio all night long. So when I couldn't sleep I'd get her back good with my own rendition of the Carpenter's song, "*Close To You.*"

I kicked, stretched out, pressed my knee, poked an arm, whatever was the biggest part of me at that time at anything in her that was, "*close to me, to bring her,* " the most discomfort. It was like being on a wild roller coaster ride at the Santa Cruz Beach Boardwalk of emotions. You'd never know where you'd end up.

My emotions weren't the only thing fried on edge. The Palestinians were running their own coaster ride of terror on the world. Not jacking cars, but airplanes. It was called Black Sunday. Three hundred air passengers were turned into three hundred skyjack hostages. Thank God it was still His Day, and they came out all right. But there was no mercy on the planes or the runways. They went up in a blast.

The Munich Olympics were supposed to be about the competition of the world's best, but rather, the world watched its worst, calling it Black September. Instead of running the 200-meter, eleven Israeli athletes had run their last race. By midnight German police in a helicopter attempted to free those who were left. All turned to dark chaos and when the bullets ceased, flags had to be draped when they should have risen. Mark Spitz did bring the gold home, seven times.

One night Michelle couldn't sleep and decided to listen to her favorite Al Green records, "*You Ought To Be with Me, Still in Love with You,* and *Let's Stay Together,*" over and over again. Then she drank some old cheap Red Port wine to help her sleep. Maybe being in a young, strong womb is good, but when attached to an immature mind, that could be a volatile combination. I was on cloud nine and kept her up all night for that. I let her experience some of my confusion. That night I tried to kick her kidneys out.

Toward the end of Michelle's pregnancy, it got worse. Mack figured since Michelle was already pregnant, he could have all the sex he wanted whenever he wanted. In my later years I learned that's all it was. To a real woman who really desires to be loved, that's not much. Michelle went along with it at first, but when I began to grow inside and her thermostat finally settled back to normal, something started to happen. Mack began to take out his frustration on and in Michelle. He would come and get on Michelle, breathing all hard, sweaty, and smelling from whatever he was doing. And whether he had won or lost on the streets, he'd get it out of his system on her.

Intimacy lost its emotion, and turned into an enema. Pleasure lost its passion and the bed became more of a grave than a resting place. The art of lovemaking crossed over to breeding, and the sheets began to cry out for mercy, "Some Tide and bleach please?" One time, Michelle asked him to stop because she was feeling sick, but he wouldn't. He told her, "I just got to get this one off." Michelle held her breath and went numbing cold, freezing her thoughts into the wall with its water-cracked portraits until Mack finished. She never had to wait long to thaw out though. He jumped up and rolled off of her as if he were getting up from some fight. He shadow boxed, and paced the floor as if he were in a boxing ring.

Michelle pulled the covers up over herself and watched

him. Her heart ran like a wild horse, troubled as if the devil himself had walked in. Whatever she had prayed to never come had just arrived. Mack was pumping his life in her. Some of whatever little good stuff from his momma, his emotions, his mind, his will, his desires, his anger, everything. Mack was fighting back. Not just on the street, but now in her womb.

"I'm Mack!" He paced the floor talking to himself. "Nobody is going to run me no mo'. My baby not going to live with no daddy on the run! He's going to be a warrior, a true soldier, like Big Mack." Mack paced like a lion in a cage.

Michelle said, "What's the matter, Mack? What are you *doing*?"

"Naw baby, my baby ain't going to have no sucka for no daddy!"

Michelle's voice cracked. A tear shimmied down the corner of her eye like a firemen down a fire pole. "Mack, you not no sucka...please baby, calm down...what's the matter?"

"I'm just gearing up for round *two*." Each step caught small sifts of breeze and lifted his long jerry-curly shag off of his shoulders like a buck-wild horse, fresh out of the stable.

"Round-two? What's this *round-two* stuff, Mack?"

"I'm about to get in it and show you that Mack is yo man!"

Mack became aroused again. Then he jumped in the bed on top of Michelle.

"Mack, please, not now?" Michelle voiced cackled with the fright of a chicken in the third packing container moving through the chicken plant. "I don't feel good. Can we wait for a little while?"

But Mack didn't care. Even the same setting doesn't make the same mindset. The bed you've played in can be the bed that can hurt you. The more Michelle begged him to stop, the more forceful he became. Her protector turned into her predator, ramming a world only concerned about its own pleasures, now pointed at Michelle's heart. The room shifted from rest to rage. Horror caught the sweet sleeping place on its back. Mack was hearing something in his head that seemed real empty at times. Something he always wanted to hear – forced submission.

As he came to a climax, he slammed his fist next to Michelle's head. Then he looked at Michelle, who was trying not to look him in the eyes.

"Look at me!" he shouted. "Look at me! I want to see what my baby's eyes look like."

His eyes were white, his pupil stuck between a rare moon mixed with lava.

Michelle looked into those two hollow bowls. It was if Mack could see right through her eyes, her heart, into her womb, and *right at me*. From her womb, I felt him. Everything that was going on in his mind and all that was in him was identifying with something in bits and pieces, to make up me. My DNA was looking at itself through this microscope of madness. Wonder if it likes what it sees? Not!

"Get off me!" Michelle yelled. "Negro, get off me *now!*" Mack rolled over and Michelle ran to the bathroom, trying to sit on the toilet and vomit in it at the same time. But this sickness was not a pregnancy sickness, it was a defiled sickness. A boundary was crossed, the forbidden thing was touched.

Bent forward, Michelle could see through the slightly open door. Mack was rolling over as if to get a good night's rest. He had just finished cleaning himself with his T-shirt.

"Oh, no you don't!" Michelle yelled. "Get up! Because you gots to get out of here!"

"Ah, baby," Mack said, rolling over.

"And I hoped you enjoyed yourself because me and you in the bed is over, Jack!" Michelle yelled as she wiped herself quickly, then turned and vomited again. "Whoever you think is in the bed with you, it ain't me. And until you find out who it is, that person, I will not be! *So get out!*" she roared from her guts.

Mack rolled over slowly, picked up his things and walked

31

toward Michelle who had just come out of the bathroom. He grabbed between his legs, bumping her to the side and walked out.

From then on Michelle had bad dreams.

One night she dreamt about how she and I were walking through a green pasture. The sky was blue and beautiful till two gunshots went off, and in a split second, it turned pitch black. We all were on the run through a warehouse with somebody shooting at Mack. Ever seen a baby running in your dream before? Especially when he's jam'n! It's funny as heck! The scene jumped and we had just got to the stairs at Grandma's house. We pulled at the front door when it turned into a locked vault. Boom! Boom! Boom! Mack got hit from behind. From the thrust we all went down, spun out with our heels in the air. I'm stretched out with Mack's blood as a new tapestry on me.

When Michelle saw it, she started screaming because she thought I got hit, too. Michelle woke up screaming for Grandma, who rushed in the room to calm her. Man, when you're inside yo momma and she is going through it, you don't get the chance to order up which video you want or even put it on pause. Whatever's on the screen of her life at that time, you just got to hold on and eat whatever's being served. That happened a lot in sequels, but the worst one was last night.

She dreamt she had to go to the funeral for Mack. She figured one day she had to, but when she got there Grandma was up at the coffin crying. Now, Grandma got love for everybody, but Mack is not going to draw nar-*ra'* tear from her anytime soon. Michelle walked up and there lay Mack. Loud seventies' pimp suit and hat, platform shoes with the toes out, and all. He was a sad representation of Superfly.

Then the picture went in 3D-horror right in front of their eyes. The room stretched and narrowed, the curtains on the wall turned to psychedelic wallpaper, the ceiling light turned into a disco ball, the coffin started to shrink, and Mack did, too. When it stopped shrinking there was me, her baby. Pimp hat, suit, baby *Stride Right* platforms with the toes out and black mustache. Michelle woke up screaming for Grandma. Grandma came running, but knew that something was really wrong, because Michelle could not stop shaking. Now you know if Michelle was shaking, my world was jiggling like an earthquake. Grandma started praying, praying hard. Michelle was seven months pregnant with me at that time.

About two weeks ago one of Mack friends got killed in front of the liquor store. [Straight out, I'm warning you about standing in front of liquor stores, hear me!] His funeral was on a Thursday. Michelle didn't want to go, because of how Mack and his friends showed out at their boys' funerals. Mack came by about 11:30 am (late as always) with a three-piece, pin-stripped suit with a ring around the collar, right out one of the Sixth and Market soul-brother stores. You can straight tell this brother don't go to nobody's church. He was smoking a joint, the smell of Right Guard deodorant over funk, a beer, and to top it off, a dingy do-rag on his head.

"Get dressed, girl, we gotta go," Mack said, shaking his hand low by his thigh. The old pimps in the neighborhood would do that when you see them talking and taking money from their prostitutes.

"Mack, you know how I feel about this?" Michelle whined.

"Dis' my boy, and we can't disrespect my boy." The sweet smell of marijuana hovered over his suit as vapors off a lake during sunrise. He kept rubbing his hands. I believe that was a sign of bad nerves. So to keep the peace Michelle went, but asked Mack not to force her to go up to the coffin.

Mother Nature didn't have to do anything different with the balance of the world. Just a tilt for one moment was all they needed. This was one of them "strange sunny days" in the neighborhood. Now, for some people, that may have suggested, "Let's go to the beach, let's fly a kite, or have a glass of white wine." But the sun on our side of town was sweating and leaned off to the left, as if it had sipped a bit of the Rocky Mountain Coors. For Mack and his crew that meant, "It's hot! We 'bout to drank the corner liquor store out, and tear something up!" You almost couldn't give them sunshine without them running wild.

The funeral would be just how Michelle pictured it. The boys were in full force with their own Jingling Brothers and Black-A-Bum-Crazy Circus, of the funkiest kind. Taking over a service was typical of them. They always tried to make a party out of a sad situation, totally disrespecting the family with loud music, drinking, and cursing. I really believe they were trying to cover their own fears, pretending the guy was still alive. Mack told Michelle about one funeral he went to. He and his fools made the mortician prop the guy up and put a joint in his mouth. Mack was talking about it as if he were proud. Even as we drove up, the brightness over the mortuary held a "welcome to madness" smile over it.

At the chapel entrance, some family members were being escorted out because of the chaos inside. An old lady was limp in the arms of the mortician. One hand full of tissues as she held her chest, the other arm flung out with the power of a vice-grip to her purse. Michelle's eyes were crazy-glued on her. She froze. Mack's stupid self snatched her by the arm forward. We found out later that was the grandmother. This was the third grandson she had to bury in the last fifteen months.

As they walked up the isle to take a seat, some nut had a radio up at the coffin blasting the guy's favorite song, and dancing with an unseen female demon. Mack walked in talking loud, slapping hands, and hugging everybody as if he were really the mourning type. The smoke from the joints and cigarettes swirled in formaldehyde danced with each other like drunken guests in King Arthur's court. Every mouth and taste bud that ever touched marijuana was struggling from smacking. The morticians, now they had sense. They were nowhere to be found.

Michelle looked around. The parlor was a gallery of swinging mirrors. All these young girls sat, many pregnant, with kids from this wild cavalry. Some girls had babies on their laps with a head start on us, just trying to survive their mommas and daddies drama. All of them temporary stunned, paranoid, slowly rocking from side to side from the powerful venom's strike of their personal choices. The results, oozing down the black-thread veins of their fishnet stockings. Many had on the same old glitter and rhinestone party dresses, with the backs out, under them hot funky rabbit coats that shed at every shake. They kept them zipped up, not to show their overloaded portable milk bottles, each one wondering, who would be the next honoree to stand over their baby's daddy's body?

The dead guy's girlfriend had just left from standing at the coffin with his son in her arms. The little boy had a tux on matching his father's. As the girl was walking away from the coffin, the baby was closing and opening his hand like babies do when they are waving bye-bye.

One of Mack's buddies, who Michelle couldn't stand because she said his breath stank like boo-boo and was always up in her face when Mack wasn't around, gave the so-called eulogy. He looked as if he had just landed from another planet. A big old "Cat in the Hat" hat on, joint in his mouth, a beer in one hand, and a Bible he found on the front seat of the mortuary in the other. Boy, if my grandma had of seen that, she'd have killed him before God got to him.

"Brothas, sistas, and friends, we are gathered here to say bye-bye to J.P.'s old yellow stupid behind! Who had his stupid-self in the wrong place, at the wrong time, probably doing the wrong thang, in the wrong way! Now somebody tell me I'm right!"

The crowd yelled back, "You right!" like they in church too.

After quoting some old pee-funk message he said, "So I'll

end on this note, Ah... J.P., yellow boy, when ya get to Hell, save a freak for me! Ha! Ha! Ha!"

His haunting laugh gave Michelle the chills, so you know who got them too. As everyone made their last pass by, some of the people were kind of shaken up by what they saw in the coffin. Mack made Michelle go up. She kept pleading with Mack, but he bent her finger back. The pain caused her to open her mouth wide enough to swallow a hard-bun sandwich whole. He jerked her out from the pew. Right before they got to the coffin, Michelle began to feel nauseated, so did I. She started to put her hand on her big belly, yet when she got to the coffin, she tripped. She touched it, and her belly, at the same time.

She passed out, and went down hard. Man, I thought the Titanic had sunk again. I hadn't turned yet in her womb, and one of her breasts hit me on the top of my head. "Whop!" But something else happened. When she touched the coffin, something spiritually negative happened. Whatever was in the coffin was knocking at the door of her womb, and trying to room in with me now. I-A-L-N-B-I-H!

I...Ain't...Letting...No...Body...In...Here!

From that time forward, Michelle could not stand the sight of Mack. She had "straight hate" for that brother. Every night for a week, in some shape, form, or fashion, we relived that funeral. The smell, the sound, the sight, and I couldn't shake that titty hitting me on top of the head either. It didn't help that Michelle, with all of America, had lined up for hours to see *The Exorcist*. Grandma had people at the church praying for us. When Michelle would fall asleep on the couch, Grandma would read the Bible and rub her hand on Michelle's big belly. She got some oil one night and prayed until that sick funeral stuff got off of us. The nights got better.

At 10:20 P.M., October 15[th,] 1973, just days before the full-blown OPEC Oil Crisis, the Yom Kippur War, Nixon finally releasing those Watergate tapes, and America's first introduction to the word "inflation," Michelle was up late doing some research for nursing classes. Her water burst. When she went to get Grandma, she noticed red lights flashing going fast down the street. It was an ambulance.

Grandma asked if she was going to call Mack.

"Why?" She looked at Grandma all crazy.

Grandma shot back, "Why shouldn't you? It took two to make this baby, and I wasn't there when it happened."

Michelle knew she better leave Grandma alone with that word-for-word stuff, and as much as she needed her now, too? So Michelle called Mack, and like always, it took him a while to get there. Since he lived so close, Michelle asked him what took him so long. He said one of Joe Young's boys they called 'Petty D', who was known for hammering folks for pay, "Got paid in full." The police had the street blocked off. Mack was sweaty, musty, and nervous as usual.

Grandma drove to the emergency room and parked right next to the ambulance that carried Petty D. As we walked past the open doors, a mural of blood covered the floor, and walls. Immediately a water main of pain broke, and that flood hit Michelle all at once.

Grandma knew all the nurses, so they took Michelle in fast. The gurney had to roll straight through the blood Petty D had lost. Mack helped push Michelle down the hall. Somehow he transferred back into some kid at the skating rink, criss-crossing his dirty tennis shoes through the blood. A doctor looked at him and said, "Are you all right?" Mack didn't look up, just kept pushing Michelle to the room. It was next to the emergency room of Joe's boy.

As Petty D's blood pressure dropped, Michelle's would rise. As his breathing began to fail, Michelle's breathing would increase. The harder the doctor's pushed on his chest, the harder Michelle's contractions came. Until in sync, as the young man heaved out his last breath in death, I took my first breath of life, and cried. There was some kind of spiritual transference.

Everything my daddy thought he was, my mom is, and some things that young man will never be, were somehow in me. Michelle lay there totally exhausted, drained, as if she had been rescued from a fire, but glad to see me. I was glad to see her in my own little way too.

On my birthday certificate my name is Emmanuel Charles Harris. My daddy put a.k.a. "Little Mack" in the corner. I guess that was supposed to be a joke.

The city certified it that way.

My grandma calls me, "Emmanuel." Since she knew neither Mack nor Michelle could take care of me anytime soon, the last thing Grandma wanted my mother to do in emotional silliness was to give me my father's last name. My middle name was after my grandfather, because he followed the Bible in leaving his children's children an inheritance. He never knew me, but he left me money, and Grandma said some other things that I would only understand when I get older. She always told me, "He loves you, from where he is."

The nurse cleaned me and handed me to my daddy. The first thing he whispered was not "Hello son," but, "That was for you, boy! Because yo daddy's no sucka."

Wow, my first gift from him, a war.

Chapter 3
The Piper's New Song –
The Groove I'll Never Forget

In 1978, Grandma first told me this story. I was about five years old then, but it's still fresh in my mind. I see its plot played out in our youth today. Many simply think that it was just a fairy tale. But the fairy didn't pay attention to the warning signs, and turned down the wrong ally. Somebody took her hostage, stole her horse and buggy, and put a new flavored twist to the waters of our imaginations. San Francisco was rocked to its core. An atmosphere of the impossible hovered over the City by the Bay, where the unthinkable not only could happen, but just had happened.

Not even its Golden Gates, Cable Cars, or Rice-A-Roni could calm the tension of the unexpected. Mayor Moscone and Supervisor Harvey Milk had just been murdered by one of its trusted own. And if that wasn't enough, the news reported that Jim Jones had just gone berserk on the People's Temple members in Guyana. Michelle visited that church one time, and had some friends who went to Jonestown. She said that church was too much for her. The people were acting like this guy was God. I think that was why Grandma stopped her from giving me Twinkies, and wasn't no grape Kool-Aid to be brought in the house, ever again.

Even the children weren't safe from the imaginations of fear on their little minds.

Grandma came home from work tired. Her feet were hurting. Michelle ran her bath water, music blasting from KSOL on the bathroom radio.

"Girl, turn that mess down!" Grandma yelled. The sound must have jumped out the window. Then she turned sweetly to me, her baby. "What are you doing up, young man?"

"Waiting for you to talk to me?" That was my way of telling her, "Tell me that story again."

"After this, you get your little behind in the bed, all right?"

"Yes, Mama."

I had a little chair I'd sit in when I first started walking, and Grandma taught me how to sit down. If need be, the hard way. She always said that the best protection for the behind is to be sitting on it when told to do so. Now, you know as the baby, after a few failed test runs, my curiosity-hearing-aid going in and out, and Grandma's black slipper catching them cheeks, I finally got the hang of it.

She sat down and looked at me over her glasses, shaking her head, and reached for the broom. She'd pulled a loose strand of straw to use the top for a toothpick, and left it hanging out her mouth. My eyes would be locked on that strand as it rolled around the tip of her lip as she spoke.

Then she'd start by saying, "A long time ago, there was a little town that had a big nasty problem. The whole city, every house, had rats, just like some of the houses close around here. Now, we can deal with some mice, but we can't handle no rats."

I was cheesing from ear to ear, because she would make it so real.

"And couldn't nobody in that town do noth'n with them rats. Rats in the morn'n, rats at noonday, rats watching television with you. They was bold. They just pull up a chair and sit down; start digging in ya popcorn and drinking yo soda like you do me when I leave the room.

"So one day, this soul brotha came in town, playing this horn. He was called, Da' Soul Piper, and man, he could play. Aaaw, dat boy could play!"

Grandma told the story like she liked it, too. She'd be snap'n her head, and pop'n her fingers when she would say, "Da' Soul Piper." I just knew he was coming in the door any minute.

"When he got to the middle of the town, he sat his horn down. A rat came up, snatched it, and ran off with it. But before the rat could get out of sight, he pulled out this beautiful, little horn and started playing a tune. The rat stopped, right in his tracks. That rat turned around, and walked back up to the guy while he was playing and said, 'Man, dat sho sound sweet. You got me, boy. You got me.' That rat was swaying, back and forth, like a drunken man. Now, up in a window, the Mayor was watching. He ran down the stairs where Da' Soul Piper was.

"Mayor said, 'Saaaay maaan, how you do dat?' Piper said, 'There isn't anything this pipe can't get rid of when I play it. And by the way, the rats seem like they run'n thangs here. I saw two of them buggy-jacking some of your folks up the street.' And as the Mayor turned his head, there they go, running, across the street from the buggy, in two mink coats, money falling everywhere!"

I couldn't help but bust out laughing. "Don't laugh yet, I'm not through yet," Grandma would say. Then she'd really get started.

"Piper said, 'I could help you get rid of the rats. For a small fee of course.' Mayor said, 'Small fee? That ain't no problem. Just do yo thang man, do yo thang!'

"So Da' Soul Piper told him he would be back in the morning, but would take this rat with him, because he had some groove in him. He started playing, and walked toward the open gate of the town. That rat was following right behind him in stride, as if he was dancing with Queen Elizabeth.

"The next day early in the morning, the piper came back. And remember that rat that left with him? He came back too! Dressed like one of Earth, Wind and Fire in they early days, with some Prince glasses on."

Now I didn't know who they were, but Prince was Michelle's boy. At this time I was laughing so hard, I fell out of my chair.

"Wait, don't fall out now. I'm not done yet!" Grandma said. I knew I had to get all my laughter out now, because the end was not funny and was all too real. It reminded me of the look in a family's face. They wait for the plane, carrying the coffins with the body of their soldiers that was killed in combat, coming home from war. Yes, they are heroes, in every sense, but where's the real joy?

"Well, Soul Piper came in backed by his new side kick Razzy Rat on the bass guitar, right up to the Mayor's house and said, 'Mayor, we're here for the job, get the check.' The Mayor told them, 'Finish the job because I'm on my way to the credit union right now!' So Da' Soul Piper and Razzy Rat struck up a tune, and they were jamming. Awe, I mean they were going! When the rats heard that music, they were coming out of everywhere you could see. There's one, coming from under your chair!"

Silly me, I looked to see. "Where?"

She looked at me and frowned. "Boy, now you know yo' grand-momma don't got no rats in here." Then she went to close the story out.

"Soul Piper started walking, still playing that tune, and all the rats followed him right out of town, rocking and moving to the music, never to be seen again. All the people looked out their windows, and seen the rats were gone, and started shouting like they were at church. So a little while passed, when Da' Soul Piper and Razzy Rat came back in town. They went to the Mayor's house. Soul Piper yelled up, 'Hey Mayor, I'm back to get paid!' Rat tapped Piper on the shoulder, and bucked his eyes, like he reminding Soul Piper, he here too. Rat yelled out, 'Yeah, we back to get paid, we back.' See, Rat was caught up now. Started smiling, and took out his wallet, because he bout to get paid.

"The Mayor looked out the window, looked down the street to see what had happened, put a toothpick in his mouth, and said with a funky attitude, 'How much you say you charge, boy?'

"Soul Piper kind of looked at Razzy Rat disappointed, like to say, 'Here we go again?' Soul Piper said, 'Well, since you got an attitude, I'll charge you at first-class rate for my services. I want everythang!'

"Mayor batted his eyes, picked his nose, and said 'Ah, maybe I miss unnerstood you? You didn't say, everythang, did you?'

"Then the piper spelled it out. 'E-V-E-R-Y-T-H-A-N-G!'

"Mayor got irritated. 'Look, come back tomorrow. I'll take it up with the trustee board, and we'll have a little somethin'-somethin' for you.' Under his breath the Mayor mumbled, 'Huh, talk'n bout everythang; boy crazy.' Piper said, 'Okay. But if you don't pay me, I'll bring the rats back, and change my big fat fee!' 'Yeah right, son,' said the Mayor. Then Soul Piper walked up, real close to the mayor, looked him in the eyeballs and said, 'That which is dearest and valuable to you, shall dance away to my tune.' Then as he and Razzy Rat walked away, he started playing a slow, soul-chilling tune. It sent chills down Mayor spine; ol' Mayor tried to shake it off.

"Then he went to his trustee board, and told them what Da' Soul Piper had said. They got loud. They said, 'Piper won't get nothin' here, junior! Just give him a twenty-dollar check, and put a ten-day hold on it at the bank.' One old trustee bit his lip. 'Ah, if he gives you any trouble, call me. I'll jack him up! Ain't jacked nobody in a longtime, need to know how dat feel again!' They all bust out laughing. But ain't gone be laughing too much later.

"Well, the next day, Da' Soul Piper with Razzy Rat was at the Mayor's house again. Piper went to the door, hit the doorbell. Mayor's doorbell had that old King Henry the VIII sound. Mayor came to the door. Piper said to him, 'You got my stuff?' Mayor answered, 'Dis it,' and slammed an envelope in the Piper's hand! Soul Piper opened it, looked in, and leaned over to show it to Razzy Rat. The rat started shaking his head.

"Soul Piper said, 'Well, guess I got ta do, what I got ta do, right Mayor?' Mayor said, 'It's on you, playa.' Piper turned to the rat and said, 'Let's go, baby, we won't trouble ourselves with this mess, but oh, Mayor, would you permit us to walk through town, and play just one last farewell tune, as they say?' The Mayor just pointed his finger in the direction of the middle of town, and the Piper started walking, vvveeerrry slow.

"Razzy Rat stepped over to the mayor, said, 'Man, you shouldn't play with dat man's money. Guess we all got to learn like I did; because we all pay Da' Piper. You can put that in ya' pipe and smoke it.' Razzy Rat started walking away, hitting some hard, slowww, deeeep, licks on the bass.

By this time I was scared, and sleepy.

"Grandma, I'm sleepy now. I'm going to sleep with my momma."

"Okay baby, good night."

I walked over and kissed her on the cheek as she rubbed her left leg. It was swelling at the ankle. I remembered Michelle talking on the phone to someone about Grandma taking some test for that.

When I got to Michelle's room, she was rolling her hair and singing some off-the-wall song on the radio. I got in the bed, but was scared to close my eyes because of the living proof at the end of the story. As I was fighting my sleep, fatigue placed a sleeper hold on my eyelids. I could barely see Michelle sneaking a puff from a cigarette, and dancing around the room. She didn't fully blow the smoke out the window. It settled low like hands around her waist, as she twirled around. This set the stage as I drifted off, into that present nightmare.

My dream lifted me out of the bed, through Michelle's smoke-made escalator, right where my grandmother had left off. I stepped off, right in the middle of that town. It seemed like Razzy Rat was about ten feet away from me, and he was big.

He stopped, and looked at me. "Hey, you Ms. Harris's boy, ain't you?

I nodded.

He pointed at me with his pinky finger, a big old cubic zirconium on it. "You, and all the other kids, will be the payment on the debt owed!" Then he walked away.

I wanted to run, but my feet turned like Pharaoh's stone feet on a statue. Then there he was, "Da' Soul Piper." Suit sparkling, hair laid, glasses tight. He stood on a gold crate in the middle of town, and raised his hand to the sky. These big old giant Vega speakers busted out from the ground out of nowhere. They farted out a hard, moving, funky beat that made something happen, down in your soul. My heart was pounding, in rhythm with the beat.

Then I noticed something. All the children were coming out of everywhere. They were all moving to the groove, and something crazy happened. We all had little mousey features. The music was loud, jam'n, and yet something else was odd. The grown folks couldn't hear the music. You could tell by the expressions on their faces. They just couldn't hear it.

Soul Piper turned to the rat and said, "Rap-Rat!"

Razzy Rat snatched the mic and took off saying:

"Because your daddies forgot to tell,

Who brought them into, all their hell?

If they had understood, and paid the Soul Piper like they should,

I turn to you, this next generation,

To die like dogs, across the nation,

To hate one another, without a reason,

Get your guns, boys, it's hunting season!"

We all screamed as if we were at a concert. Brothers slap'n high fives, girls were drop'n and back'n them thangs up, and we was riding them booties like no tomorrow.

With the Soul Piper and Razzy Rat stepping side by side, they led all of us kids to a beautiful battlefield. As we entered the gate, some of us were given beautiful guns. Some were given drugs in candy wrappers, and some were given stacks of money. All of the girls were given mini-skirts, thongs, and condoms. As the girls passed this big old mirror, they'd stop and look. A blast of wind would come from the floor under their shirt and skirts, and their breast and butts began to swell. The boys were hollering, "It's on, man! It's on!"

The music was getting louder, and Razzy Rat hit another riff:

"We got you all, he is big hog,
He got the gun, and she's a female dog
Now you all can't leave this pretty grave,
Because you all are now our slaves,
He's got the smoke, she's got the drank,
Shots from the car, some rob the banks,
Some will freak, another will cry,
None can leave, you all shall die!"

I was crying in my sleep, but couldn't wake up because of the most frightening thing. With every leap of our wildness, the atmosphere began to move in slow motion. All the kids were singing along and some guys started cocking their guns. I began to recognize these were kids I knew from the neighborhood.

Smoke started to fill the field, and somehow I woke myself up at about 5 a.m. I turned and saw Michelle taking off her Afro wig, talking to someone on the phone. I used to wonder how she did it. She'd have a little hair in the day, and then this big old Afro when she went out? Hey, you get what you pay for at Westwood Pharmacy. She had just got back from a party. She stayed there in the room with me until I went to sleep before she left. The radio was still on right above my head. She used to put me to sleep that way when I was a baby. All night at the head of my crib that crazy music played, so it flowed right into my blood stream.

Thank God for Grandma though. She was medicine for the

snakebite. She played gospel music to me, the old hymns. I could hear her early in the morning washing clothes. She'd be moaning those old spiritual songs. When I'd hear her, I'd get out of bed with Michelle and get in her bed. Then she'd come back to get in her bed, and see me in there. She'd never put me out. Just cover me up, and keep on moaning songs. She said her father would sing them in the fields. Those songs could chase away the worst nightmares.

She left her religious station on the radio. Dr. Franklin would be preaching. She'd be saying, "Yes, Lord," in her sleep. When I couldn't sleep, she would lay her hands on my head with some oil and pray. Next thing I knew, it would be daylight. I'd be sleeping so good I'd wet the bed. Waking up in the morning was still like a step closer to the Soul Piper's real world. His tune was everywhere, except in church; the Piper couldn't play his song there. In the neighborhood, I could see the kids, even some of the mothers and fathers, under the control of the piper tune.

That same week, some kid shot at the police. It hit the front page of the news. Michelle was reading it and told Grandma. She said the boy said that he did it because he had heard a song saying, "Got to be the bigger bear, and somebody got to pay for the license." Grandma asked Michelle to explain what was the kid talking about when he said, "Someone had to pay?"

Michelle said, "Oh Momma, he's talking about that new song by the group R.E.P.I.P. You know, that song you make me turn off when we in the car?"

"I, PP, I, what? Girl, I thought that was some of you all's new style of panties," Grandma answered laughing.

I found out later in life what that meant; it's P.I.P.E.R. spelled backward.

47

Chapter 4
Desensitization Doses:
I Don't Feel You Anymore

I can still remember the first time when I really did some damage to myself. I'll never forget the first time I did damage to somebody. I try to forget the first time somebody damaged me. I found out that *blow after blow,* it does something medieval and motivating in you. It destroys you, and strengthens you, with the same pain. Yet, I guess both have the same end. It kills something inside.

I thought I felt a lot of pain in getting a whipping when I was little. But when I was twelve, I ran into a fire hydrant riding my bike and busted my kneecap wide open. Two of my friends carried me home and Michelle took me to the emergency room. I did like Grandma said to do when you can't handle the situation, "Call on Jesus!" And I did, louder than San Francisco's Tuesday noon-warning horn. Grandma was there working when I arrived and got so upset, throwing her hands in the air screaming, "Lord Jesus, help me, help me!" Then when she saw the blood, she went down with the impact of a meteor. The nurses had to pick her up and carry her out, while the doctor reconstructed this major mess where I decided to drive into the unforgiving street appliance. I had to stay off of it for two weeks. Grandma spoiled me the whole time with gov'ment grilled cheese sandwiches galore. After that, all the other bumps and bruises weren't so bad.

I was growing more tolerant to pain, but didn't know it.

Michelle stopped whipping me so much after I stopped crying when she did whip me. She'd just curse me out when Grandma was not around. That did hurt my feelings for a while. But after some time enduring *blow after blow,* many threats but no action, her hot breath and few flying sprinkles in my face, it was nothing.

Michelle let me spend a lot of time with Mack though. Whether this was good or bad, only time will tell? But he loved his boy. Even with his craziness and all, he came and got me every time he could.

We would see Joe Young and Joe-Joe, his son. Mack would say, "See him? When you get the chance, beat him down like a sucka!"

In the old'n days (*listen to me talking like I'm some old 'G' or something*) like the late seventies, early eighties, families would get into stuff and let one kid from each family fight it out. After that, it was over. Joe-Joe was bigger than me and had a reputation of fighting like his daddy. But Mack and "Little Mack Pack" (better never let my grandma hear anyone call me that) ran just as tough in the neighborhood too. Our fathers were the main ringleaders, main jailbirds, dope dealers, head busters, and instinctively, we walked the same knucklehead paths. I used to wonder if we had any choice, or was this just our destiny. And with nearly an entire neighborhood thinking like that, they expected it. Sounds kind of funny. We never heard of what happened to the bad father-and-son's business, just the good ones.

For a young kid, I experienced my own and almost somebody else's share of madness. Michelle and I went to a friend's house and saw the girl's boyfriend pull a gun on the girl. The first time it happened, I jumped on the couch behind Michelle, and screamed. She turned around and told me, "Be quiet, boy!" This guy really wasn't going to do anything. And with all his ranting and raving, the girl just sat there, looking at him like he was crazy. Then she'd cuss his stupid butt out! And with all that wolfing, he didn't do anything. After that happened four or five times, it didn't faze me anymore.

I got use to seeing guns because Mack carried one.

One day, here I was playing down the block and knew at

any time I would hear with my peanut head, "Boy! You better stay your behind from down that street!"

Now, you know I got some Mack-track in me, and I still can't hear too good sometimes, at least Michelle. Saturdays was at full throttle, which lifted all our experimental instinct of what "we could get away with," without our mothers seeing us. I had a friend Bernard, who we called Bammy. Bammy found an air pistol and we'd shoot at stuff in the yard. Bammy let me take the pistol home (*stupid me*), because he knew he would get in trouble for having it at his house.

I thought, woo... I better get back home before my momma sees me.

I'm walking home, picking up pebbles and eating crab grass when a car pulled up and stopped. It was Joe Young and Joe-Joe. Joe-Joe got out and walked up on me with his fist balled up. Everything slowed down.

"What's up, dude?" I said.

Joe-Joe stood there locked on me. He didn't say a word. He just looked back over to his dad in the car as if looking for some sign. Then he turned and cold-cocked me right in the side of the head. It knocked me to the ground. The blow was hard and stunning, because he had a padlock in his hand. It hit straight metal to bone. I felt like I was in the freeze-frame game at school. I had the chance to think about what I was going to do before I hit the ground. My mouth was bleeding, with nerves jumping up through the roof of my mouth, as if I had bitten an electric cord. My eye slammed shut. I felt no pain.

Just one thought ran through my mind: Get back in the game!

As Joe-Joe stood over me, I yelled at him, "I ain't no sucka and my daddy told me to beat you down!" Blam! I rushed him with a wild Ronny Lott hit on a Super Bowl Sunday. My force to his chest popped his neck like a sizzling chicken wing, scraping his butt on the concrete, knocking him flat. His legs and feet were bent over his back, looking like a face-down question mark. I blasted him, stomping my Adidas into his head. His hands took most of the blows as he tried to cover his face.

Joe Young was still sitting in the car looking straight ahead, revving the motor and yelling, "Joe-Joe, you better get up and run-nat sucka! Run-nat sucka!" like he was getting off on it.

Joe-Joe got on his feet with his hair full of dirt from the bottom of my shoe. His eyes were watery, dukes up from the little boxing he was taking at the Boys Club, lips tight red like Marilyn Monroe with a reaction to a bee sting. He knew he had his hands full.

A small crowd formed as we tussled for a while, till I pushed him away. All of a sudden, out came that air pistol. I beat him with it first, then backed off and pointed it at him. He froze. It was like I was back in the living room of Momma's friend's house. You know; the argument, the fight, and then the gun. I knew it was an air pistol, but he didn't. Knowing what someone else doesn't know? Uh, that's funny.

It did something on the inside of me.

It was power! It felt good!

Joe Young started reaching for something while trying to open the car door. The police were pulling up, sirens and all.

"Joe-Joe, come here!" Joe Young yelled. But Joe-Joe didn't move.

"Put the gun down!" the police yelled with their guns pointed at us. "Drop it! Or I'll blow you away, now!"

I dropped the gun.

"Lay on the ground, both of you!"

So we lay on the ground, face down. Joe Young slumped down in his seat.

"You! In the car! Put the keys on the roof and come out with both hands in the air!"

Joe Young put the keys on the roof with his left hand, and

got out slow with a big doo-doo eat'n grin on his face. He lay on the ground as Joe-Joe and I stared eye to eye. Our faces showed our pasts in blood, our eyes telling the present in tears, the pistol between us, maybe warning our future.

I could see a lot of people out of the corner of my eye, but it was all the guns pointed at us that worried me. I saw the shadow of a policeman as he crept up on Joe Young. Another cop slammed his knee into Joe's back, patting him down. He found a nine-millimeter on him and like always, the negro gots' to put up a last-minute struggle to show off before being put in the police car. The officers slowly approached Joe-Joe and me. They told us not to move so we would not get shot, and we didn't. We both could see this cop crouching slowly toward the air pistol when, "blam!" Compare it to the shock of an un-invited ninety-plus-year-old stripper at a convalescent tea party. The pain we felt when those cops put their weight, and knees, in the middle of our backs as they handcuffed us was unbearable. I slammed my eyes shut so hard, the lids burned like they got dipped in Tabasco sauce. The cuffs cut through my dirty wrist, but I would not dare cry in front of Joe-Joe. I had seen cops drop a lot of brothers, and brothers drop a lot of cops, too, but it's a whole different game when you're in it.

They put him and me side by side in the police car. I guess we couldn't hold it anymore, and both like on cue started crying like two lost cubs. Our grandmothers were going to find out now, and that was more painful than the cuffs.

The police were no stranger to us. We knew their names, their cars, and their days off. Some cops were regular customers of the dope dealers. Others gave information before the raids would come, but most were too stupid to listen.

When my grandmother came to pick me up, I really started crying. Now, I don't know how bad Joe-Joe got it, but my grandma would *teach, preach, and then beat!* It was like she got the Holy Ghost too. She'd get that Bible, and then find in there some part talking about God said, "foolishness is in the heart of a child, but get a rod and beat it out," or something like that. It was funnier how she used my butt as the exit. Then she read somewhere else it said, "If she beat me, I wouldn't die." I'd be hollering like I was dying.

When we got home, Grandma would be crying about this time. She told me about when she was in Alabama. She and two of her cousins went to the place called "A Jook Joint." Now, you know me. My juvenile mind at the time, I was thinking, you mean Grandma was somewhere smokin' a joint?

Young minds really do catch on to things slow. Her last name before she got married was Magner. And because of her family name, she couldn't just go anywhere, and do anything. She said she didn't even have to get out of the car, and knew her mother was going to find out. She also knew she was going to get a whipping. She was eighteen years old. She said by the look of the crowd at the place, other people knew she wasn't supposed to be there either.

Grandma has some removable teeth too, and took them out. This one was going to be a bad one. And when she bit that tongue, oh lord, you knew what wasn't far behind next. She talked about how they didn't have a phone, but when they drove up, her mother was standing outside. Her mother asked her what was she doing around that place. She couldn't say a word. Then she said that her mother made her go get "a switch off the tree" and "*stripped down to her bra, slip, and panties.*"

Then my grandma got up, walked outside, and pulled a switch off the tree from the backyard of the house. It was glowing! My eyes almost popped out of their sockets! With tears in her eyes she told me how one of her brothers would plead with their mother not to whip her, but her other brother said, "Beat her Momma." Then she got right in my face with her front teeth out, hot breath, and yelled, "*And my momma whipped me; eighteen years old and all!*"

A horse must have kicked her out of the gate because she started whipping my behind and I was hollering! She whipped me till she got tired. It was like I was butt naked too! Grandma used that switch with the accuracy of a seasoned pissed-off lumberjack. Every swing whistled, and cut the wind through my jeans like hot grits! Michelle came in all big and bad. She tried to stop Grandma by jumping between me, and that live wire. I got the chance to see Grandma shift gears and kick it up another notch on Michelle. She whipped her so bad till Michelle blasted out of the room like *Apollo 6*, breaking the high heel on her new shoe. On top of that for punishment, she made me stay in except for school for two weeks and put a dress on me when I got home, daring me to take it off. So you know I wouldn't go anywhere near the door.

That was the worst whipping I'd ever got in my life! But guess what! The Holy Ghost must have got on her again, and I did have a way of forgetting really fast. She woke me up that night, and must have thought I was thinking about doing something else stupid, and *whipped me again*! I was good for six months. Michelle was, too.

In those next six months, I saw something that changed my life.

Hot summer nights in the hood were free-entertainment nights. Just go where a bunch of folks were hanging out – a picnic, the corner store, in front of somebody else's house – something was bound to happen.

My daddy would pick me up, late, but he did have my bag of candy. His cassette player blasted his anthem. It was Rick James' *"Ghetto Life,"* in his day. He mesmerized me by playing a beeping-beat on the horn when he blew at a fine babe walking down the street. The tape rolled right into the next hit, *"Don't Be So Hard To Get!"* Me and him in the car bobbing our heads in sequence singing, "Um-paw-paw, um-paw-paw-um," like the midget on the *Wizard of Oz*. The Crusader's *"Street Life,"* was his theme at night. Some of Mack's friends who were drinking and gambling got into a fight, and started shooting at each other. When silence finally came, two were hurt and two dead. I was in the car with Mack in front of the place right before it happened. Mack went inside, started cursing and hitting people. I snuck up to the door and peeked in. It was the first time I had seen someone right after they just got shot. It wasn't a movie, so I had something new to brag about to my friends.

One of the guys near the door was shot in the head. Every time he breathed, the blood would pump out. A cold feeling filled the room. The feeling of knowing you have no business being in the woods, at night, with no light, wood, nor matches.

Mack yelled, "We got to do something! Get them up, and put them in sheets! Clean up the blood, fool! Nobody can know we been fighting amongst ourselves."

The other guys picked the dead ones up and put them in a car. One nut ran in with a water hose, blasting water everywhere, roof, carpet, and all. I was standing in the front doorway watching. The water and blood flowed under my tennis shoe, mixing into designs, forming a streaming waterfall at the end of the porch.

Then Mack said something real crazy. I used to wonder why Grandma used to tell me, "Don't grow up talking like your daddy." This is when I found out why.

Mack's mouth was twisted and his eyes glazed over as if they were polished with furniture wax. "We got to make this look like Joe Young's boys did dis! Man, them punks been trying to get one of us for a long time, and if they would have got the chance, they'd did it like dis. How you gonna just walk up on us and kill us? They would have been bad with it too. They the kind of brothas that would dog a brotha', then leave a brotha to die like a dog. Them some cold cats!"

Brothers was standing around, faces all balled up resembling a mighty midgets' football team whose dope-fiend uncle just ran away with their uniform fundraiser money.

He kicked in again. "And you know, if they had did dis, they'd be out there talk'n loud, and disrespecting our mommas!"

He got to talking so crazy, that I thought that Joe Young boys did do it. By the time he finished, all Mack's buddies were pumped and acting like they were ready to take revenge. One of the guys yelled out, "Let's go get them niggas!" And this was one of the ones who actually did the shooting.

Some west wind must have blown in and Mack somehow came back with a little sense, before anyone did anything else to complicate the matter. This gave me some hope for my future.

"Look y'all, I said, we got to '*make it look*' like they did this. This our mess, fools, so don't get crazy."

This is when I learned that "beefing or having a beef" had no boundaries. It could erupt anywhere, between anyone. Cross town, down the street, or in the next bedroom. Some were small and all was needed was a little sense to spring up in someone's mind. It was over. Other beefs exploded with shrapnel metal ripping and falling for years, splicing even the innocent into its hateful unforgiving arms. People getting hurt because of something their brother or sister said, did, didn't do. Over something that means so much to us, being disrespected. I believe cows going to the slaughter never thought about mentioning them (beef) could cause so much destruction.

Mack had the guys take the bodies, put them in a car and drive them to an open lot. They shot up the car to make it look like a drive-by. I saw something in Mack that I remember in an old B movie, *Gangster Fantasy*, one of Michelle's bootleg Beta-Max videos she hid from me in the closet. Two days later, it was in the bay area section of the newspaper, four-line max: "Two men shot in Lot. Police reported that a vehicle with two men was found in vacant lot. Car and men were riddled with bullets. No suspects."

Mack was pissed off, talking about it should have made the front page. What did he expect? Heck, we ain't news no more. Reagan was in charge, at least Jessie Jackson ran, we had just got past the Falkland War, and the Space Shuttle Columbia had just went up in smoke. I found later, that people only care for so long when you keep doing stupid stuff to yourselves. After that, as long as it doesn't reach their neighborhood, they don't want to even hear about it.

When it was time to bury Mack's boys, they were meeting and talking about how they were going to put on this big show at the funeral. But at this one guy's funeral, it was a whole new ball game. To all of our surprise, the family of this boy was not having it at all.

At the doors of the church the preacher stood waiting for us as we walked up buzzing, resembling a swarm of bees at the wrong hive. But you know they do make "spray" for us. The preacher had a big can of it, enough to choke us all out.

He said, "This is God's House, and you will respect God's House. And if you can't respect God's House, in God's way, I have some men of God here. They will lay hands on you." The preacher looked slowly at each one of us straight in the eyes and did not smile. "And if they can't cast the devil out of you, they'll beat it out. But either the devil, or you and the devil will leave this place!"

Some deacons were standing by his side and when we got inside, there were plenty more. They were nice, smiled, but those smiles had the hint of "we will tear a patch out yo behind" look in the corners of their lips.

So we all went in like we had good sense and sat down. Took them hats, do-rags, and them dark glasses off too. One of Mack's boys didn't get there in time for the preacher's greeting and came in clowning. In mid-step, those deacons were on him so fast he didn't know what happened. They snatched that nut right up out of his shoes.

This service was different. The huge church was filled with a presence unfamiliar to us. A brightly lit ceiling with stained-glass windows welcomed in the sun's grand colors, and flags from every nation swung in signs of victory. The powerful choir sang and people stood lifting their hands, some with tears pouring, like the end of rainy season. But they weren't crying for the dead boy. They were like, happy in God. We were definitely in the minority here.

Then that strong old preacher got up to the podium. Even the air paid attention. His robe straight, fitting tight around the chest, glasses on the tip of his nose. It was clear he could handle himself in any barroom brawl or board meeting. Now, I remember at Grandma's church folks be walking in and out, or going to sleep. But this wise old fella's presence had presence. He peered over his black steel spectacles straight at the crowd.

He began to preach.

"I don't think we have any better witness that the Bible is true, then this young man lying here before us. This is proof, for the Word of God says in The Book to the Hebrew, chapter nine, verse twenty-seven. *"It's appointed once for men to die, and after this, huh, the judgment'."*

He'd be pausing a second between certain words to give the people a little time to get their 'amens' out.

Then he jumped back in again. "But, I want to tell you...that I did not come to preach...about this young man...because his life...preached...its own funeral for him."

"All right, preacher!" went all through the crowd.

"For you see...neither you nor I...can blame other people...no other race...for the death...of our children. These are...black men, dying by black hands...in black neighborhoods...and the only one suffering...is black folks...somebody don't hear me now, black people."

"You say that, preacher!" yelled a woman.

"Go head, sir! Come on here!" an old deacon rang out.

The cheers rang out as if they were daring him to shift gears and this train was moving with him.

His voice took "a tone" with his preaching.

"I did not come here...huh, to talk about death...but I came...to talk about...the good news...of life!" As he was going for it, a pretty lady with a big nice butt tipped over to the organ and gave him what Grandma called, "some running music."

"Jesus Christ," as he'd paused and took a deep breath, "came…that you might…have life." Then he made the old-school Baptist roll call. That took the place into overdrive.

"Cause he's a doctor… in the sick room!"

The crowd was gaining strength. They stood on their feet.

"He's a lawyer… in a courtroom!"

"Yeah!" The crowd answered.

"When I'm hungry…"

"Yeah!"

"Oh yeah…He's the bread…of life!"

With so much power in the room and no breakfast, I looked up for a sandwich to break right through the roof. I could taste a big fat burger with onions, and a lot of mayo. But this power in the place slammed my imagination back in my seat and right back in the message.

"And when I'm thirsty…come on, somebody…he's living water!" the preacher shouted. His specks vibrated on the tip of his nose.

"Living water, uh?" It was hot, my throat was dry, and so my mind crept back up to the roof again. I could see a ten foot tall cold glass of Kool-Aid with a lot of sugar. I heard of crack addicts having visions, too, but this was heavy.

The whole place was going up! Mack and his friends' eyes bucked out like fish out of water, and scared to move. The parents of the guy who died, in front with their hands lifted, told the preacher, "Preach on, man!"

One old lady was dancing. But not like in the club, but with the *Holy Ghost*.

As the preacher took it up another step, he pointed his finger at Michelle. She was crying, with her hands in the air. I looked over and went close to touch her, but she was like an electric outlet. I didn't want to get shocked. So what else could happen?

The preacher stopped, pointing in the air like he was talking to God, then started a song out that turned the party out!

"When I think about of His goodness, and all he's done for me! When I think of His goodness, and how he set me free! I could dance, dance, dance, dance, dance, dance, all night!"

The preacher took off running, the music took off running, and everybody in the church was up. The only thing that was missing was party hats, confetti, and balloons. I found out later in life after I came to my own experience with God, they where *Dancing in the Spirit*. I looked over for Michelle. She was gone! Like disappeared! She had taken off running down the isle. I looked around at everyone going and almost passed out myself. Some of Mack's boys were crying, some standing, clapping, some looking shell shocked. One of the guys was rubbing his face and arms, like something was on him.

"Mack, get it off! Get it off me, man!"

"Fool, ain't noth'n on you!" Mack tried to whisper, but was breaking his neck trying to get away from whatever was on that guy. He stood back and gave that brother some space to nut up. Something was on that boy and he wasn't going to stop until it was off. He got up and took off to the front where the preacher was. But the preacher saw him coming. Before he could say a word, that preacher laid his hands on that boy's head and started praying.

"In the name of Jesus!" yelled the preacher.

That cat hit the floor, bam! He was O.U.T.! I lay down in the seat and curled up in a little ball like a baby. The church celebrating was the broadcast on Grandma's radio tonight. Mack couldn't take being in an environment he could not control. He grabbed his do-rag, and like the silver ball being slammed by the bumpers in a pinball machine, buffaloed his way out.

The preacher let them go for a while, and then he calmed the music. He gave a life-stirring appeal to those who wanted to give their lives to Jesus. One by one, people raised their hands. And there was Michelle, on her knees right in front of the coffin in tears, make-up running everywhere (and *that* had never happened before) and shoeless. She had danced right out of them. Even some of Mack's boys raised their hands, snatching them do-rags off, and listening as if they had just got their hearing back from being deaf.

Dripping in sweat, as if he had walked through a waterfall, that old preacher led those standing and those near the coffin in a soul gripping prayer. The rest of the people in the pews prayed with him for those receiving Christ. Michelle, the loudest one of all, who was being held up by the sister who had been on the organ, made a change that would be the beginning of something different for her and me. It was something better, and something that was finally out of our control. Michelle used to talk about how sometimes when things were bad in our lives, it was like "having to walk through a grave yard, and feel somebody out there calling your name. You feel something bad was going to happen to you, you don't know why, and you can't stop it."

But after that service, she quit saying that.

The preacher stood there, a handkerchief covering his mouth, as a lot of people lay out on the floor. He said, "Leave them alone. God is working on them now."

The father of the dead boy got up in tears, pointed to the coffin, and turned to the crowd.

"This is my boy. I tried the best I could. And if he didn't know the Lord before now, it's too late! He could have known him as Savior, but now, he may have to know him as Judge. And to all of you young people here – if not his life, at least let this boy's death bring some of you all into the reality of Heaven and Hell. Stop this foolishness, and come back to God. For it's His power, His glory, and His kingdom. Because whatever you choose, it will be forever."

He brought his wife to his side as they stood before the

coffin. She turned to him and softly rested her face on his chest. As he whispered something to her, she looked up in his eyes with a radiating smile. They bent over the coffin, and kissed their son for the last time. He reached up and closed the coffin as the music played, took his wife by the hand, and the crowd followed him out.

We went home, and Michelle shared what happened with Grandma. Grandma shouted all over the house, "Thank you, Jesus! Thank you, Jesus!"

Michelle was so excited she took me down to that friend's house, whose boyfriend pulled a gun on her to tell her what happened. So happens, Michelle's friend was at the funeral in the back on the other side of the church. She gave her life to the Lord, too. Boy, they were just hugging and crying.

A few minutes later, the ex-boyfriend was at the door. They had broken up for the thousandth time. But from what Michelle said, this time was it. His bushy natural was wild, tangled, like sheep's wool with an Afro pick perched up. Looked like a rooster. Lips dry as the Sahara Desert, cracked, with white stuff on the side of his mouth and eyes red as tomatoes. But strangely, he was kind of quiet this time. He said he had quit his job at Crocker Bank and sold his car. He was leaving town since they wasn't going to be together. Then before she could say a word, out came the gun again and he started going off. But I think it blew his mind when she didn't curse back. Man, it threw me for a loop!

He stood there, shocked, shaking with her response. She put her arms out to him. He dug deep in the valley of his throat, pulling up from that sick green meadow at the cusp of his neck, and spit it in her face. Then he opened the revolver and took some bullets out, spun and slammed the chamber back in the gun. He pointed it at her chest.

"You know what? This is pimp game here, and one of us got to bring this all to an end. And guess what? Since I got the gun, ha-ha, guess that makes me the shot caller. You'll get yours first!"

But before pulling the trigger, he switched up again. He put the gun to his head. I was confused.

"No! Why you always think you got to be first? People like you ain't first, with a powerhouse like me."

Then he opened the gun again, spun the chamber, slammed it back in. He's got it back at her chest. "I'm picking now. Here! This-what-you-get!"

He squeezed the trigger. Click! Nothing happened. Yet the empty sound changed the temperature in the room. Its echo gripped the walls of a midnight hallway, but the intent was explosive.

The red exited his eyes. They turned white. Then he put the gun under his chin. His vocal cords swallowed a refrigerated chill, blowing out hopelessness.

"You know. It's still my choice, right baby? I guess I finally get it. I was the real fool? You can see me go. I hope you glad! "

He screamed and pulled the trigger.

Boom!

The rich darkness was amplified. The magnum's cannon ignited, releasing the firing pin to slam, connecting dead center to the primer head. The explosive powder chambered with the power of a thousand horsemen launched the hollow-point missile, escaping out of its casing at one thousand fifty feet per second. It spiraled, being etched and engraved by the walls, as it barreled toward the covered exit.

It was instant 4th of July. But this was November?

With the contact of external ballistics, his chin surface disappeared in the implosion. The entry dug a black hole, shattering his lower jawbone like porcelain. The top of his head exploded as the projectile exited through the ceiling, crashing right into the bottom of the stove leg on the next floor. The lady upstairs was so used to the noise that she didn't even stop cooking her chicken. His mouth became like the Nile River, pouring its morbid contents over the banks of his lips with rapid force. His body jerked stiff, his bowels split, blowing feces down through his socks loading his shoes with wet red stinking carnage. He fell like a sliced cedar of Lebanon. Blood poured from the ceiling, like morning rain drops on my head. He crashed right at my feet.

Michelle and her friend screamed. Grabbing his limp body, her friend was crying for him not to die like this. Michelle picked up the phone and called for help. I'm just sitting there, motionless and now more desensitized as ever. Emotionless; I don't feel anything. As blood pumps from the exit of his cracked head, it puddles into the rug, and runs under my feet. I took my fingers and touched the top of my head where the moisture landed. I looked at my hand.

I wondered, what kind of funeral will this be?

Chapter 5
Home is a Rural Maze,
With No Exits!

1988. Jessie Jackson attempted to become Mr. President one more time. His chant rang as he tried to teach us, "Keep Hope Alive!" I was a tenth grader at Balboa High School. Grandma said something about being glad for anything positive that had a face like mine on it. Yeah, right. Radios blasted in the quad during class-change periods. Some of us had the forty-five dollar Jerry-Curls, and for others who couldn't afford to go to the shop and had to do them at home, they wore K.D.'s (kitchen dew) scary-curls.

Lunch was either a hard-bun sandwich at the corner store, Tic-Toc's on Ocean Street, or the school beanery, which wasn't bad. They had fat chocolate cake and cold milk. We would be cursing in the halls, until you got anywhere in the vicinity of room 321. It got quiet then. And we would act up in every other class, but not this one; biology. I'll never forget him.

Mr. H. Hortan. To us the 'H' meant, "He'll handle it right there." He had a reputation better than some of the baddest guys in the hood, and he knew it like the back of his hand. I found out later in life that he knew it so well because as a youngster, he helped make it 'the hood.' Michelle had him as a teacher and warned us not to test him because he came from what they called, 'old school.' But you know us, you can't tell us nothing 'bout no old school!

Our boy Bammy had to test the waters. He was one of the few guys we knew whose daddy lived at home. But it was funny, his momma was big and young, but his daddy was old and still tried to dress like he was young. He'd be done up like a funky Christmas tree with some gold-rimmed *Kango* glasses and matching hat turned backward, a *Members Only Jacket* with nylon pants, the works. You could tell Bammy something, he'd believe it, get pumped up, and go and do something stupid. Yet, in the back of our minds, we'd kind of felt it could be dangerous to play with Mr. Hortan. He had what was termed his greatest statement: "I refuse to tolerate disrespect from a child."

One day we told Bammy to reach in Mr. Hortan's briefcase. Touching anything without Mr. Hortan's permission was "disrespect." Mr. Hortan had his back to us at the board. We thought he didn't see what Bammy was doing. Bammy's hand was good and in when, "slam!" Mr. Hortan dropped his weight in Big-Time Wrestling style on that briefcase lid, right on Bammy's hand, and locked it. Almost cut the boys arm off! Bammy's holler went so high it turned into a Swedish yodel, "Yaaa-heee!" That momentary screeching sound felt like it ran forever. We sat there too scared to move. When Mr. Hortan opened the briefcase and let him lose, Bammy snatched his hand out. Then my boy messed up. He got up in Mr. Horton's face, well, as tall as he was, in Mr. Hortan's chest. I'd seen Bammy pull this on his momma one time when his daddy was gone for awhile, and it didn't work then. But today, this was his 'being broke from that' day.

Mr. Hortan grabbed him around the neck, took him off the ground, and pinned him to the chalkboard. Bammy's whole body imprint was a chalked shadow. Dust flew everywhere. You know as I look at it now, we should have considered that Mr. Hortan wasn't a small boy, excuse me, small man anyway. Bammy's eye's (which were all that could move) rolled toward us as if he was trying to communicate something. Come and save me? The pressurized grip was causing his eye sockets to extend to their limits. But Mr. Hortan said sternly, "If any of you young people even think about moving, I'll break his neck, then yours."

Now, our little crew around school had a reputation for rat-packing folks. Sometimes we'd push kids around, other times we'd just circle one in and he'd give up the money. But every now and then, we ran into some kid who wouldn't play that, like this small stick of Korean dynamite named Tim. We tried to pick on him at the beginning of school. He did a spinning roundhouse-kick and kicked the ice cream right off the top of Johnny Butler's cone, and landed flat-footed. Brother never took his backpack off. We figured it was better to have him with us, than against us. He was our Bruce Lee, and loved him some sistas.

Mr. Hortan's warning gripped our throats. None of us moved. Actually, we froze like cold ducks. Our butts were so tight in those seats, if someone would have farted, the class might have blown up. Mr. Hortan's eyes were fixed like flint, veins popped out of the hand that gripped Bammy's throat, and a white starched shirt that showed straight muscles up to the neck. It was the most professional intimidating sight we had ever seen. Bammy tried to struggle. Mr. Hortan's grip squeezed tighter. Awe! We heard it when it tightened a notch! Bammy eyes could be compared to a thousand watt light bulb.

He dropped Bammy to the floor and told him calmly, "Young man, take your seat."

Bammy staggered like 'Too Drunk Dennis' at the corner store to his seat and sat down. He was grasping for air, holding his throat and his chest. Both vital organs were probably highly pissed at him for what he had put them through. The impressive finger painting of Mr. Hortan's grip was still on his throat. He had our full attention now.

"If any of you young people have a problem controlling yourselves, I will help you exercise self-control and self discipline. If you want to tell your parents that there's a teacher who will put his hands on you if you approach him in a threatening manner, and they have a problem with that, tell them to come see me directly. I've got what you need to succeed and I've been where you are going. I refuse to be part of the problem, and you are my project and the solution. You will learn in this class."

Well, not a parent showed up to object. Mainly, because none had the guts to even try to justify our behavior. And if some of our parents showed up clowning, it wouldn't take long before they got their hats handed back to them with truth from Mr. Hortan.

He never had a problem out of any one of us again.

Toward Bammy's end of high school, his dad died. Mr. Hortan, without anybody knowing it, helped Bammy's family with the funeral and took Bammy under his wing. The future held something great for Bammy, today better known as Bernard. He's somewhere practicing medicine.

One day we had an experiment with mazes. The woodshop class built them, easy and hard ones. We had to train mice how to complete the mazes. The experiment went well until Mr. Hortan brought in this funny maze with no exits. He had us all standing around watching the mice. After a while those mice that easily completed other mazes began to show signs of what Mr. Hortan called "confusion." One mouse we named "Bandit," was the leader. But when he couldn't find any exits, he began roughing up the other mice. The third day, we got scared. The mice began to fight each other. When one would remain in one place not moving, the other mice would attack it. It got so bad that we had to keep them apart.

Mr. Hortan said, "That's what happens to mankind when he has to survive in the same kind of environment." I thought about that very hard. Then he took a poll. "How many of you young people have ever traveled out of the state of California?" About twenty-eight of us were in the class. Four others and I raised our hands. "How many of you have been in another city in this state, but more than one hundred miles away?" Out of those other twenty-three, ten raised their hands. "How many have been fifty miles away?" Three more raised their hands.

"Okay, how many of you have never been out of this city and all you really know is your neighborhood and downtown?" Out of twenty-eight kids, ten raised their hands.

Mr. Hortan paused, the corner of each eye filled with one glass tear. "You young people who have never been out away from this city may be affected by something called Mental Environmental Limitation Delay."

One of the kids in the ten said, "What's that? You saying because we haven't been no where, we don't think we somebody like other folks, like we weird or something?"

"I'm not saying you do, I'm saying you may be affected and are unaware you are," answered Mr. Hortan

Mr. Hortan walked toward the maze and called us over. "Take the mice in the maze. When they had a place of entry and exit, they were fine. But when their exits were taken away, they began to fight amongst each other. Their senses of escape have been removed and unbeknownst to them, they have to escape even if it is from each other."

While Mr. Hortan and the other student were talking, I looked out the window and went off in a daydream about our vacation last summer. Grandma and Uncle Big Toe took Michelle and me to Alabama for a family reunion. It was my first time being a long ways away. Michelle always took me on the bus to other cities to visit, but this time we rode in Uncle's cozy van. It had big tires and big windows in the back with the psychedelic colors on the outside.

I didn't know that there was that much world to see! That van crossed a lot of land, which led to some big cities, and right through some Indian reservations. It took us five days to get there and we stayed in some nice hotels. Uncle spent big money on us and called up room service. You know when you're not used to nothing, you try to order everything. He traveled a lot and ate all kinds of food, stuff I had never heard of.

When we got to Alabama, it was countryyyyyyy. And I

mean country…Cows, old barns, ants, and oh lord, it was hot! We tried to stay with a cousin for one day who didn't have an air conditioner. Michelle and I couldn't take it and complained so much that Uncle put us in a hotel. At one cousin's house the toilet was outside and they called it 'the-out-house,' and now, I'm tripping!

Man, I swung the door open and the funk rushed out! A big old horse fly came out and Michelle and I went running. And check this out; if you had to use the bathroom at night, they had "Da Slop Jar!" It was a pot, covered with a towel, and a little water in it and if you had some, a little bleach. That's it! I walked in one time and saw Michelle sitting on it and got sick. I couldn't take it. I ran, got a camera, and took her picture on it. She started hollering for Grandma to get me. I was gone.

Uncle Big Toe and Grandma were like kids back home. He showed us land their dad owned and it was a lot. He told us hopefully he could start something on it and maybe we could keep it going in the family. I kind of snickered under my breath thinking, I ain't living in nobody's country. All I ever heard of the country was the KKK and to stay out of it.

The bell rang, pushing me out of my daze.

"Tomorrow we are going to open some wounds in our society," Mr. Hortan said. "If you want to stay after school, I'm taking whoever wants to stay late home after our trip. We are going to see our own society in their mazes. How many of you young people will be going?" Almost all of us raised our hands. He put his hand up to his forehead in happiness and shock at the same time. "Well, I'll bring my van. Maybe I'll need two? Get your permission slips signed and bring them back. Dinner is on me, have a good evening."

We all screamed, "Yeah!"

On the ride home for once, my thoughts sat me down quietly on the bus. I began to explore how my maze ran to Grandma's house. The bus I caught went a certain way. Not just a certain route, but because of the neighborhood, a certain way. In our neighborhood, we had certain drivers, mainly black, not stopping in certain places because of the activity on the corner. It was the first time I noticed that the drivers sat behind a plastic shield with bars across, somewhat cage-like. Very straight, un-talkative robots whose mission was "just get to the end without any trouble." I peeked over the shoulder of someone reading a newspaper and looked at the pictures. For once I decided to do something different and at least read the heading of what was going on other than my ten-block world.

'Pan-Am 747 explodes over Lockerbie, Scotland in possible terror attack.' Huh, where is that?

'Magic and Lakers unstoppable in Detroit,' Go Magic, that's my boy.

'China Celebrates Year of the Dragon.' Enter the Dragon, yeah, I liked that movie. Man, I wanted some shrimp fried-rice now.

'*Hustler Magazine* hustles Jerry Farwell out of $200,000.' Got some fine white girls in them centerfolds. None of this ain't got nothing to do with me. I'm back to pictures again.

As I rode I saw Joe-Joe standing out by the liquor store where his daddy used to stand. The boy was in the exact same spot with his hands in his pants scratching himself, probably with some dirty drawers on too. His daddy was in prison.

A few blocks away was my stop. I got off the bus right in front – guess what, a liquor store. I looked up the block, a liquor store. Walked down the block and turned the corner. The smell of urine invisibly hooked around me and, another liquor store.

Once home I decided to do something different instead of sitting in front of the TV. I wanted to find all the liquor stores in my maze. After I drank me some Kool-Aid, I got on my bike and hit the streets. Almost at every turn sat a liquor store with a bunch of folks standing outside. Some pickled and stanking, some puffing and leaning, some just standing there in another place and time in their minds.

Okay, Emmanuel, what next? Let me see how many beauty parlors and barbershops were here? Around the blocks, about half as many of them as liquor stores. How many banks? Now everybody had money on the first and fifteenth, what we call "Mother's Day." (*Give the motha' his, and this motha' hers, and so on.*) I almost rode for an hour before I found one. I guess we had settled for the local pharmacy where Grandma pays her PG&E, the check-cashing places that charged an arm and a leg, and the corner store for our banks. The Arabs would cash that check for you in a heartbeat, believe that.

Now with all the guns in my neighborhood, many I had personally seen, I knew there would be a lot of gun stores, but I couldn't find one. I rode for two hours till my calves hurt, but still no gun stores. No gun stores? So how did so many get here? Maybe the stories about 'the train' were not so far fetched after all. The mid-night vans just showing up? Un-locked? Full of weapons? Maybe that wasn't a lie?

Tired, I started home. My Mondays are my Tuesdays with the same old faces, standing and sitting in the same old places, doing the same old thing since I was small. Shots fired a few blocks over, I flinched but wasn't scared, sirens going, police on the street.

And with all the foolishness on our part, we stayed for supposedly 'safety reasons' in our own mazes. To protect ourselves from whom? Why go anywhere else for excitement and mayhem? Here, we create our own calamity.

The next day, only ten kids had permission to go. "Get your things," said Mr. Hortan, "and remember we are not going to the zoo, nor are we from the zoo, nor are we going to the White House. We are going to where we live, but I believe we will see it in a different light from now on."

We walked to his van, which was bad! And there was plenty of room.

He hit us with something that was new to all the fellows.

"Gentlemen, open the door for our ladies."

""Psss! Our ladies, baaa!" I said

"And you wonder why other people disrespect our mothers and sisters?" Mr. Hortan's eyes were wide, flashing for the dare of a foolish answer! "Men, until you learn to respect your own women, you'll never respect each other, you'll never respect yourselves."

I said, "Yeah, you right."

"You are right, who?"

"You're right, sir."

"Thank you, young man," Mr. Hortan said with a smile.

All of us knuckleheads rode in this custom-made van like the kind in a low-rider magazine. He had soft music playing and a microphone to speak through so all of us could hear him because we were talking so loud.

"Aaa, Mr. Hortan! How you afford this kind of stuff on your old school pay."

"Emmanuel," he answered, "do you mean to state correctly, 'How can I afford this vehicle on my salary?'"

"Yeah, that's what I was trying to say."

"Well, there are many things that I do or did in which none of you know about. Like having a master's degree, taught in college, having my own business, and owning property in some areas."

"Wow," the whole vanload sang like a choir.

As we drove along he shared some deep things with us. He pulled to a stop sign and stopped. He looked in his rear view mirror and took a deep breath, which caught all our attention. "You see, I set my wages in what I want to give the school system for my time, talent, knowledge, and effort. I don't settle for what they decided to give me. I'm in demand. So the only one who can put a limit on what I am worth is me, and I declare, 'I have no limitations!'" With that kind of knowledge being poured out, we couldn't say a word. Just rode in the van looking stupid.

As the van went down the road he said, "We'll go see a

Latin maze."

Carla Gonzales was sitting in the front. "Yeah, that's my maze, *hombres*," bobbing her head and popping her gum, thinking she bad or something. Now, she fine with a big chest, but she was young and stupid, too. When she talked, her nose was always up like she smelled something and eyes squinted as if the sun were in her face. She was loud and never wore a blouse with sleeves. Sexy hot, make-up strong, but looked just a little musty. We never smelled her, she just looked it. We heard she was going with this old dude with a lot of tattoos and did anything he said. Last week we saw her riding with him in this low rider when she was supposed to been in school. She slipped up and said he named her his 'mid-night snack,' but by the expression on her face she may have not been ready for what was required to be served on the menu.

You know Mr. Hortan had to bring her back to reality, too. "Young lady, will you be able to get out if the exits get closed?"

Her crazy smile went soft, and the smack of her gum leveled out because she could pop it.

As we drove through, we saw the same thing in all the poor mazes. Liquor stores, gunshots, violence, and people out on the corners. Nothing was different except the color of the skin. Foolishness was foolishness.

Mr. Hortan hit us with something new. "I'm going to take you to a rich maze now." He drove for awhile until we got to the hills, twisting and turning. Big dark trees stood reminding you of soldiers in armor guarding the road then finally up to this big gate. Lights so bright we could barely see who was coming up to the window. It was a security guard. When his shadow cleared and our eyes locked in on that big .45 on his hip, all of our hearts dropped down into our shoes. I guess we expected him to tell us all to get out and lay on the ground. He walked over to Mr. Hortan's window and said, "Hello sir, are these your students?"

74

"Yes, these are all mine," he answered.

"Okay sir, have a nice evening." Then he looked at us and said, "Enjoy yourselves. You students have the opportunity of a lifetime to study under this man!" Then he walked back to open the gate.

We all started looking at each other. I guess this was the pearly gates in heaven Grandma talked about.

As we drove, we saw houses that were out of this world! Mr. Hortan showed us where different entertainers, movie stars, and rich folks lived.

When we pulled up to this big white mansion with pillars, all us kids yelled, "All Wowwwww!"

He turned around and looked at us. "This is the only time I'll let you people scream in my presence." Then he looked at the house. "Wowwww!" We all burst out laughing.

Mr. Hortan got out of the van. "Everybody out and make yourselves at home."

He got out, but didn't anybody else move! We were stuck.

He walked over and looked in the window. "Did you hear me? Get out people!"

Carla, whose lips were poked out like a puffer fish and looking like she saw a ghost said, "And go where? In *there*?"

"Yes, my wife is waiting to see all of you. Let's not keep her waiting."

So we got out.

Tim, my Korean buddy who was just as black as us said, "Hey, don't forget to open the door for our ladies."

"Yeah, you right, Tim," all the boys said. And that's what we did.

When we got to the door, Mr. Hortan rang the doorbell. Man, you would have thought you were at an old white church when the church organ wiring went berserk with all them kind of bells ringing. Then this Spanish lady answered the door. Her Spanish English was tight. "Are these our lovely children?"

I whispered to Carla, "Is dis yo momma?"

She whispered back, "No. But I wish she was."

"Yes, these are all our children," Mr. Hortan said.

"We've been waiting for you all." Then she started kissing and squeezing our cheeks like you do fat babies. I guess we were in so much shock, we didn't mind.

As we walked in, I thought we would need bibs to put under our mouths to keep us from drooling on the carpet. Beautiful paintings, vases with real flowers in them, and mirrors everywhere. You'd see yourself so much, you'd almost get scared. We went down a marble hallway into the big ballroom. Wrong. It was the den. And they had it set up as an all-you-can-eat place too! People to serve it too!

"Young people, gather around," Mr. Hortan said. "I want you to feel at home. I'm not worried about anyone taking or breaking anything. Wherever you want to go and look around, just feel free, it's okay."

"Thank you, Mr. Hortan," we all said together.

"Oh, my God," a soft voice said behind us.

We turned around. It was a beautiful woman. I mean she was a new Lena Horne knockout!

"This ladies and gentleman, is my wife, Mrs. Hortan."

"Wow, Mr. Hortan, I didn't know you had it in you," I said. "You got a bad one."

"No, I got the bad one," Mrs. Hortan said as she put her arms around his waist.

"Mr. Hortan, ol'wild boy! Oops, that slipped." I covered my mouth real quick. Everybody looked at me. I felt as if I was about to be stoned.

Mr. Hortan looked over his glasses and winked at me. "Okay, son."

"Well, come on, let's have a good time," said Mrs. Hortan.

And that's what we did. Mr. Hortan had people in white serving us food and everything. Mrs. Hortan had some of her professional friends style all the girls' hair, put make-up on them. Man, she had them girls looking good, even the ugly ones had it going on. After we played and danced, we went around and toured. We asked a million questions, and Mr. Hortan gave a million answers. He was a literal walking-history machine. He had purchased a lot of things, some were from slavery time. We asked him why. Then Mr. Hortan sat us all down in the den and *talked to us*, not at us.

"When we are at school, I talk to you not to degrade you, but so you can receive what you need. My life's desire and goal is that you get the necessary tools in life so you do not just survive, but also succeed. I understand who has to receive in my classroom, and it is every one of you. This is not about me. I've got what I need, and it's not money."

I said, "Not money? You got to get paid? Then what you here for?"

"I'm glad you asked that question," answered Mr. Hortan

He paused a second. Something was going on in his mind. The time machine of thoughts sent him back to pick up specific needed fragments of information for us, even as Jesus once told his disciples after feeding the multitude of those following him for the wrong reason, "pick up the remaining fragments." Why, Lord? That none be lost.

Mr. Hortan did not want us lost.

His waving finger was a ready pen, his forehead tight and wrinkled pressing to push something forward. "Any person who works, especially in teaching and is just there to get a paycheck, is there for the wrong reason!"

"Wait, wait, wait!" Tim said with his mouth twisted, one eye closed. "You mean to tell me that if a person is working to get paid, that's not the reason to work?"

"No, Tim," Mr. Hortan said. He got down on one knee real close for Tim to hear his heart beat. "Listen to what I said. Working to receive is not the issue, but the reason for the work has to be defined and the motive clear."

Tim's pupils were clear as a freshly polished hallway. He was open.

We were all shell shocked not knowing which way Mr. Hortan would go. He clapped and blew in the space between his thumbs as he thought how to get his message across to us. Then all of a sudden, it hit him.

"Let's take for instance the medical profession. A doctor must put care or health care first, then payment for their labor. They receive pay whether or not their patients are healthy or not, but the focus is to care for their client's well being. Life and death are many times in every decision they make, and most people continue with one certain doctor their entire life because of the care they receive. A trust is built over time and even when that person dies, the family believes their doctor has given them the best care humanly possible. People go to a medical specialist despite the cost, because the care is for their benefit. You must have a reason why you do what you do, and it must be to first give, and then receive. A giving heart must be the call, not just receiving. Care. Giving. They will always pay for themselves."

"Well Mr. Hortan, why do you work?" Tim asked with this real straight face.

That statement penetrated Mr. Hortan right in the chest. The passion of his heart reached into Tim's hopeless eyes. He paused again. "Because I owe my people and your people, my community, my parents, my ancestry, and my heritage everything. What was done for me so I could get out of my maze, someone paid a serious price. Some lived long enough that I was able to personally honor them, yet many died before I could give them their just due. They did it so I could ride anywhere on the bus, even though many of you all still feel it's cool for you have to sit on the back of the bus. Today, I chose to ride the bus. I choose if I will give up my seat to someone. Sometimes I do, other days everybody got to stand. It's always my choice. Somebody died so I can make my choice. To go to college, to excel, to do what I do, it cost somebody everything."

His words were showers to the souls of us kids who didn't know we were dying of thirst. "I can't afford to ever forget that. I owe them, and I owe you." He turned and looked Carla in the eyes. "What I mean when I say, I owe you, is I owe you the truth. About letting you know what's out there. How the young man you're dating means you no good. On how he's using you, child. How society is not for, but against you. And if they can keep you in fear, scared to leave because of the system of your own foolish wars among yourselves, keep you in your own little corners because you're concentrated, closed-in like rats, you will fight and devour one another. And as long as you're fighting each other, they just come in and clean up the blood when it's over.

"So I'm here to let you see life from a helicopter point of view and to give back. Not so some of you can make it big and then just leave and forget where you came from, but to go back and rebuild what you've once destroyed. If you don't learn this, we die from the inside!"

Mr. Hortan slowly dropped his head. You couldn't have bought the silence in that room. The melody of the night was the light drops of rain on the window...

79

Chapter 6
Both My Wolves Hollered,
"You Set You Up!"

Even with all of Mr. Hortan's concern and teaching, some of us still decided to catch on when we felt like it. And guess who was the leader of the pack? Me! I was eighteen years old, out of school, not by choice, and you know what my problem was, I knew everything. You couldn't tell me noth'n! I was a pretty mixture of my momma and daddy, had a little-yokes-on body you could see through my *Members Only Jacket*, and in my mind "the world better look out for me."

Michelle and I moved out near Woodrow Wilson High School off Mansell Avenue about four months ago. No conflict with Grandma, just that Michelle was doing okay, and now she wanted us to go for it on our own.

Now, you know we had to make one emergency return to Grandma's house when that eviction notice just magically appeared on our door. We had to learn that people weren't playing when they said, 'pay or quit.' Michelle quit, so we had to git. Thus, paperwork was posted on the front door. Michelle played it off. Right till them sheriffs was at the front door.

You could hear them banging loud on the door, "Boom! Boom! Boom! Boom! Boom!" but Michelle was told by some crazy girl (she didn't hardly know) not to answer it. The girl said, "They ain't gone put you and yo boy on the street. You just play sleep and they'll go away. That's what I did at my last place, girl."

Well, they may not put you on the street, but they will escort you and your stuff to the curb. That locksmith popped that lock, and they were up in the house strong. We didn't have 'not a thing' packed, because again, we didn't think we were going anywhere. But I found out something–legal papers don't lie. You can play like you don't see or hear them, but they are saying something. Them sheriffs was very nice and gave us all of fifteen minutes to get whatever we could carry. We had to get the rest later. Yet embarrassing as that was, the next time we did it right. So pay yo rent!

I got a piece of a car from Mack before he went to jail. Remember that big cover up when those guys got killed years ago? Well, it got uncovered. Somebody in that so called "so-tight bunch" unraveled under pressure. The police in their investigation picked up Mack and about four others. I went to visit him on the sixth floor every weekend. His attorney told him he would be out soon and he still was talking that same old talk. How he'd been framed and how he was going to sue the system. He's always got a new way of running thangs, and still at war behind bars. Going through the visiting process was sick, because the police treat you as if everybody's a criminal. And a whole new breed of people coming to visit inmates acted like they got some crime in them. Ghetto visiting ghetto, ain't nothing nice. As much as I denied it, I got a kick out of people noticing me.

"You just like yo daddy."

This big iron door goes 'pop.' Here came my daddy. Walking with that old pimp walk, county-jail hair wave, dressed in all orange. His under-the-mattress pressed pants on looking like he a Florida fruit tree, caged in through six inches of glass. We'd start out talking loud and never checked the volume.

"Little Mack, when I get out, me and you going to kick it like real partners," Mack said.

I answered back with a grumble in my voice, "My name is Emmanuel. You know my grandma never like anyone calling me Little Mack. Man, why you do that? Don't spoil it every time we talk!"

"What you mean 'spoil it when we talk'? I call you who

you are. Do you know who you talk'n to, boy? I'm yo daddy."

"Yeah, I know who I'm talk'n to. So why you trying to always roll up on me like I'm some punk. I come down here and every time you either go squirrel, or skunk on me. You too busy talking about the next hustle you thinking about, or how they treat you because you locked up. Don't put that on me. I see why nobody come see yo mean behind and you talk'n to me crazy?"

Mack sat back and went into full pimp mode. "Look Mack, be cool, because you talk'n to Mack. You can't get away from who you are. I know you been listening to some people trying to tell you about other thangs in life, but this is life for you. You better look at it good, because I'm you and you me. I'm all up in you, yo blood, yo electric bass, yo walk, yo salty taste. It's me, you ah Mack rat!"

Mack's mug face stank. Heat and mist seeped through his teeth and his lips sprayed puffs of hatred into the atmosphere. His words cut across his viper tongue with precision. "Listening to ya momma and grand-momma talk that crazy stuff about you growing up and being somebody. You is somebody, boy!" as he slammed his hand on the table, "Me!"

My eyes locked, my tongue curled ready to strike back.

"Momma and Grandma still call me stupid for running down here to see you all the time. Got to go check on my daddy? The pinned-up pimp."

Mack spit blasted out like acid all over the glass. "Ya momma crazy, and Grandma ain't noth'n but an old b—"

Before the "i" drove off the tip of his tongue, I slammed the receiver down in his face. It was on! The other visitors had begun to end their visiting calls quickly because they knew the sitcom episode coming next. Mack jumped up, slammed his phone down, and slung curses at me through the glass. I jumped up and started cursing him back.

"You can't talk about my grandma, dude! I'll kick yo a—"

Before I got the last word out, them deputies rolled in

there with military style and power.

One deputy on Mack's side told him to calm down, but he wouldn't. He snatched his do-rag off, and started cursing the deputy. "This ain't no L.A. and ain't no Rodney King up in here! This Mack! I shocks it here!"

Then he grabbed the phone, and used it as an axe against the window; his face and mouth evolved into a fireball of rage. The deputy said something on his radio. Mack went off. So they went off. Four, five, six against one, and that fool knew he didn't have a chance. See, it was hype in the jail to have other inmates know you fought a lot of cops. They drug him out, probably whipped his butt too, like Rodney King. The one he should have got when he was little.

Two deputies came to me and told me to leave. My chest flailing, mouth stretched out of contusion like the Riddler. But I saw the whipping they had put on my dad. Needless to say, I opted out of a full confrontation. I just eye balled them and farted loud as I hit the button before getting on the elevator. Left them police a little somethin to remember me by.

I left angry as a bull with hot sauce in his eye. And I was pumped. Mack taught me never let anybody sucker me. So I didn't know how to take it when he did. Now, all I wanted to do was hurt something or somebody. I was out the jail and ready to leave when I see a little light left on inside of my yellow 1978 AMC Pacer Station Wagon.

It had the style as if a giant had stepped on it, making the headlights buck out. My battery was too weak and it wouldn't start. Got to be more careful! Had a job interview set up by Mr. Hortan and guess what? Missed that! He had warned me that if anything got me off track I'd miss it, and oh, my God, if he wasn't right! I couldn't graduate off stage and had to go to summer school if I wanted to get my diploma, too.

So I ran to the bus stop to get on the bus. No money!

When the bus pulled up, I just walked up on it and stared at the bus driver. He looked at me and turned his head, never saying a word.

I went and pounced down in a seat.

I was pumped. All the people on the bus knew it. A man sitting toward the front of the bus looked at me too long.

"What you looking at, old man!" I yelled. He turned his head quickly.

"What's up, what you want? You want some of me! Here it is! Anybody wants some! Get some!"

Nobody moved as I stood on the middle of the bus twirling around with my hands in the air.

"You know me!" I started pointing at them as I danced doing the robot. "You, you, you know me. What's my name? What's my, my, my name?"

People so scared they played like they didn't hear me. One dude didn't raise his gaze up off his newspaper.

A high rush hit me. I was in control. I was in power. "Hey, bus driver! Stop the bus!" The bus came to a slow stop. "I'm getting off here! Remember this face! Alls yous peoples have a nice day now, ya hear!"

I jumped off the bus about ten blocks from home. I turned and waved at the people on the bus as I started walking home with an old 70's pimp walk.

"Hey, Little Mack," somebody yelled.

"What's up, baby!" I yelled back, pointing in that direction.

Mack had a reputation here, and whether good or bad because of him, I got respect. His name was my protection, but what was I to do with his, our life?

"Lil Mack running thangs!" somebody else shouted out.

I threw the '60s' power sign up, smiling inside. I was pumped. A high pump. Mack used to play this song in his car "Superfly" and I was feeling all of that right now. I needed Mack in me when I hit the streets. He dealt with life in the moment, and because his moment could change at anytime. Little caught him off guard.

The only problem with that was someone else always controlled the climate, which made him always have to adjust, keeping him just one step behind. To him life was fun and wild, but he was never in control of it. Even when he was calling the shots, it was because of what someone else fired. I was now living in reaction of his actions. And I was still walking.

Everything goes up in size with years, even me. The '90s showed some might and madness of its own. The west coast offensive dream-team Forty-Niner's lost to the punk New York Giants and wasn't going to Super Bowl XXV. That took much of our little chump change, but the U.S. was showing its strength in Operation Desert Storm.

General Colin Powell was at the helm and all of America stood in respect, knowing this brother was handling business. "Take out communication." That's all we can remember. Boy, shut them dowwwn! Wasn't about color then, just kick some butt coming and going. But just land that emotional airplane because local chaos still show our other ugly hand. L.A. tried its best to clear the air and indicted four cops after the almost live electrocution of our boy, Rodney. Never thought a hundred dollar camcorder could put a billion dollar metropolis on trial.

The world of horror took a shift from the screen and went too real beyond any writer's creativity with Jeffery Dahmer and his *literal appetite* for cold boy prostitutes. That freaked us out and had us scared to eat Spam sandwiches for months.

Grandma used to warn Michelle all the time about letting me watch the *Pee-Wee Herman Show*, until he got caught messing with himself in the theater. Even the Supreme Court had its night behind the shadow with the hands-on deal of Clarence Thomas and Anita Hill. Everybody, no matter at what level, had some freak in them.

We were coming home from church one day and it started raining ashes. The Oakland Hills were up in flames and the fire departments were unable to get enough water to it. You would have thought it was Christmas with snow flakes falling in San Francisco.

We sat silent in front of the TV when Magic told the world he had AIDS. AIDS, what was that? Everybody from the too young to the too old who had been playing under the covers uncovered, was at Grandma's clinic the next day. And I was still walking.

About two blocks away from my house on Silver Ave was a store. I was thirsty but didn't have no money. I ought to go in and just take it. But I had a little sense to know that everyone was not scared of us, and if this store had been in business here for any length of time wasn't because of us running in and taking things. Muhammad got something behind the counter to handle anything or anybody who came in that store acting a fool.

Next door was a house with a guy looking out of the second-story window.

"Lil'l Mack, ah, I mean, Emmanuel!" It was Dace, a well-known dope dealer and friend of Mack. The dude was known as one who could not be trusted even in the most crooked of deals. "What you want, man? You need a little money, little man?"

"Yeah," I said.

"Look, go in the store. Get me an Old English and get ya self somethin. Tell him to put it on Dace's tab."

"So it's like that, hum?"

"Just go in and don't forget my drink, boy."

So I went in the store. "Dace sent me over to get some things. Put it on his tab."

"Okay, just bring it up," said the man behind the counter.

I got Dace an Old English and got me a bunch of junk.

"That's comes to eight dollars and fifty-six cents." He handed me the bag and walked away. I thought, is this how it is?" Man, that was too easy.

When I got to Dace's house, he met me at the door. He

looked in the bag, looked at me, pulled out his old English, and crunched up his nose with that one gold tooth showing.

"Look's like with yo appetite, you need a job, baby?" He smiled like The Grinch That Stole Christmas. "Dace and yo daddy always talked about setting up a business for our boys. Wan'na work?" He walked over to the window and sat on the ledge looking out. "Make a little money, make a lot of money. Drive a raggedy car, drive a new ride. Have one woman or a whole sack of freaks for the week! So what' cha want, little man?"

I looked up, sucking my bottom lip in. I had no money, the broken-down car my daddy gave me, and just met this new girl named Sandy. I saw her one day toward the end of school with little Mexican mama Carla who helped introduce us. She gave me a little four-one-one on Sandy, so I wouldn't make a complete fool out of myself too fast and blow the whole rap from jump-street.

The first time I called, I made a little small talk with a suggestive song playing low in the background. *"Tonight you can get it, get it, get it, girl. Anytime. Tonight is fine."* Now you know me, the Mack-a-doe-shish straight shooter, I kind of asked Sandy in a round about way about sex.

I felt her walk right through that phone and cut that line with a straight razor. She made it very clear she wasn't giving up no booty, to nobody! Told me it was a sin and after her first baby, she wasn't going through no-moe baby-daddy drama again if she wasn't married. So I backed up off that conversational piece quickly. I had to respect what she stood for. Really, I didn't have a choice, so I'd had to take whatever place I could get with her for now, which was nowhere.

But I didn't stop me from being me.

"I'm in, man."

"All ride. Come on, let me get you started," Dace said.

So I was on my way in the drug bidness. At first I was just the pick-up man. Pick up this and take it there, pick up there and take it here. The job was to just make sure everything got to where it was supposed to. No dope better not wind up missing and no money better either, or you'd wind up missing. You'd be some new mats on somebody car floor. That's if they found some traces of you left! This taught you your first and valuable lesson of the game: "How to look out for stuff." And it gave you a new taste for more.

After a month Dace said, "Now, I'm going to let you make your own money because I promised ya jail-bird daddy I'd look out for you."

I jumped back. "What's all this, you ripping at my dad, Dace? You know you wouldn't be doing that if he was here." I kind of checked him a little.

"All right, little Mack Piz-zack. I know you got yo daddy's back, thick'n thin. I'm just making mention of his present-day incarcerational situation." He made it sound big, so I let it go. He pinched between his eyebrows and got serious.

"But you got to stay off other people's property. Other people have crossed me, Mack, trying to grow beyond their means. Hear me on this fly, don't cross on other folk's bidness, there's plenty for all us where we at."

"Yeah, I'm ready for that. Time for me to show them how to do it."

"You really think so? Show them how to do it?"

"You know, the Mack way. My daddy had a few tricks up his sleeve he showed me." I winked at Dace. "Time to bust a move in a new way."

"Careful, lit' Mack, careful, this game been here way before you were running around in your daddy's balls. Ain't no new tricks here? Only thing new is how to get caught slipping. You got to respect the game, youngster; got to respect the game."

"Yeah, right."

As I was getting ready to leave, I opened the door and Dace snatched me by the arm hard. He pulled me nose to nose to him, looking me straight through my eyes. I could feel his thoughts bogarting through my goals of getting paid, pushing around the furniture of big profits on top of fat living in the back of my head. He turned real hard.

"Don't cross nobody, boy, and remember the party and property lines. Because whatever you get, you bought yourself," he said, his hot breath in my face. The smell of fresh fried fish ran up my nostrils and took a slide down the back of my throat. He was so close I thought he was going to kiss me. Folks warned me that when he was high, he went whichever way the wind blew that day. I almost was the fan.

"What's that 'pose to mean!" I snatched from his grip.

"Well, if you do, you'll know the expense of it, by the bite out your a…hole! Don't forget to say to 'hi' to all ya boys you haven't seen in a while too, if ya do?"

I felt my heart stop for a moment as I held my breath. What was he about to do next?

Dace licked his middle finger like a lollipop till it dripped wet and touched the tip of my nose. I frooozzze!

"Yep. Whoever gets you, will get a good one. Go boy, get out of there, little baller, and make yo money!"

After leaving, I almost threw up. Thank God he didn't pinch me on the behind.

"Boom!" I was out there now, hard, dealing, and making money. Based on the hours you chose, you could have money coming hand over fist. I got money in every Converse box in my room. Every now and then when most of the clientele was in custody for a minute, business got slow. Sometimes you could put your feet up, twenty-four hours later, you couldn't take your shoes off.

But I "so-called" got some bidness standards too. I wouldn't sell to pregnant girls if they showing, unless times got real hard. Ducking the police, packing for safety, I was rolling.

Michelle asked questions why I wasn't going to school. I just told her I got this good job, but she looked straight through me. She knew that if I wasn't making no eye contact with her, I got a lie in my pocket.

Then things started to happen. I got a new car, and a few toss-ups honeys while trying my best to keep it from Sandy. But I got something I didn't expect. An addiction to money, power and danger. Found out people do anything for drugs. Whatever you say do, that's what they did. There was a girl who let a guy roll over her foot with his car for some dope! That sounds crazy, but she put her foot under that tire for a twenty shot! Me and my partners be shocked and cracking up at the scenes. Man, we had people fighting each other. Just throw a rock on the ground and "Pow" big-time wrestling. Stealing from they mommas, robbing people. It was a shame to say what some of the girls would do for it.

A girl we called Jiga-momma came up one night about two in the morning with her baby in her arms. Only a diaper, T-shirt, a thin sheet on the baby, and trying…to buy…some dope.

"Take this milk," she said. It was milk she got from the WIC program.

"Go home, and take your baby with you, fool," I said, laughing as I turned toward one of my homeboys.

She started rubbing all over herself, talking about, "I'll do you, just let me put my baby in your car."

"Jiga-momma, get out of my face before I slap you out!" I said, leaning on my car.

"If that's what gets you off! Just come wit' it," rocking and swaying about to pass out. My boys were standing 'round, hunching their shoulders. Then she reached and put the baby in my car! She went too far!

"Girl, get that baby out of my car!" I yelled and slapped her. But she kept on coming, and coming, and coming like a Bozo Classic Clown Punching Bag.

I stepped back. "Here! Here! Take it! And I threw about ten rocks on the ground. And like an electric shock, she hit the floor with the accuracy of a Bloodhound and got them rocks in about two seconds. Got up, eyes clear as a bell, and kissed one of the rock to heaven. "Thank you, lord," and walked away switching them hips like she was on a modeling runway.

All I could do was lean on the car in a daze. This was my money, my hook, and my power! But I saw something else, they got power too. They got heart, needs, demands, and diligence. Through pain, they hunt in the night until they find their own light.

More guts than us to stand in places and spaces to find their next hit. Death to them was a low priority. They'd get what they want and survive, and me, Boo-Boo the Fool in the middle. Can't win, can't lose. So I decided to go home. But when I got in my car, there was her baby sound asleep and she was still on the corner.

"Hey fool! Come get yo baby!"

She strutted back over. "Oh, I'm that fool. I'd lose my head if it wasn't screwed on and my baby's, too." She snatched that baby up like a rag doll and was gone back in a blanket of darkness in a flash.

Wonder what kind of war that baby had to fight in her womb?

When I drove up it was late, but all the lights were on in the house.

That should have been a warning sign, but I was a little slow in picking things up like that. Michelle was home, but I thought she was working with Grandma at the clinic tonight. *There I go, thinking again.*

When I hit the door, there she stood. On the table open was one of my Converse boxes with all my *Miss Hong Kong Honey's Magazines*, dope and money in one hand, and a small Billy club in the other, which didn't catch my eye at first. I used to wonder how Mack got the dent in the side of his head. But I later remembered I'd seen her go after him one day with it when he had slapped her. He never did that again.

91

"Emmanuel, what's this?" Michelle asked.

"What it look like!" I answered with my smart mouth.

WHA-POW! I got a Mack dent! She hit me right upside the head. I hit the floor, my brains rang like Big Ben, and blood gushed from my nose and lips as if I had kissed a moving BART train.

"Boy, don't make me kill you tonight!" Michelle screamed.

I whined like Baby Huey, "Why you hit me, Momma!"

Well, I was scared and dared not move or try anything.

"Emmanuel, after all I've done for you. Trying to give you the best, feeding you, clothing you, not bringing men in the house in front of you! You could at least respect me enough not to bring this mess in my house!"

Then I started talking crazy. "Well, how you expect me to live! I got to have mines, too. What's a black man suppose to do in this neighborhood?"

Michelle took a few steps toward me, swaying from side to side. "Emmanuel, tell me? What's a black man suppose to do, come on, black man?"

I had to come up with something good now. I started signaling for the wolves over the fence in the back of my mind to come on. Those fellas were always back there doing something they had no business and could come up with some doozies of a lie under pressure.

"If it's good," said Michelle "you can stay, but if it doesn't add up, you'd better beat me to the door." She was flat footed. That meant this was serious, real trouble, and with the wrong word, it could turn to a knock-down, drag out.

So I got up and heard one of them wolves say, "Mack, start the old soul-brother routine. She'll fall for that. Yeah, go-go 'head, boy. "

Other wolf said, "Yeah, there you go, dog. That's a good one, nat's a good one."

But she stopped me before I got to shuffling. "No song and

dance, Emmanuel. No time for games now."

Wolves got quiet, looking at each other and giggling. "Oh, she ain't play'n."

For a little sympathy, I made myself stumble and sat in the chair nearest the door, just in case she went off. Then in mental chaos, both my wolves started barking at the same time.

"Do this, Mack!" One jumped up, raising its hand like it was in class.

"Naw, do this, Mack," the other responded looking at the other one crazy.

I thought, *one at a time, you nuts!* I focused on Michelle with my good eye. "Momma, a young black man ain't gonna make it out of here unless he making his own business. I don't know whether you know it or not, but times is rough out here, and Mack and Dace talked about us young brotha's taking over one day to make this place a better world."

Michelle's bright skin turned red, her bottom lip was rolling out like carpet toward the floor. I thought, oh, I'm sinking. One wolf ran over and pushed the other wolf aside: "Think, man, think! Go medical on her. Yeah, that'll work, dog!"

"But Momma, some of that money could be used to go to the clinic to help people get off crack. You know the government let it in. We don't got no factories making no dope here."

Michelle's eyebrows rose, so I thought I had a plug in. I'd let this wolf bark for a little while more and work this with a little shoe shuffling to add some feeling. "They the ones that's really pushing drugs in our county. See momma, if they take that money and put it in education, then people like me would stop selling crack and people would get off crack."

Michelle cut it. "Emmanuel, did you hear what you just said? If you really listen to what you're saying, you'll confuse *you*."

And she was right. The more I talked, the crazier I

sounded. I rolled my eyes to the back of my head toward the wolves. *You guys are not helping this at all!*

Michelle walked over to me and pressed that club at the peak of my forehead. My hearing went into high recognition 'save your behind' mode.

Her voice went cold as if she were talking from an ice box. "I can't speak for the government, and I can't speak for the crack user, but I can speak for you." She paused for a moment. "You can't sell drugs and live here. The money you take is the money mothers get to feed their children. Last time I looked, you surely don't look like no savings and loan, or the check-cashing place. Choose now, your mother or your drugs." She backed up about five feet holding a clear plastic bag; in it, crack, pills, and about four grand.

I started walking over to her. As she reached out her arms as if to embrace me, I snatched the bag and ran for the door.

"Momma, I'll be back! I'm just going to sell this and quit, but I'll be back."

I slammed the door behind me. I watched to see if Michelle was going to come after me. But she didn't. I heard her hit the floor crying and praying. Praying so hard I felt it. For a moment, I couldn't move. I could hear her calling on God not to let her boy die in the streets.

"What boy is she crying about? I'm Little Mack, and God ain't gonna let nothin happen to me. Okay God, just let this be the last time and I promise next week, I'll quit selling dope." If God heard that, I was in trouble.

I got in my car and started driving as far as I could. I decided to get my hustle on so I could go on a spending spree. Maybe I could get Michelle some nice stuff and she'd forget all about how I got it. With the four grand in cash and enough dope to flow to make another three, I decided to make a fast big sale. So I had to go where they bought big, but it was where Dace had warned me not to go, on other people's property.

But I was little Mack. I didn't care.

I drove to the corner of Mason and Columbus. Rich folks bought out there. This was where the well hooked-up party suppliers sold. We would hear about young white folk falling out at the parties and dying because they took too much dope. They'd be out on the dance floor with that stuff in their system on top of alcohol, moving to that wild music, shaking and flipping like Sockeye Salmon heading up stream and all of a sudden, pass out.

I parked my car and got out. I stood there for awhile. A black Mercedes R500 pulled up.

A voice came from the Mercedes. "Yo' man, got something for sell?

"A lot, dude. You got a lot to spend? Look like you roll'n big, Mr. Mercedes Bens?"

I was looking up and down the street, totally out of place. He pulled his car around the corner and I followed. I could see two white-boy figures through the tinted windows. They were listening to some old off-the-wall rap.

"Let's see it?"

I pulled out twin plastic bags full of crack and pills. I showed them from a distance just in case they were the police. Dude on the driver's side open the armrest between the seats. Full, stacks of money. My mouth flipped opened and I was blinded. Twenties by the pound, calling my name. He slammed it shut and patted on the leather rest.

"Here's your money, drop in the stuff, hustler." I reached in the car and dropped the dope in the passenger's lap and backed up quick. The driver opened the armrest.

"Get your money, dealer, so we can get out of here."

I reached in again and leaned in over the passenger. He grabbed me and the driver slammed a cuff on my wrist trying to lock it to the steering wheel.

"Police! You're Under Arrest!" as the driver tried to pull me in.

The other grabbed my jacket. I drove my sled hammer

forearm right into the driver's jaw, "Poom!" His glasses dived off his nose getting out of the way. With my body twisting in an alligator death spin, I broke the passenger's grip.

"Get off me!" I yelled as I bolted with handcuff still on one wrist toward my car as one of the guys got out to chase me. But no white boy was a match for a brother low-running from the law.

I got in my Chevy I-ROCK and now, I was rocking it. They were on my tail, pushing that Mercedes to the limit. I could hear those crying hound-dog sirens as I blasted through intersections with lighting speed. Ninety! One hundred! A hundred and ten! I'm rocking that car to get to the 6th street freeway, but they started to cut off my path. Lights came toward me. I turned off Evans down 3rd street when I ran over something and the left side of my car dropped. Both tires were blown. Ten cars with fire on top and sirens were behind me. All I could see was my momma on her knees, crying out for her boy.

My window was down and the air blew so hard in my eyes that my tears knew what was coming. They ran over my ears, diving off to the back of my head. I was losing speed because I couldn't get traction and could clearly see that 3rd was blocked by the police. So I made up in my mind if I go out, I go out like General Custer. Both blown tire squealing in high soprano, sparks shooting like the 4th of July, and I was *literally* hanging out the window posed like Napoleon going down in the *Santa Maria*. The late night owl crowd stood on the street corner cheering me on: "Go, lit' Mack. Run them police!"

Yeah, right. My car couldn't take no more. The engine was crying, "Man give up, before I blow up!"

I pulled to the side right before I got to the stockade of police cars and like my daddy, tried for a last-ditch run. There were two police, had to be brothers because they were already on my heels, and a police dog. I took off, but there was *no* shaking these cats. Then they let the dog loose and it was over.

That dog was on me so quick I hollered, "Mommaaa… mommaaa…!" It snatched me down like a rag doll and commenced to tearing my behind up. They finally got the dog off me. One of them with his heel on my neck told me to lay still.

I began screaming, "You set me up, you set me up!"

He leaned down, got right in my face with spit flying, "Shut up, punk! *You* set you up!" He pulled the cuffs I still had on around to the other arm, and pressed down until my wrist bled. I cringed in pain because I was now face to face with the side-affects of my addiction. The one no one ever tells you about nor anticipated.

When you're addicted, you've sold yourself, your wolves turn into poodles in high heels and devour each other, and everyone closest to you pay the bill out of your behind, for being on other people's property.

Chapter 7
Young Pit Bulls of the County Jail. In Tennis Shoes?

Even the toughest of them got to cry sometimes, so I used this time in the police car to get all of my tears out before I got booked in. Some kids like me without a dad in the home would always be talking about, "I want to go live with my daddy!" Most of the time, it was because they were mad about something their mommas wouldn't do or give them. Fools didn't understand that their moms were doing the best they could with what they had, and extra, was a privilege, not the norm. Well, not by choice, I got the chance to be incarcerated with mine.

Being locked up was nothing to a soldier like me, till my Grandma came to visit. Lest you were a seasoned convict with almost no heart, you'd see the baddest of them break when the grand momma's had to see you behind bars. So ironic, this was one of only two places that slowed you down enough for someone to see some of us in a controlled environment. The other was the mortuary.

I was the first reason she had been in any place like this. The corner of her beautiful hazel eyes always told the story of what she was dealing with. Sometimes they held crystal sugar drops as she smiled and slightly comforted them as they softly rolled into a blanket of tissue. Sometimes her tears were waterfalls of thanksgiving, as she would stand in church or anywhere talking about God and all his goodness as she raised us without her husband. Then sometimes they poured as a broken water main flooded of pain and disappointment, unable to be controlled. In those cases, the one that broke in and unleashed the controlling valve never asked her permission.

They were the outlets of her heart.

They had already brought us in the visiting booths when Grandma and Michelle arrived. The door slammed behind Grandma and she jumped. There was one seat, one phone, two visitors per inmate. As Michelle sat down with major attitude, my gaze went straight through her and fixed on Grandma. That old brown cotton coat, the usher's annual-day button still on the lapel, always buttoned to the top, her hand gripped at her collar. In panoramic view was the wear and tear of her grandsons' life on her face, with deep puddles of worry in those eyes. And I saw something that hit me at my core. A cut on her lip.

"Hi, is it Emmanuel or little Mack? Which one of you is finally here?" Michelle said with major funk on her breath.

"Yeah, so what?" I answered hard, quickly.

Michelle started getting loud. "You know what? You better check yourself now before I put this phone down, and me and momma will go home!"

"Cool, I'll stop, but you started it, Momma. I just don't know what to say. I'm here. What is there to say? I done got myself in some stuff and I guess I got to pay the price now."

"Oh, you so much you're paying prices now? The price for what, Emmanuel? Trying to be a big-time dope dealer, Mr. Mack Jr.? If you're paying so much, why you the one blowing up my phone, crying about you need some soap?"

"All right, Momma. I should be home soon because I know I ain't gonna do much time. One dude said his cousin in Texas got a year for every rock they found on him. Thank God this ain't Texas. I'll be back flowing soon."

"Yeah, back soon, and to do what?" Michelle covered the phone with her hand. "Did you look at your grandmother's face?"

My eyes flashed toward my grandma again. I was lit. I was hot. A thousand fire ants were on me. I locked in on her lip again. "What's the matter? Somebody touch my grandma?"

"No. What's the matter is she's so worried about you that you're not the only one doing time. She's locked up, too. You touched her."

I touched my lower lip and pain ran across my mouth. I had forgotten that it got busted when I got arrested. The stress of my life was wearing, draining, and unplugging the portholes of life on my grandmother's ship. Every phone call about somebody seeing me, every late night Michelle called her not knowing where I was, every time she saw another young man come in on a gurney with holes in his chest, she saw me. Her vessel was taking on water fast. God could only hear her May-days.

"Wait! I ain't finish talking to you, boy?" Michelle said.

"Momma, don't flash on me again!" I punched back.

Just as our voices began turning into blow horns, Grandma touched Michelle on the shoulder. So softly she posed to Michelle, "No, baby. No hollering. Let me talk to my boy."

"But Momma, he trying to do that Mack stuff with me and I ain't having it!"

"Stop, Michelle." Her voice still, ever so calm. "It's okay. Let me talk to my Emmanuel."

Michelle looked through the glass with daggers. "You'd better not upset her!"

"Give Grandma the phone please and go somewhere," I said with my lips twisted like a jack-o-lantern.

Michelle handed Grandma the receiver and walked away from the window. It took Grandma a little time to get herself together. She looked at the phone for moment, and turned those eyes as she reached for me, touching the barrier shield between us. Every emotion was wrapped up behind pharmacy-bought reading glasses.

"Emmanuel, how are you?"

I dropped my head. I broke.

"Pick your head up son, and look at your grandmother."

I lifted my big nugget head, but my gaze was still floored.

100

"Look your grandmother in the eyes and talk to her."

"Yes, Mama. How are you, Grandma?"

"Loving and missing my grandson, Emmanuel Charles Harris, that's how I am. I believe every day that God would keep his promise to his grandfather, and that he would be just what God created him to be. You're not some wild animal running loose waiting for the hunters to capture you. You're Charles Harris's grandson, you are Emmanuel."

"What does that mean, Grandma?"

"What does what mean, son?"

"You say to me, you are Emmanuel. Who is Emmanuel? I'm locked up in jail around all these other fools. Everybody here got a song and dance, just talk'n loud because here, you can be anybody you want to be. At the end of the day, a grown man tells you to shut up and go to bed. One day looks just like the next. If my bunky didn't have a calendar, I won't know what day it was. I don't know, Grandma? Tell me who Emmanuel is?"

"Emmanuel, your name means 'God is with us,' that's what that means. Your name means God has come down to be with man. When people see you, they ought to see God. You're not God, but people should be able to see God in you. That's who you are."

I sat there dumbfounded.

"I don't know what to say?"

"Then don't say nothing and listen, Emmanuel." She reached in her purse and pulled out this old wallet looking like some Indians made it. "See this, my father gave me this."

I could see some writing on it, but it was fuzzy through the Plexiglas.

"Can you see it?"

"A little."

"Read it to me."

"The Lord is my Sheppard I shall not want, he makes me lie down in green pastures, he leads me beside the still waters;

he restores my soul. He leads me in the path of righteousness for his name sake"

Then Grandma starts to quote it with me:

"Yea, thou I walk through the valley of the shadow of death, I will fear no evil, for Thou art with me. Thy rod and thy staff, they comfort me. Thou preparest a table before me in the presences of mine enemies, Thou anointeth my head with oil; my cup runs over. Surely goodness and mercy shall follow me, all the days of my life. And I will dwell in the house of the Lord forever."

I couldn't take my gaze off the wallet.

"This is who I have committed you to, Emmanuel, the Lord. He made you and gave you to us. He will take care of you. It's time for me to go."

"Grandma, could you put some money on my books?"

She giggled. "You know, I would take money out of my house for your college, and yo grandma still pay her PG&E at the pharmacy. But don't you ever think I'll pay folks to go to jail. You better eat that food if you have to choke it down and spit it back up. Oh, and God ain't gonna put no money on your books either, so don't ask him."

"Visiting time is over," came across the phone and the line went dead. Grandma slowly put the receiver on the holder as she kept the wallet pressed against the window.

Then she took it down slowly with the care of a dove and put it in her purse.

I got my next real schooling while leaving Eight-Fifty Bryant. I had the chance to sit next to an "old G" on the bus to Bruno. He was talking to another young knucklehead sitting across from me.

"You, young boy, so keep ya mouth shut when you get out here. I know you going to put on the hard face and dat's needed somewhat to survive, but don't be running ya mouth too much. They'll tight'n ya little foolish butt up if you do. And don't be around all that craziness because if you get ya dumb self caught up in something you didn't do, you should have did something, fool, because you going to have to pay the same price as the fools that did it anyway. And since you were stupid to be over there anyway, you will get what coming to ya from the police. So why go down for something you didn't do, and ain't got noth'n to do with you. Unnerstand me, junior?"

The youngster nodded.

"And don't get up there and nut-up either or they'll give you something that will have you sleep all day or marching in the same spot at night don't know where you at or who you are? Have you there looking stupid and somebody might think you cute. Then you wake up with some big guy standing over you, ready to put his thang in ya booty. And don't get caught all up in that Rodney King stuff either. They act'n a fool in Los Angeles, but this ain't Los Angeles and these deputies out here ain't LAPD. Let them fools who want to get caught talking about that riot do that, and see what happen to them. You just keep to ya self and go home on yo TX date, not their's. You hear me, junior?"

The young guy nodded again and kept his mouth shut the whole ride. I could see this vibe was messing with his mind, but he was trying to get it down the best he could. He and other little youngsters like me had our little mugs on, but not too thick to cause it to get checked by the real convicts. That 'old G' wasn't talking to me, but I heard him loud and clear.

The bus blasted through a corridor from under the downtown jail and cut a corner spitting concrete like dust, hitting the 6th street freeway with the veracity of a stolen ambulance. The roof melted oozing over our window that turned into spiked bars. That San Francisco scenery faded to gray as the fog miser from the coast welcomed us in Dracula style, under its cape of darkness. The sun waved goodbye after being snatched backward through the clouds. This threw us over to a new regional drill sergeant of cutting winds and cold. The so-called experienced inmates at this were still talking, but a slow numbing silence was gripping the throats of most of the lies being told about, "Oh, this ain't a bad ride. You should have seen when we had to go to Quentin."

The freeway threw us up and dropped us at will. Broken springs cut through the meat on every impact of our butts to the seats, which broke away chunks of concrete on both sides of our transporter, till we were on a one way road with bottomless cliffs on either side. The airplanes out of SFO screamed toward us and transformed into flying Phoenixes of terror. Boeing blazing bats in afterburner grazed over the open roof, blowing ashen messages in the clouds. "You got what you asked for! Want ya mommas now, boyz!" right in our faces. Our driver sped because we were late to Frankenstein's wedding. He grinned and slammed every shifted gear, sparking lighting from the sky. As the bus rounded the corner off Sky Long Drive, it took a big dip to the left. We lost our breath when we caught a glimpse of the top hat of the facility. Silence slapped everybody. The bus backfired, "poom!" and we all ducked. The exhaust rose up, being released from hell's chimney and the driver deliberately slowed the bus so the back draft could seize our noses and throats, trying to choke us all to death.

As we approached the front gate, I caught my real first glimpse of the world-renowned Bruno. She was lying there waiting for her man to arrive. Her front entry stair and doors were a centerfold pose. A 1920's rejected showgirl that got struck in the face by a semi-truck. We had the distinct pleasure of that not being the entrance for us. She breathed slowly in and out like a bull with emphysema. In her outer jaws were six rows of concrete teeth called tiers, smiling like a manual typewriter. When she inhaled, she drew in the bus toward her snake-curve thigh, then blew us down to a lower big-butt-cheek custody gate. It even smelled like booty. Her army-made chicken coup was strapped and reinforced to detain all entrees, human or animal, until she decided it was time to leave. This was the real live haunted castle from Transylvania they forgot to tear down, full of swept-away souls. Every trash-bin raiding raccoon, fake bush, and petrified buffalo stood still, hypnotized under her cape of historical darkness.

A deputy stepped up on the bus. About five foot five, Hispanic, buffed, uniform tight as if he had been blown up in it, face and eyes flat as a mat. No love for nobody here. You could feel him, like a Cholo hit man gone straight.

"Gentleman, follow the man in front of you and keep your mouth shut. Welcome to San Bruno." Nice, but chilling.

He had our undivided attention with that Cobra black shotgun with scope on his shoulder that was as tall and talking louder than him.

I thought deep inside, man, how you gonna miss with that?

Now, you know some of us still couldn't hear. For them, you saw dark gloves reach out and snatch them out of line. They straight disappeared. I'm processed in, strip searched, pictures taken, fingerprinted, orange clothes, bedroll, raggedy underwear, soap and razor, one roll of toilet paper, a box lunch with just enough to starve on, and on my way to 5 North.

Before I could make it to my cell, the talk was out. Mack knew I was there. The jailhouse stank. Noise, noise, noise! Sounds like a freight train in idle or ghost moaning because of wasted time. For the first timers, we all glad to graduate from Juvenile Hall and proud to finally get to Bruno. At least I think we are? We never knew it was the seduction just to be in her that had all of us hooked.

On my way down the hall to the stairs, somebody slipped me a kite (a note) from Mack. "You see Joe-Joe/beat nat sucka down/we all count n on the Mac Pac/scene set at high-9/just get n nat behind/ The Mack."

The last time me and Joe-Joe locked horns was about four months ago. We fought at a garage party, tearing everything up till the father of the girl who owned that house pulled out a pistol. Folks almost killed each other running out the back door. Days after, I saw him when I was driving, standing on the corner. As I sped by I yelled out, "Next time, only one man will walk, boy!"

As I looked in my side-view mirror driving away, I could see Joe-Joe smiling, standing in the middle of the street with his hands in the air suggesting, "Come on." His Glock was showing stuck down in his belt. He got popped the same day by the police, threatening his girl with a baseball bat. He had never hit her with it, but he had put his hands on her before.

I hate brothers beating on a female, so I had it in for him when we touched next. Rumors gave life to jail time and word had it that bets were made. Even Joe Young, who was in prison, knew about it.

As I hit the tiers with about ten other guys, it was like a neighborhood family reunion. We were slapping the soul brother handshake so loud you'd thought firecrackers were going off. "Aaa...! Aaa...! Aaa...! We here!" Yeah, we all were there.

Ray-Ray, Dank, Ski-Bobble, Pissy Pee Jr., Boo-boo, and B-Love looking like the jailhouse Guru. He was toe-up and acted a fool on the streets, but would get in jail and had his little Malcolm X glasses, Three Musketeer mustache with the twist at the ends. Brother was all cleaned up, always with a book in his hand. He was stupid, but looked heavy behind bars. Who else? Mac' Clammy, little Earl's cousin who we all thought was dead, Galaxy, Mims-lee, the twins Tilt and Twon who swore they were so fine and nobody couldn't tell them apart. Yeah right, if it wasn't for the massive differences in the sizes of their heads. Weed Mike, Ricky Wild, Marcel, and Pidgin who was bow-legged because his momma didn't get his feet fixed when he was a baby. He was fast, but drug his feet so it looked like they were writing something. One-Eyed Ron, Sweet-T, Lover Lance, Nut-bucker with his stupid self, I mean everybody!

Was this what Dace was talking about? I looked up. Willie Wonka? Oh no, him too? His real name was William, but he got that name because he never brushed his teeth and his mouth looked like he'd been eating chocolate, Bustler the Hustler who always had a hustle going on, and my God, the man, Jake the Terror! They had to keep that brother in Adseg (Administrative Segregation). You'd know when he was out because a woman would always come running from his house half naked, no shoes on, and screaming for her life. Brother was always doing too much, trying to express himself.

If you didn't know where they were, we found them. By the way they looked, they been here for a long time. Brothers wasn't looking half bad, gained that jailhouse food weight, arms all yoked, haircuts and everythang. Fellas never worked on them legs though, so they all walking around like swollen midgets. It's a shame how some people look better incarcerated than out on the streets? The place was like a half-and-half order from the Chinese restaurant down the street, half of the tier was from my side, half from Joe-Joe's side, including him. Housing deputies? You boys slipping on the housing cards again.

They put all of us youngsters together, running around, blowing in the phone for free calls and learning from the immature older cats how to booby-trap the gates with a comb during cell checks for the deputies. They'd tug to pull the door open and "Siff-siff-siff-siff-siff," comb teeth would blow out like arrows from a Medieval Moorish aerial attack. Deputies would get a good poke right in the neck. Every now and then we'd get an eye, too. At night us young bucks weren't tired and somebody would bang a beat on the wall while his cellee rapped a song. That's why they'd put most of us youngster on the lower tiers. A deputy would run up fast and yell, "Shut up!" Things would get quiet for a minute, then "boom-boom-tick, boom-boom-boom-tick."

Then this voice deep within the darkness descended through the concrete floors from up top rang out. "A, youngstas. That's enough!" The whole place would go silent and stay that way. It was no deputy voice either, and you knew

107

to shut up for real then. If you didn't, the word would get out that you wouldn't mind nobody. And with that kind of immature jail conduct, the tier had its way of making it very hard for you to survive.

Not everybody had a conflict to settle, so they were getting along until we got there. Most of the time in county jail, they had a way to let matters get settled without everyone getting locked down, called one on one. Nobody broke it up and the winner walked away. The other, the best way he could. Many knockout artists would try to jump in the shower to wash their hand wounds before the tier deputy found out. For the cat whose face was the canvas work, if one of the 'old G's" had a little mercy, they might say to the deputy, "Aaa man, there's somebody bleeding back there," but that was rare.

Sometimes it got too heavy on the tier and brothers just rolled themselves up. Be standing there with his bedroll, sheets, zoo-zoos and wham-whams in a plastic bag at the gate waiting for the deputy to rescue him. As soon as he'd get out the gate, would start "talking head" from the other side. Brothers rolling out was famous for selling wolf tickets during their exits.

Other times, someone would do something stupid like stealing. The roll up was vicious. A couple of trustees done checked him good (beat his natural behind and I mean one of those whippings you don't soon forget). They'd roll his unconscious butt in them blankets and lay him on his mattress at the front of the tier. Everything left after payment and theft would be propped up there with him, lying on his chest. Deputy would just 'find him' and everyone on the tier acting as if nothing was going on. Fellas playing dominos, working out, watching TV, and ain't seen nothing. Inside Bruno, like disease in the body, it's her blood line for cells to judge each other.

Get this on the wide-view screen of your mind because the screen is set.

There were two sides to the jail and five floors. North side went to yard from 11:00 to 1:00. South side went out from 1:30

to 3:30. Today though, when the North side would go out, they were to start a ruckus out in the yard. We knew that most of the deputies would go out to control it, and that left the tiers to the inmates.

This day it would be Joe-Joe and me. These fights were not the arena fights with the crowds cheering, but silent not to attract attention too soon. People just kind of stand there in a frozen portrait as the fighters locked in. The second day I was there, that was the time. The T.V. watchers at the front of the tier were listening out to hear the radio transmission from the deputies' radios. Most new bootie deputies kept their radios up too loud, trying to play SFPD. They talked too loud and left a lot of their private information on the desk just in eye view, so we knew who passed, failed, and who was on the waiting list. We heard everything going on in the jail.

"Code-three yard! Code-three yard!"

Gates started to slam, keys crashing on the deputies' hips as they ran down the stairwell. You could see out the window from your cell what was going on in the yard. Many of the black inmates had squared off. Even the Whites and Mexicans were in on it. Shirts off and a lot of finger pointing.

The more people involved, the more assistance needed. The goal was enough undisturbed fight time for Joe-Joe and me. We knew with the stand off, it would take time for the deputies to talk it down and safer for us rather than everybody in an all-out brawl. That way nobody got extra time or caught a bullet from the 'can't wait to use it' rifleman in the tower. Every time you looked up there, he waved, pointed at you, then pointed the rifle toward the fence. We all knew what that meant; a dare for you to run toward it so he could put a round in your back. I haven't yet met anyone who could outrun some hot lead.

All the cells were open on the tier. When I came out my cell, Joe-Joe was at the end of the tier walking round with some of his partners. His hands down in front of his pants, scratch'n his balls with the crack of his butt showing. Stanky hands, punk! That was a direct sign of disrespect. I walked toward him and stopped to tighten up my tennis shoes on the bench. That was another sign of a beat down in progress.

Earlier when they opened a new jail across the way, deputies in that open dorm-like facility had to learn quick how to read these "something wrong" jail photo clips from the inmates. Note this, when you see everybody lying on their bunks, looking at the ceiling, their shoes or work boots on, and it's light out? These fellas don't have insomnia and their feet aren't cold. Something big is about to jump off and ain't nobody want to be caught sleep, sliding, nor slipping. It's going to be a long night for the deputy who didn't notice all them locks missing from the footlockers either. Hello!

Then what happened next were the six steps of what I call, "Young Pit Bulls, No Chains, In Tennis Shoes."

Some fellas would bring their dogs at the yard down the street called "the pit-pit." I always wanted a pit bull, but my momma and grandma had no love for me on it. Never had, never will. Grandma told me, "If it didn't have a job and can't clean up behind itself, it won't live here." She added when I got grown and had my own place, I could have ten dogs if I wanted to. They could cook my food, iron my clothes, drive my car, and write checks out of my checkbook for all she cared. Then she'd say, pointing, "As long as you, Emmanuel, have personal problems with washing your own behind, don't bring no dog talk up in here no more!"

And I didn't. She was probably referring to the smell of my underwear and the lack of the use of water on my part, but I dared not ask her.

Some of my friends had dogs and you'd know it before you opened their door because the whole house smelled like dog. The dog really was just a macho piece to walk with. You could intimidate folks with it when you were a chump on the inside.

Now the dogs' is us. Joe-Joe and me. Young, primed, the fumes of madness hovering in our minds, explosive, and out of control. And you know with all those elements in effect, there's usually a punk-hearted crowd with hot hungry breath to ignite this fire.

ROUND ONE: LOW LIFE VEGAS: All through the jail like cats at the slots in someone's homemade fighting ring willing to win at any cost, everybody was betting something. We heard some heavy rollers bet up to a grand. Some fools always betting phone change, pictures out of the Jet magazine, or their breakfast and lunches so they could get fat on somebody else. Vegas never ended here because the debt collection was the next bet for many who couldn't pay. If there was too many hospital runs for too many unexplained injuries from one tier, payment was being made. Even on the streets, Dace had a pool going. Folks put one or two dollars of their SSI or welfare check till payday. Found out he had a grand on both of us. Then I also found out about the big betters.

It was social economics vs. the judicial system. Society says, "I'll keep him down, or better yet, I'll teach him how to keep himself down." Judicial system says, "I'll keep him institutionalized and make the state pay for it." Were brothers like me in the plans for a better America, or were we a disease left to die on our own? By my exposure to the elements of my limited view of life; the odds were against me. But with my grandma and momma praying, and God hearing them, the odds were for me. Life was so short and I gave everyone a reason to waste my time. The odds were against me. Yet I had not fulfilled my purpose and destiny that God had promised my grandfathers in the slave fields. The odds were for me, ching-ching, ching-ching.

Today I've watched people with that same look on their faces on my many trips to the real Las Vegas.

What I hear you think is that "I go often", and yeah, you're right. They get me, too. Everybody thinks as soon as they get off the plane, I'm about to wear them out! Vegas, you have been waiting for me, and here I am!

Yet the truth is nobody wins in Vegas. We go there, stay in our upscale room (depending on what hotel) like we have actually bought this one bedroom mansion. All we got it for and really can afford, buddy, is three nights max. That's why if we take our kids we put them in the same room with us. Let's admit it now, our credit card is the real strength and stretched to the max for the hotel, right? We have a little overtime stash and some bill money that shouldn't have been brought and can't afford lose, but we try it anyway.

We start out at the tables on the first day because remember, we will beat Vegas. By the time our blood pressures eases as the chips go from one side of the table to the other, we rescue ourselves to the nickel and dime slots now, big spender! It's close to gone by the second day. Kids begging and whining about going to the arcade, and they spend just as much money as we do. That's why I can't stand taking mine with me. Hey! I admit it! Now your heart is not beating so fast, huh?

We've eaten at the big expensive buffets, tipping was still cheap until money gets low, then everybody's at the six dollar and ninety-nine cent place. You know it by how long the lines are. Don't be embarrassed, you see them, they see you too. Then at the end of day three, we are out in front of the hotel with all the other frustrated broke beetles hollering at the kids, trying to figure out how much we have left to tip the cabbie and get to the airport on time. And the doorman just waves us away until our next something-for-nothing itch hits again. No matter where you are when the dice rolls, you never know what's coming up.

Joe-Joe and I were now the faces on the cards and the main event. Never really calculated that someone else is trying to win off of us, but we were too young and stupid then to realize it. Yet before you can think, the pit boss grabs the chips. All bets are in!

ROUND TWO: LET'S DANCE: Before the owners/masters (if you can refer to them as that) let the dogs loose on each other, they let them stand staring at each other. They'd rub their sides, messaging-in tension and fire, the best chemical for an explosion of flesh. Heads low, slowly swaying from side to side in a temporary daze, silently dancing with no motion. Not even given the opportunity to hear the sound of 'La'Fool's Do'De'Death' funeral march, until you popped the chains.

Joe-Joe and I circled each other like vultures. The wind beneath our young wings was full of stench from the dead carnage that might come from this encounter. Joe-Joe tore off his shirt, throwing his hand up toward the sunlight coming through the broken cell window. Clinching his fist, he pulls power from the ray. City or county clothes, don't mean nuthin' to him. He had a big bear chest, but still a lot of baby fat around his belly. He balled his fist and started hitting himself on the chest like hammers. "You gonna get this boy!" His chest turned red and swollen.

I spit back. "Son, please! Yo nipples look like you had a baby, Joseph."

Everybody cracked up, but didn't laugh too long to have Joe-Joe turn on them. I whipped the extra slob off my lip and struck an old Mr. Universe pose, flexing my young tight physique. I was always running, Grandma and Michelle cooked well, and blessed with my fast metabolism from my grandfather. Thank you. Even if at first I didn't use it for the right reasons. Every inch of me was dangerous. And he knew it.

Every step our feet took rang against the walls with time moving in slow motion. The atmosphere was not on our side, eye balling each other, stalking, and waiting for the right moment to strike.

A thousand pictures of fights ran through in our minds. Karate, soul-brother movies! Ali! Frazier!

We heard rap songs of killing and gangsters on the FM stations of our minds. The songs have traded in their sound for blood. They've blown up the stage for this sideshow on the tier as we revved our engines. Without a doubt, these cars were going to crash.

The stalking became a dance of Roman armies circling in battle. The sound with every footstep thundering in unison, trying to out emotionalize the other, to study and strip the other, to intimidate and annihilate the other. Two voodoo dolls casting hexes, cursing one another, young cobras with poison not just in our fangs, but also in our own systems. It's been seen from the beginning of time, Cain killing Abel, David defeating Goliath, Christ dethroning Satan.

Who will take the fall into forever? The victory is won, but with a price even the victor must pay. We seldom consider what the price of victory will cost, so we dance around the fine print till we sign the checks in blood.

Joe-Joe and I were at Donna Summer's *"Last Dance."* Well coached for years by the streets and willing to defend the honor of being respected. Performing in a coliseum of the non-respectable standing around us, we called each other out to the floor to perform 'the jig of pain.' We were strong enough to kill, and yet the song played that we were killing ourselves slowly. What? You can't hear the music?

ROUND THREE: INSTINCTIVE FIGHTING. OKAY, WE AIN'T PLAYING NOW! Joe-Joe took a little karate at the boys club and began a stagger step he learned from watching the old karate movie Drunken Monkey. He lost his footing slightly.

"Blam!" I rushed and stuck him into the plaster with a world-renowned Oakland Raiders Jack Tatum forearm neck breaking hit. It was on! It was hot! Any contact informed that part of the body it had been touched. If you've ever stiffed your gardener without paying him, this was a mirror of the results of what your lawn would look like.

We slammed together and wrestled twined like mating boa-constrictors in the everglades. Applying pressure, squeezing, trying to drain the other of life with grips of endurance. Then we broke for a second to let the breath of life finds its way back into our bruised minds.

The slugfest began. Take some, give some, grab, slam, kick some. Then back to the old boxing stances, trying to get some in from a distance, as we picked the next piece of meat to put on the grill of pain.

"Stick and move, baby, stick and move," somebody slightly whispered.

I caught a solid punch to the ribs that pushed my box lunch to the upper floors of my lungs. I went down. He rushed me. My back received a wake-up call from the edge of one of those steel tables. The pain plowed through muscle and slammed into my spine. There the fight took that ugly swing. An evil spirit descended coughing up living-death of what a fight truly was and does, hurt. All the inmates on the tier knew it and an informal hush hit the room. The encounter was no more movie-style acting, but hands turned to hammers with punishment and mayhem. The sunlight closed in through a cracked window spotlight on us. The stage of our performance had turned to a graveyard of un-forgiveness. The mouth of the earth bellowed open, yearning to eat either at the slightest slip. Every move gave and took something from us that it was unwilling to give back.

With the piercing in my back, I heard myself say, "He's really trying to hurt you." I was still down, bent back, yet my mind shifted gears. Something on the inside began to bang on that door that I really needed, yet didn't need to be opened. It was that blank something in my mind that didn't necessarily kick in immediately. My thoughts attempt to compute before it crashed from the blows as the screen within my head smashed against the floor.

"I'm in it. No, I'm not on? Yes, I'm on! I'm in it! I must

do something because I am in it!"

Time to reach in and get the tag-team member you loved to hate. Why hate him, because he could really do the job you couldn't do, the job you wouldn't do.

Here he came, the Mack in me. Come on! In all your dark glory!

ROUND FOUR: FRESH FLESH! When pit bulls fight and blood starta to flow, those cats really start going at it. Before I could get to my feet, the top of Joe-Joe's shoe caught me up under the chin. My bottom teeth leaped through my top lip. Blood spurted with the force of a fire hydrant inside my nose and mouth. I turned my face to avoid his kick again. He kicked me in the back of the head and then stomped me in my ribs. I then understood the sound of the sizzle when some pork ribs hit the hot grill. I rolled under a table to the other side, and then got on my feet. I spat. Something white with a pool of blood came out while I bent over from the pain in my midsection. Then fuel kicked in. Little Mack showed up.

In one power sprint I turned into Ultra-Man, ramming him backward against the table. I grabbed that full bush of nappy half-dread, half-dead natural, and started slamming the back of his head against that steel, which rang in his skull like London's Big Ben. His neck was strong, but I had Mack's strength. I got one good knee to the side of his head, which stunned him, then fired off a multiplicity of them thangs straight in his noggin. His head responded like a speed bag.

When he pushed me back, he turned, and I kicked him between the legs. He went up like a ballerina on a rocket, and down like a rock, grabbing his balls and screaming. While his mouth was wide open, I took a step back and returned the best roundhouse kick I could to his face. Blood shot on the ceiling in-lieu of the broken water sprinklers as he flipped backward. The crowd breathed hard. But this bull wouldn't stay down long.

As the fight went on, some hushed "ooowws" erupted at

every hard blow. Joe slipped on the water near a cell door and I ran to stomp him. But he grabbed my legs and flipped me to the ground. He got me from behind in a scissor wresting move with his legs squeezing my neck. I felt myself going out. I bit him on the thigh till blood filled up my mouth like a faucet. He screamed and began to pound me in the head. The sound of congas and jack hammers in reverb bellowed through my ears. Every strike was intensified as my head rebounded off the tier concrete floor. I was losing consciousness. My chest was a fireball and every breath, a combustible fume. Joe's thighs were logs and I was the lumberjack that fell under them in the water. The stench of sweat and blood were bench-pressing the fight to the final rounds and the stand-off outside was taking too long.

The pits bulls were in the middle of the street at full steam and no one would dare pour any hot water to break them up.

ROUND FIVE: POSITION: LOCK DOWN! I saw a lot of pit-bulls fight. During the fight, the smarter and stronger dog finds a weakness in the other's reaction. Then he'd get ready for the final blow. They have the ability to lock their jaws with deadly pressure yet have no knowledge to unlock it. It's brutal. It's finishing.

Joe-Joe and I had been wrestling, hurting, and hating the fight that now had turned against us. I had always got a kick out of watching others bump heads over silly issues, but when your own strength is the fire, the cost of the fuel is expensive. We both knew we couldn't go on much further and the penny-paying crowd was looking for all their monies worth. It had to be a classic finale. For all that was done, these fools standing around would have never paid to see a legitimate match. But any free gut-wrenching episode that didn't involve them was great. I never knew how we exploited ourselves as 'sport' until 'I am' the game. And whether you win or lose is not the objective to the tier hustling-customer. "Just give me pain, horror and blood so I can go eat my cheese burger." But what was the payday for the gladiators? Were we to find out?

Joe-Joe's got me from behind. I was on my stomach on the floor and he was on my back. He pulled my hair and took me by the neck. He slid that big arm around my neck like a vice grip and braced his head against mine. I could hear him wheezing because of his asthma. I knew where he was going; LOCK DOWN!

It was necessary in the '50s, '60s, and '70s to hold the strength in the Civil Rights movement. "The man is trying to keep a brother down." This was and is true. But I've learned there is an agenda behind everything. When "the man" is not around, whom do we blame? Is he still forcing you and me to each other's throat? Did he make you attack me? Has 'the cause' to be free evolved to the place where we have the right to tear up our own and everything around us? Did the Klan change colors? Did Jim Crow teach us anything? Our ancestors pervaded through some of the bitterest time. Posted signs: No Dogs, Negros, Mexicans. Have we chosen to grovel in our own pits now?

The tier had chosen sides, blacks against blacks, whites extremist against the white liberals, Mexican Northernism against Immigrant Southernism. Charlotte Hawkins Brown stated, "External constraints must not be allowed to segregate mind or soul," and now with me and Joe-Joe's actions, this crowd behind us, we eat'n crow. Didn't he die?

Crow's etiquette prescribed that "a black male could not offer his hand (to shake hands) with a White male because it implied being socially equal." The early inventors used those hands to dig out from those impossibilities and give society some of its greatest inventions. People such as Benjamin Banneker and the making of Washington D.C., Dr. Charles Drew and open-heart surgery, and even in the late '60s, Marie Brown and the first video home security-system.

We babies today have turned our hand to be weapons against each other. Police would yell, "Show us your hands!"

Creative hands turning cocaine into crack, and transferring it 'by hand' into others' hands, and now our babies from those hands are born addicted with shriveled hands.

Crow said, "Black men are not supposed to offer their hand to a white woman, not supposed to eat together, not to light a cigarette to a white woman." We went to the totally opposite extremes. We have got black and white girls half naked in our videos, eating barbeque, and not to even speak on how much weed they smoke. Jim Crow dead? Better think again. Oil and economics, America? You do the math.

The pit bull was locking on the other to kill it. With my alligator twist, I got one hand between his arm and my throat to breath, but this boy applied pressure. My one free arm grabbed, reached for anyway to unlock this jaw. Anybody got a key?

ROUND SIX: BEAT HIM OFF! : When pit bulls lock for too long, you got to use something to pry their jaw bones loose. A stick, tire-iron, something that won't break. Many a master who really cared about their dogs would stop the fight rather than let their dog suffer for long.

"I'm out, man. Get him off my dog!" shouted a master.

"What?" answers the other.

"I'm out, man, get him off my dog!"

"Right. Yo dog's a punk."

"Whatever. Stop the fight. I'm out."

Maybe the real Master was looking out for us both.

As Joe-Joe was on my back breathing hard and spitting blood on me he said, "I'm going to break yo neck, cause you a sucka!" we heard behind us, "Code-Three! Five-North! Code-Three! Five-North!" With all those fools watching us, who was watching the door? The deputies were coming down the tier in droves! A herd of armed gazelles had been let loose and they were about to get revenge on the hyenas.

One of them said, "Aaaa! He's trying to break his neck!"

At full speed, they hit the whole crowd! POW! Everything standing fell. Remember the knowledge from the 'old G' on

119

the bus? Well, none of these fools heard the message.

Hats and bats! We didn't take into consideration them sheriffs would be still suited up from the yard mess. They were whipping us like there was no tomorrow. One grabbed Joe-Joe around the neck with a mini-baton. Joe-Joe locked in with him. Before I could get up, they were whipping me, too. Like when pits lock down, the only way was to beat one off.

And that was what they did. Quite well, I must say.

As the fight kept escalating, the deputies were as fire ants that rolled out of a disturbed fortress. Some guys hollered, "Momma, Momma!" The mace became the conductor of this mad symphony, and it stopped everything. We were gagging, deputies, and all. When the smoke cleared, all the inmates were either cuffed or locked in their cells. And there was Joe-Joe, one cuff on his wrist and the other to the bars. But he was reaching for his throat like he couldn't breathe. I was cuffed face down, one eye opened, one eye closed, facing Joe-Joe.

Then he started reaching for a deputy.

"Hey!" the deputy yelled, "he can't breathe!" Three other deputies ran over and Joe-Joe started shaking crazy. I could see something in his eyes, fear, and a cry for help. As they uncuffed him, he passed out.

"Code-Three! Medical! Man Down! Man Down 5 North!"

"Get medical up here quick!" a deputy radioed.

It looked like a picture of Vietnam when help arrived. More deputies than I'd ever seen. Captain and Lieutenant came too. All the inmates were hollering, "Get him out of here! Take him to a doctor, man!"

Oh, now we care?

It got really quiet as the medical staff got off the elevator and rushed down for Joe-Joe. Blood was everywhere. Joe-Joe's body was jerking and blood was coming out of his nose. The nurse tried to put something on his mouth, but couldn't get it in.

"His trachea is broke, get an ambulance!" a nurse yelled.

His eyes were rolling around his head as they put him on the stretcher and rushed him down the tier.

"One love, Joe-Joe, stay strong!" an inmate yelled.

Another yelled, "Don't die on us, baby. Young boys don't die young!"

On my stomach I could see a blur down the tier and watch them waiting on the elevator. A nurse tried to give him mouth-to-mouth.

"Hey, don't put your mouth on him. He's bleeding!" a deputy yelled.

"It doesn't matter about the blood. If he can't breathe, he'll die if he doesn't get air!" she answered.

As the elevator came up, one of the cool deputies screamed, "Hurry Up! We can't lose this boy!" They piled on the elevator.

Some inmates were in their cells talking about the fight and what they would have done. The ones who had enough sense to miss all the madness were either on the toilet, or asleep. One crazy guy still stood in his cell door not moving, not speaking.

And there I was still lying there bloody from head to toe. No one ever asked me how I was doing.

One nut yelled out the window, "The scores is in: ninety nine, one hundred for Little Mack, hundred, ninety-nine for Joe-Joe; the winners and still champion, the deputies!" The jail inhaled and everybody started laughing, and like clockwork went back to normal.

Hurting, bleeding, and beaten, still covered with blood, I couldn't even lick my wounds for the cuffs. And Bruno, she continues to breathe, slowly. This historical whore got me down and nobody couldn't tell us not to be with her.

Chapter 8
Repairer Of The Breach:
Let That Be The Reason!

I lay there for about an hour until they came and got me. I stayed on the medical ward for two days. My injuries were too bad and they told me I was going to the hospital tomorrow. Next to the ward I was in, I found out the nuts and crazy inmates had bet their medications on the fight. They'd been hiding their meds under their tongue and selling them for top dollar. Um, like most places in jail, you always could find out who the winner was here. He was the one who'd almost overdosed on dope that was not for him.

Medical just pumped their stomachs, and sent them on back to their cells. They were just as high and happy as j-birds. I had wondered where Fed-Ex Man was. He was in here on the ward too. This brother must have had some major experience with that company. As long as he had a Fed-Ex box in his hands, he was fine. But if not, he would be downtown screaming at the top his lungs, cursing everybody out in sight. There he was asleep, quiet as a mouse, Fed-Ex box under each arm. I guess medical knew the best medication for him.

Mack faked chest pains to get down and see me. He asked the nurse could he speak to me for a minute. "One minute, that's it." The first thing out of his mouth was not, "How you doing, how's your momma? Are you hurt?"

"Did you win that money for me, boy?"

I looked at him. I turned my head and tried not to cry. "You...you bet on me?" I was so weak. I could hardly speak because of my teeth and lip.

"Boy, you money! I pumped a while in yo momma to get me a young buck like you! You here to take my name and run my game, let them know there's a real Mack in the house!" He grabbed between his legs.

I called for the medical staff. "Nurse, he's bothering me. Could you get him away from me, please?"

"Boy, what's wrong with you. You mines, sucka'!" driving his barreled fist into his palm repeatedly.

"Yeah, maybe that's what wrong with me!" I turned my head from him.

Mack really went into his gangster role, stepping toward me like a giant in sludge. "You know what? You ain't noth'n but a little punk! I heard Joe-Joe beat yo punk butt down! If it wasn't for the police, he would have had you." Those barreled fists were walking toward me now.

I yelled out to the deputy in the ward, "Hey, can you get this dude away from me!"

"Mack, back to your cell," the deputy told him. This deputy was a big white boy and didn't take no mess from nobody.

"Sho, massa deputy!" Mack answered. "I'z go'n." He turned and walked out. He didn't have enough man in him to say bye, just walked out. But I could hear him out in the sally port area talking loud: "Yeah, little Mack pack handled it for big daddy." And you know how we do it, all of his buddy hollering and slap'n each other high fives. I turned over to try to sleep, but my broken ribs made it hard.

All night I had nightmares. I could see Joe-Joe's face and eyes, crying for help. I saw myself in court being charged with attempted murder. My childhood Soul Piper and Razzy Rat were judges. But I did get a little relief that night when it was time for medication. A nurse told me that Joe-Joe was okay. She said, "They had to operate on him, but he's fine. He's just pissed because he's still chained to the bed." We laughed.

As I fell back asleep, I could see my grandma praying for me. I saw Michelle crying and I started crying in my sleep when the sleep started to get painful. Man, this dream was getting too real. I woke up and was in some real pain. I went to the bathroom and had blood in my urine and stool.

"Nurse, I'm bleeding and starting to get real cold."

A nurse came in the bathroom and checked me. "May," she said to the other nurse, "he's bleeding internally. He's got to go out now." They sent an ambulance, red lights and everything because my blood pressure was dropping. They took me straight into surgery. The only thing I could remember hearing some nut say before I left the jail was, "He gonna get paid."

When I woke up, I was on the jail medical floor at the hospital just for the jail folks. Pregnant women, guys who got shot, nuts, and even some rich folks who couldn't survive in the jail. Guess who else was there? Oh lord, Joe-Joe. He couldn't talk yet. They had him hooked up to a lot of machines and still pulling at those cuffs. He wouldn't leave the tubes alone when he was awake so they gave him stuff that kept him out.

After surgery, the doctors encourage me to get up and walk as soon as I could. So I'd walk the halls. Sometime I'd walk down and look in at Joe-Joe. He'd just be lying there still, almost dead under the heavy medication, but that machine showed a strong heartbeat. I laughed under my breath. Negro too mean to die.

On the fourth day there, Michelle and Grandma were able to visit. I couldn't look in their faces for a while. I had stitches in my upper lip, my rib cage, and the back of my head. Normally you can't receive anything during a visit, but a deputy was cool enough to let my grandma give me some tapes from the old preacher who preached the funeral where Michelle got saved. I promised to listen to them soon.

Then she'd moan a song. It made me remember when she used to moan while she washed clothes. She told me about her daddy singing that song. I never knew how much you could miss something like that, until you tasted it again.

"Grandma?"

"Yes, Emmanuel."

"Moan that song again."

Her face lit up like a Christmas tree. "You remember that song?

"Yes."

She smiled. "I use to hum that to you when you were a baby."

Then she started. She hummed and sang till all the people started coming down the halls. Many were looking in and some came in and sat right on the floor. An old wino started rubbing his eyes saying, "Boy, dat sho' sound good. I ain't heard nothing like dat since Momma passed." Even the nurses who knew Grandma came in.

As Grandma ended that song, one nurse came up and put her hands on her shoulders.

"Mrs. Harris you remember when you were working midnights, you'd sang up a storm and made our nights just fly by. When we'd lose a patient, you'd sang and lifted our spirits. Go on, girl! Sang a good one like—"

"'Amazing Grace'," I said.

Grandma's eyes heated up like fresh peach cobbler and she started singing. I mean as they say in church, "She brought the house down!" Everybody was crying, nurse, inmates, everybody. I thought I even saw a deputy drying his eyes.

Michelle was shouting, "Thank you, Lord."

After Grandma ended the song, she just stood there, lifting her hands in the air, tears streaming down like a leaking roof onto the bed. I put my hand under them as they fell and counted them like drops of gold.

Grandma said softly, "Thank you, Lord …for my baby; that we didn't lose him. Lord! You're so good, so kind."

Folks said real softly as she prayed, "Yes, Lord."

She turned to me. "Well, I got to go." She kissed me on my forehead. "Listen to these tapes, please."

"Yes, Mama."

Michelle lay on me crying as everyone left the room. All the inmates sniffling and crying talking' bout, "Man, when I get out of here, I'm going back to church." Liars.

Michelle kissed me and looked me in the eyes. "Emmanuel. I love you. And you're going to make it, because half of you is me. So you got some good seed in you. That other half of ya daddy, well, with prayer, God will make good. It's time for it to grow now." She dried her eyes and walked away.

About an hour later I walked down the hall by Joe-Joe's room. I stood there. His head was turn away from me toward the window. As I began to pass the room, I heard his weak voice. "Hey man, I heard your grandma singing. She can still blow."

"Yeah man, all she know is the Lord. You all right?"

"Yeah," balling up his fist in anger. "If it wasn't for those punk deputies! They cracked my Adam's apple."

My side started hurting, so I sat down. "Joe, I saw the look in your eyes, dude!"

"Man, I couldn't breathe, dude." He got excited and started to cough. The monitors started to go crazy.

"Yo-yo man, don't hurt yourself."

He calmed down and slowly got himself together.

"Yo, Joe got a question for you?"

Joe-Joe looked at me.

"Why you hate me, man?"

His eyes flared red and he bent his lip in. Then he caught himself. "Why you hate me, dude!"

Then it happened. We both were like goose, stuck on stupid.

I said, "You know what? I can't really answer that question? You know, Joe, it's like you know you're not suppose to hate, but like only with us, it's the thing to do."

Joe-Joe shook his head and said, "I remember one time

when I was little, me and my daddy was riding in the car and we saw you and Mack. My dad said, 'I hate dude!' I'll never forget this as long as I live because I asked him, 'Why, daddy?' Man, I'm just a kid. I don't know nothing but some cereal and cartoons in the morning. My dad, he looked at me with his lip hanging almost in the middle of his shirt. It took him about two minutes to come up with something. Oh, then he said something stupid like, 'Ah, that's the way it's suppose to be, brothers suppose to war against brothers, so the white man won't mess with us.' Like fighting with each other gets folks' respect. Man, dude. The more and more I think about it, the stupider and stupider it sounds."

We both kind of laughed.

Then I looked him in the eye. "Then why we hate each other?"

Joe-Joe lay there silent. "I don't know, Mack, I really don't know. I guess we just do." He gazed out the window.

"Meal time!" a nurse called down the hall. I got up and walked toward the door. Joe-Joe whispered, "Yo Mack, so where we go from here?"

"I don't know, Joe, I don't know? Is there anywhere else to go? I do know this, I damn sure don't want to go where my daddy's going. Can't be like him, grabbing his balls, in and out of jail, living on other people's time."

"Me either!"

Just as I turned out the door Joe-Joe hit me with something that almost made me trip and kill myself. "Yo Mack, I think I should let you know something. Your daddy bet against you, and I thought that was the lowest mess in the world. Even before me and you got into it, I was messed up over that."

I stopped in my tracks and couldn't lift my head. By this time tears were flowing on the inside. "Yo, dude. If they get you up, come see me after dinner," I said.

Before he could respond I cut the corner, holding my side and fighting back the tears. All I could hear inside was, "You don't mean noth'n to your daddy. Your daddy wasn't noth'n, and you're going to be noth'n." I didn't know how to be noth'n. Now, I really was too sick and weak as all get out trying to get back in my bed.

The nurse came in with dinner and even though I was hurting, I was hungry as a dog. Food still tasted like jailhouse mystery meat, but food is food when that's all you got. I reached over to get the tape.

"Repairers of the Breach, Let that be the Reason!"

The tape had the verse on it in the Bible so I decided to read it. A little Bible was on the table next to the bed. I started reading to myself, but I couldn't understand it because I was smacking so loud. It was saying something like, "somebody among you, shall build up something, some old waste places?" You mean we going to be rebuilding toilets? Well, that was what it said to me. Waste places? The book said it, not me! Now to me, that meant the place where folk don't got a bathroom and they just bend over or stand and piss wherever they want to? No, that's probably not what it was saying, but I was still stupid.

"You shall raise up the foundation of many generations?" I was supposed to raise up what? Wait, this was getting more confusing and calling me at the same time. I batted my eyes, trying to stay focused. "You shall be called 'The Repairer of the Breach, The Restorer of Streets to Dwell In.' Lord, we gonna be working on dams and I was scared of deep water and mentally allergic to working on streets. I didn't know much about no manual labor. I always thought that was for them Mexicans standing on the street corner for hire and in the strawberry fields. Isaiah 58:12.

I didn't understand it, but knew it had something to do with me. So I read it again. Still, I don't understand. Maybe I couldn't read and chew at the same time? But something inside knew it had to deal with me.

By the time I finished eating, I saw Joe-Joe rolling down

the hall.

This was the first time he was able to get around by himself and the deputies warned him not to start no stuff or back chained to the bed ya go. They had fixed his throat, but he was still on that watery food.

He rolled into my room and tried to talk with that raspy voice. "Damn, I hate this food!" he said with his face crumpled up like an old paper bag.

"Hey, man," I mumbled with the last bite in my mouth, "got something I want you to listen to."

You know how we do, Joe-Joe got to bouncing. "What, one of them new rap tapes from T-boy on East 57th street? I ain't heard no new grooves in a while."

"No, man. It's some preaching."

"What, some preaching? Dude, did you crack your head that hard?" He laughed and covered his mouth.

"Naw man, for real. I know I need to hear it. And you do too, crazy man."

Joe-Joe stopped bouncing and looked at me. Not mean, just kind of opened faced. I handed him the Bible and told him what chapter and verse to go to. He turned there so quick my mouth was hanging open.

"Yo, you handle that book like you know what you doing."

Licking his fingers to help him go through the pages faster, he said, "Yep, my grandmamma took me to church every Sunday. And when I wouldn't sit still, she'd hit me upside the head with the Bible. So I learned all the chapters."

Joe-Joe started reading the scripture, all the time nodding. I was surprised, the brother could read. "So what you saying, Mack? Is this what the preach'n is about?"

"Yeah man and he don't be yelling at folks, it's like he teaches. Just check him out."

"All right, Mr. D.J., it's on you. Hit the mix!"

So I hit the tape, turned up the volume, and with me and

Joe-Joe's imaginations, we thought we were almost in church. When the preacher started speaking, he read the text that I couldn't read clearly and paused. Then he gave the title of his message.

"I want to speak to you today from the subject, Let That Be the Reason. The congregation's chairs squeaked as they took their seats like they were strapping on their seat belts for this one. I heard my grandma on the tape too. She yelled out, "All right, Preacher, you preach that!"

I looked over at Joe-Joe sitting in that wheel chair. He was kind of rocking his head like the old ladies do in church. Man, if he was an old lady, he would surely be an ugly grandmamma. I could see him so clear sitting there, an old lady with some white stockings on and red lipstick, old high-heeled shoes, and a loud Sunday dress with a big hat blocking somebody's view. Then the preacher hit in high gear.

As the tape played I could see myself in every scene he painted in his words. Like a skilled swordsmen, he took his time just prepping the crowd as he laid the path he would plow into their lives. His words were clear. His words had power. His words cut, and my heart was on the operating table with no dope to numb the pain or impact. He started talking about the history of the children of Israel being a people who were disobedient.

Then it hit me, pow! In a moment I was there! Wherever there was?

It was like a high-powered explosion and I literally felt as if I were outside my body. Flashing lights like the local movie show in my mind were times shown where I was at home, in school, on the streets. Somebody might have been trying to tell me right, and I was doing just the opposite.

I saw myself standing there on a stage like a giant, towering over everyone with fat money in my hands, yelling, "Ah, old fool. You ain't talking to me. Look at this money! You don't know me? How you gonna tell me what's right?"

130

And my favorite line: "Okay, what's right, what's right?" I'd love to say that real fast, trying to jam people up in their own words.

Blam! I was on top! Back in the land with the Soul Piper and Razzy Rat! The battlefield looked like Disneyland, but the casualties were not. Those two hadn't spotted me yet, so I ran in the cuts with some platform shoes, big yellow hat, and a bud of Columbia Gold in my mouth. Next, the scene changed; I was a superhero, high and flying high. I was swelling like The Hulk running my own game. Doing my own thing was taking me higher in the clouds. I pulled up a big green glob of snot in my mouth. I spat it at everyone. But like in an instant when something goes up, it has to come down.

The preacher shifted the wind in a different direction. This blew my spit back into my face which launched an aerial attack in my chest filling up like a hot air balloon. I got caught in a clothesline, wrapped up in my cape, when he talked about how whole nations were destroyed through being disobedient. I was knocked out of the sky, falling like a man with no parachute, money flying everywhere, and I slammed right back in the hospital bed. I was starting to see how 'me' not listening brought 'me' here.

Grandma told me about the time before I was born how Michelle was acting like she was hard of hearing and had the nerve to argue about it. Well, let me change that, Michelle was loud talking Grandma, and about to get knocked out was the real case. My grandfather was still alive then and was asleep in the bedroom. Grandma said she didn't remember what the argument was about, but she did remember when Michelle was about fifteen then and said something crazy like, "Momma, I had to bust my butt to get where I am today!" Grandma said before she could get to her, Grandpa came out the back room and knocked Michelle out against the old refrigerator. She slid off the door like a wet paper towel and hit the floor, legs sprawled straight out. Didn't make my grandfather no never mind, he went in the bathroom, filled up a bucket full of water, and threw it in her face, almost drowning her with it. She came out of it coughing, spitting, and swinging in the air. Grandma said she knew Michelle in all her craziness had enough sense not to hit her with any of them blows. Grandpa told her, "Where are you now? Talk'n crazy to my wife! Who do you think you are! Don't nobody talk crazy to my wife! I don't, so you ain't, ya crazy fool!"

I found out that I was not an isolated case of being disobedient. Nobody was picking on me, and I was no victim of a slave trade. I lay there facing walls that were unforgiving that had never asked me to come in. It's always the high, exciting, off-the-hook thing to do what you're not supposed to do, right? Only at first. But when you do what you're not supposed to do and get called to the carpet on it, you want to start crying then! Israel got what was coming to them because they wouldn't listen to God. So I knew I got something coming.

POW! Gone again!

The scene changed from the cash box to the courtroom. Now I was on a witness stand! Soul Piper was the judge and Razzy Rat was the D.A. Man, got to be more careful. I yelled, "What's my charges?" The jury was some of the kids in my dream all dressed up in white suits looking as though they hadn't ever did nothing wrong. "Little Mack, you chose to do wrong! Little Mack, you're a fool and ya gonna get paid!"

"What you got against me? You ain't got noth'n against me! All y'all punks!"

A door opened up and this short thing walked out. It was a cross between a predator and alien baby. It's ugly, arms and tentacles waving every direction, a dirty pamper on, chewing some bubble gum, and slobbering everywhere. It looked like little Ron's cousin who everybody said "was touched." Don't catch that brother eating some white donuts with his mouth all open. Dude, you will throw up!

"Here he is! Dis is yo baby! Disobedience!"

Oh, my God! This was what they called in as evidence against me! They ran the video tape and there we were. We had white cream all around our mouths and that thing had the nerve to pose in every picture. I hadn't ever seen this thing before, but it had been there all the time. I was thinking all that time no one had seen what I'd done. But everything was there, in black and white. Razzy Rat said to the jury, "You all have seen the evidence, as ugly as it is. Its nose is snotty, its hair ain't combed, but no matter what you say, it's his. What's your verdict! Guilty or guilty?"

I yelled out, "What!" But before I can finish the jury yelled, "Guilty!"

I screamed "No. It wasn't me!"

The Soul Piper Judge said, "Shut up! Jury, what's the penalty?"

Jury yelled, "Give him just what he gave everybody!"

I'm thinking, give him what he gave everybody? Man, my eyes almost burst out of my head! I yelled, "No, no!" as these straps came of out of nowhere, wrapped around me, and began pulling me back toward the wall, when POW! I was back in the bed, and thinking this is killing me.

The preacher now started picking his punches. He set us up by saying, "I've got four points to make, and then we can go home. Is that all right? Ah, I wish I had a witness?"

I got a moment to regain some consciousness as he gave the congregation a place to jump in. The crowd yelled out some Amens.

"Look at the text. It's still in your Bible if you haven't torn it out. Those from among you shall build up the old waste places. Yes, there are those in our midst today that are the forerunners. Forerunners in places that seem there is no hope, no future. But the Bible says...yeah...you all stay with me now...that God has foreordained those among you to build in places that have once been destroyed. Maybe my neighborhood or maybe your home, or even it maybe someone else's life. You are responsible to build up, where terror and torment were once the rule of the game."

POW! I was there. Wherever there was.

I saw myself on the operating table. The room was a mess, sticky, stuff flying around. A lot of people walked looking like Night of the Living Dead around me in the circle in the old Creature Feature movie Michelle said they used to play on Channel 2 back in the '70s. That was way before cable and all this other stuff. All of a sudden this spotlight from the sky hit my chest, and I started to open from the inside out. I screamed like a pig going to the slaughterhouse, but this other light now coming out of my chest was stronger than my cry. I didn't have anything in me, but stuff was coming out of me.

I was half Noah's Ark, half Home Depot. Lights flashing and hammer, wood, nails, and door coming out my chest. The light touched the people. The people reached toward the light and grabbed tools floating in the air. And I was still hollering. Then something strange happened, they started working and hammering. The more they worked, the better they got. Their worn hands were getting healed, but I was cracked up and getting worse.

The preacher said, "God will take your life." He paused to take another breath. "Ah, I wish I had some help here, and let your life, be light for someone else, who maybe in darkness. Church, let that be the reason!"

The beating of the hammer and the clapping of the crowd were one voice now. When I opened my eyes, those people had built the hospital room I was back in.

Was there something in me to fix all this? As much madness as I had seen and done, did I really have something to do with the solution? Before I could catch my breath again, I could hear the preacher quieting them down, saying, "Sit down, I ain't there yet."

I could feel them settling down for the next bomb.

Preacher said, "Stay with me in the text, you all. 'You shall build up, the foundation of many generations'." I could just see him just standing there in silence for a moment, letting the word work on the minds of the folks. "You are responsible for preparing and yes, repairing the next platform, for many who are unable to stand for themselves will journey upon. There are so many people who need a firm place in life to stand today. And whatever you build today will have an effect on tomorrow. Where will our babies stand if we don't build them anything to stand on? Somebody help me please?"

The crowd yelled out some, "All rights" and, POW! I was gone again.

I knew what it felt like now when those white boys were tripping on that acid. That stuff was too much for most of the brothers. We'd see somebody high off some weed or tweaking off some crack all the time, but this was whole new trip.

I was just going to ride this out. I got the chance to catch a glimpse of Joe-Joe as I lifted off in my rocket with his stupid butt sneaking on the phone, trying to call out. Totally oblivious to what was going on with me.

When the smoke cleared, I stood somewhere on fresh concrete. Then I began to sink. But I was not just sinking in the concrete; I was turning into the concrete. Children were coming. Young, naive, looking for direction. I could barely lift my head to see where my concrete path was leading them. I saw a field of something, but it was camouflaged by white smoke, making it unclear. The closer they came, the clearer it became. My eyes literally blew out their sockets when I saw it, but I didn't have a mouth to tell the children to stop. With all my might I started to shift my concrete body from the direction of destruction. The children moved fast and it seemed like my efforts were worthless. Do something! What? I wasn't used to making decision for someone else's good? I was used to doing my thing for me, but I must do something fast! I had to destroy the path they were on? What! That meant I must destroy me?

135

But if I could destroy the path to destruction, I could save the children.

The children were midway to me and the smoke was getting thick. I started to rock and swayed like an earthquake and the children started to stumble and fall to the ground. I could see the end of my concrete path. I began to turn it with everything I had. I started to crack and fall apart. I destroyed me, to destroy the end of the path. I was totally out of strength, so the quaking stopped. The children were able to get to their feet and the smoke cleared. They began running in the new direction, around a corner. I couldn't see anything; all I could do was listen. I waited to hear a shot or something. No shots. No screams. Just the sound of little feet with those black low-healed shoes I used to complain about when Grandma used to buy me them for Easter Sunday. Pitter-patter, pitter-patter, pitter-patter. They kept going and going and going.

I heard the preacher say, "God will use your life. It may have been broken." The crowd yelled, "Yeah!" "It may have been bad" (Yeah!), "but if you give that life to Him" (Yeah!) "He'll take it" (Yeah!), "break it" (Yeah!), "and make your path, a way back to Him!" (Yeah!) "Let that!" (Yeah!) "Be the reason!" The crowd went wild.

The yelling and screaming caused the concrete me to shatter into pieces and I fell from the heavens like snowflakes. Believe you-me, I was broken, I was in pieces, but I knew something about me now. Every broken piece of me was a piece that could fix someone else. The fragments of my life were a puzzle to show the way for another not to go. It's not all bad, when you figure out your life had become a classroom for others. I hoped they got the lesson.

I came to myself and turned my head to Joe-Joe. He was on the phone and got his hand over the speaker, whispering. I heard him say, "Don't worry about that noise in the back. It's just some preacher taking loud, but ain't saying noth'n."

Man, if he only knew what was happening to me. But it

136

quickly came to me as Rev. took his third point, slowing down and shifting gears but not losing a step. The church organ was on his heals, but he said, "Hold on, brother piano man, I ain't there yet. You all stay with me and don't miss this one. You! Shall be called! The Repairer! Of the Breach!"

My ears seemed ten times their regular size. The words like a military band were able to march right up in my ear hole, and invaded my heart.

"Yes, God is talking, rather he's calling you. He is not just calling your name, but he's calling your life to be placed in a place to stop the leaks." Then he asked himself a question, "Well, Rev., what kind of leaks are you talking about? Glad you asked, let me tell you; the leaks of pain, the leaks of suffering, the leaks of hatred, the leaks of destruction."

As his voice vibrated in my soul I started to fade out again. When I came to, I was swirling under water. I guess I'd been holding my breath for as long as I could and I pressed toward the surface of the water. As I came to the top, I blew out of the water like a top and landed on a nearby golden shore. It was beautiful; it was serene, just nice. There was a beautiful Hawaiian babe waiting there for me with a towel and a Long Island Ice Tea. As I reached for the towel, I heard some noise coming from the water, then all of a sudden, the water's edges began to disappear. I looked up and there was this big dam that looked like half-a-flying saucer on its side. It must have been hit by a meteor in space because there was a big crack in it with water gushing out. As I got closer to the powering outpour, the water began to turn into people as it reached the dam break, and they were being blown out like rockets.

Repair the beach; repair the breach? What does that mean?

I ran back to the Hawaiian babe and asked her where was that water going? She had her back to me and turned to answer, but she'd changed. She was torn up now. I said, "What happened to you?" She answered, "This is what you look like when nobody stops you from being flushed through the dam, and nobody cares. Do you care?"

I ran toward the middle of the dam where the break was and jumped. Why? Don't ask me. I figured with all I saw because of this sermon, the answer would show itself if I was too stupid to know what to do. As I fell through the air, I heard the preacher say, "God can use you to patch the hole in other people's lives." I was getting close to the break and I heard people screaming for help.

I used to watch the Discovery Channel and see people jumping out of planes and gliding in different directions by using their hands and feet like wings. So you know me, I'm making my move and "pow," I slam right in the hole. I stretched my body to cover the hole, but the pressure was too strong. I dug my nails into the walls and attempted to kick in a place for my feet, but I was not strong enough. So I cry out, "Give me strength! Give me strength!" All of a sudden, I turned into a giant Band-Aid. I covered the hole, but the pressure was crazy. I refused to break.

Then I heard the preacher say, "You, my brother, my sister, are the one to cover the pathway in which the enemy has used to get to the next generation. It may be painful, but stay there! It may be hard, but stay there! It may seem like the pressure is about to break you, but stay there! For if you stay there, there will be a tomorrow! Let that be the reason!"

I could hear the crowd on their feet as I held on with all my might. I looked toward the top of the dam and saw people coming out of the water. Many of them I didn't recognize, but they were saying something. I could hear in the distance, "Thank you, thank you." All I could do was hang on. I started to open my eyes. I was back in my hospital room and wondered where was this last point going to take me?

The congregation was riding this train out as one person yelled out, "Come on, sir, ya on the runway!"

The Preacher said, "Here is my last and final point then we can go home. Somebody say, Amen." The crowd yelled out,

"Amen!" I could hear Grandma shouting, "Thank ya, Jesus!"

"You are the repairers of the breach. Listen! The restorers of streets to dwell in.

You are the ones God will use to get the land back to its original place of purpose. God didn't give us this world to go to Hell in a hand basket." The crowd burst out in laughter, but started responding, "You right, preacher, you right!"

"But that He loved the world, is that right (Yeah!). That he gave us Jesus."

I could still hear the tape and I think I was gone again? Or was I? I slowly opened my eyes and I was still here. No pow. No smoke. No superhero ending. This was reality. I could see the streets I lived on and they were not safe. Not safe from the aspect of walking down them, but living on them. Was life safe itself? Would these streets, spots, turf, whatever I called it be safe enough for children if I lived long enough for them to grow up on? This was not about color or race, for everybody was doing some damage on the streets. Be it high-class suburbia or the Columbine copycats in the Midwest, Southeast LA and its Hispanic population, the brothers from dark country Washington DC to the hills of Hunters Point in the Bayview. There was some terror on all levels and I heard the preacher now speaking directly to me.

"God is calling you now to restore. Let that be the reason!"

Then with the organ on his heels, he closed out as only a black Baptist preacher can. Every time he paused between words, the crowd got their shouts in and ended with, "Let that be the reason!"

The tape faded out. Joe-Joe started to push himself toward the door. His eyes were wet, his jaw closed tight, and he tried to be cool shaking it off. Somehow when I was out, he heard something that had got him stuck.

When he got to the door he stopped. "Well, young Mack Emmanuel, since you had the tape, where we go from here? Seeing who we are, where do we go?"

I cleared my throat. "Because we are the main ones, maybe it may start with us?"

"What starts with us?"

"I don't know."

"Let that be the reason." Joe-Joe turned, slightly looking over his shoulder and rolled out the room.

Chapter 9
From Boys to Men: Breaking Me From My Favorite Blanket

I did eight months in the county jail, and Joe-Joe got sixteen months in the penitentiary. I stayed out of trouble as much as possible. For one, I was sore for two months and limited mobility made limited madness. I got moved to the second floor and worked in the kitchen with Deputy Merry-Merry. He'd go through the tier at night saying, "Hello-Hello-Hello-Hello! Lock'n doors, Lock'n doors, Lock'n doors real fast!" Everybody got a kick out of him. Down here everyone was mostly older, mature, problem free and doing their time.

Only a few of us young knuckleheads were permitted to try and fit in and learn something if we'd shut up and listen, no running around with your head all wild, and a shower without fail every night.

Deputy Merry's supervisor was a woman named Sergeant Yow, who we called (under our breath) "Yip-Yow!" She was the first, finest, six-foot Chinaman I had ever seen. And again, even with this simple normal thing, an old 'G' pulled us to the side and continually schooled us so we would understand how not to mess this good opportunity up.

"Y'all listen. For one, she fine. So be cool 'cause you have something good to look at while you do your jobs, and don't get caught staring or with your hands in your pants around her either. Two, she's a sergeant. She got the power to roll yo foolish behinds up for acting a fool down here too. Three, see them legs?" We all looked. She had some jack hammers for thighs inside that tight uniform. "She'll kick you through a brick wall, so don't play her." I think we got it.

Every day when this old cool deputy was finished with his

141

newspaper, somehow it would be on the gate. Nobody asked any question how. The trustees and tier hogs would be the first to read, then it would filter down to the rest of us. Paper didn't get all tore up, just couldn't find all the sections you may have wanted to read.

At first I didn't care, but I kept seeing the world and business sections left out on the table. Front section, gone. Sports, what was that? Movies and cars? Now you might see a little of that. But the other two sections sat there like imported foster children at a family reunion. So I picked them up one day and started reading them. I learned about stock and bonds, how this company's stock operated and the Dow Jones. Found out about the movement of finances and the who's who of start-up businesses.

There was an old Chinese man we called Grandmaster. He was in good shape, stayed to himself, and read his Chinese newspaper.

One day I asked him, "Hey, old man, tell me what that say?"

He smiled. "This not important to you." Then he pointed at the section I had. "This important to you." He smiled, and went back to reading.

He prayed and worked out alone, but would let you do his moves as long as you stayed behind him and didn't disturb him. Just get your towel and do what he did.

Some knuckleheaded inmate in his thirties, still childish, got in front of Grandmaster and acted like he wanted to spar him. Grandmaster didn't detour from his routine. When Grandmaster got to one of his moves with his arms stretched out, this nut hit Grandmaster on the hand. Grandmaster stood back and put two fingers together. The next time he swung at Grandmaster, Grandmaster tapped him on the top of his hand. His whole left side went limp. His eyebrow, lip, elbow, down to the bottom of his foot was numb. Brothers laid him on his bunk for two days because he couldn't move. Boy drooled like he was teething. Nobody even thought to attempt to call medical on this one.

Grandmaster told him, "You want feel better now?" Brother couldn't answer, just nodded. Grandmaster got a cup, put some water in it, and heated it up in the microwave. He disappeared down the tier for a moment, and then came back. The cup was sizzling and a bubbling.

Somebody yelled out, "Grandmaster! What's that?"

Grandmaster said, "Secret Lee-Kee Tea. He be fine," and smiled. He gave it to the brother, who was up the next day. We asked him how it tasted. He said it smelled like pee, but he was glad he could walk again and wasn't messing with Grandmaster no more. Grandmaster just smiled at him from then on.

One of the buffed older brothers also had a few of us young guys on the little workout routine every day after we came back from the kitchen. It was me, Rock-star who had hazel eyes and was kill'n the honey's with them. He had a big young Samoan girl who would beat his behind when he got out of line.

Spider, who was pitch black, weighing about a hundred pounds wet, had some skinny arms and a skinny head, but some big bright white eyes. When it was time for lights out, you could see his eyes before you could see him. Josh Tigura, who we called Tiger-balm, took Thorazine and smelled like medicine when he sweated, and Buzzard. He got that name because he would stand at the garbage can after chow time and eat anything left on everybody's tray. "You gon' eat dat, you gon' eat dat," is all he would say. He got arrested when somebody getting off the bus knocked his last three sunflower seeds out of his hand. He went off.

Then there was my buddy who didn't stay long named Randy, who I named Digga-Find-One. He was a redhead locked up for writing bad checks in his father's name and straight PC (Protective Custody) material. His good points, he

143

was quiet and wasn't scared to ask questions, his bad point, he was always digging in his nose and would stand there and look at it for a while.

One old gray-headed 'G' who forked his afro up in the front stiff as a garage door had warned him a few time about that, but the last time Digga worked on the food line, he found the 'right thing' at the 'wrong time.' To save his own behind, he had to roll himself up quickly that day.

Before he left, we got to know a little about each other and pulled up the shade slightly in each other's world. It was the first time I could really say that color didn't matter to me. It was a Saturday night when we got into a conversation that totally opened my mind about people with big money.

"Hey Digga, you said you was in here for writing bad checks?"

"No. I said I was in here for writing checks, not bad ones."

"So what's writing a good check then, white boy?"

"It's when you write the things and there's cash galore to back it up like you can't do, black boy."

"So you got money when you wrote them?"

"Yeah dude, it was my father's account. Man, I ain't going to jail for getting busted for running with some hot tennis shoes. It's like this, if I wrote the check, it was good, no matter the amount."

"So what's the most you wrote one for?"

Digga looked over his shoulder. "Now, this just me and you talking, right? 'Cause I can't have anyone in my business and they always say you youngsters talk too much."

I jumped back. "Hey man, don't throw me up in that."

Digga didn't flinch. "Then shut up and stop running your mouth on the phone about everything that goes on in here to whoever you be talking to, homey."

I laughed and gave him a little elbow shot. "Okay. You got me on that. How much?"

"I wrote one for a hundred grand."

"What?"

"Yeah dude."

"Didn't your daddy miss that kind of cash?"

"My dad works for the government. My dad *is* that kind of cash. Down payment on a car, partying, bottles of champagne. I was just spending to be spending. I used to do it every now and then, no more than a couple of hundred dollars. Dad didn't notice anything different, at least he never sent word of anything, and then I started pushing the envelope. "

"What's pushing envelope's got to do with spending money? What, you a mailman now?"

"Yo dude, it's just a figure of speech. Didn't you pay attention in school?

"Naw, I'm in here with you, fool."

"That means that I started to do more because I was getting away with more. I don't think the money was the issue, till I put government license plates on the Porsche."

"What? You was pimp'n a Porsche?"

"Yeah, what's the big deal, dude?"

"Man, we would die to get the chance to sit in one of them."

Then the conversation shifted.

"That's the problem with you people, man."

"What?"

"You always think if somebody's got some money, their life is the best thing in the world."

"Dude, you was spending fat cash! Half the fools in here when they had some cash were on the run trying not to get caught, and couldn't spend it because they knew they didn't look the part. Here you got money in yo family like it's normal and you say we trip'n?"

Then Digga went real deep and hard on me. He opened a door in my life I had never walked through before.

"Emmanuel, just because you've got money, doesn't make you somebody. Money can cover up more than it can buy. It can make stuff disappear. Sent to an all-boys' school across the state, paid to go away. Me and my sister sent every summer to my grandparents in England, paid to go away. My mother telling me to go in her purse and get whatever I needed, just don't come home till morning so she could be with her boyfriend, paid to go away. You don't get it, dude, because you've never had it." Digga turned red.

I tried to bring a little ease to the dialog. "Man, did any of them priest mess with you?"

He smiled. "No. But for the kids that it did happen to—"

"Paid to go away?" I said.

He threw his towel up and over our heads. "Paid to go away," he answered. "You know, Emmanuel, I had to wear shorts, sport coat, white socks in that school and all I ever wanted to do was be bad."

"What? Be bad? What's being bad to you?"

"Yeah, get loose! Get high! Have a pit-bull with one of them shut up collars on it! Not some dog that looks like it's always smiling and rode with a seat belt on. So when I got out, I got out. Partying with anybody I could, black, white, straight, gay. I just want to live. But one thing I don't understand about you, Emmanuel, is you guys fighting over some land, street, turf, whatever you call it, and none of you own it."

I paused for a second. "We live there. It's ours. That's why we protect it."

Digga's eyes cut. "You own it, huh. That's the reason the bread delivery truck and milk truck had to put doors with locks, because of you guys. It's like you do stuff just to do stuff. You don't even know why? Some guys can't even keep quiet on the BART train at six o'clock in the morning, man, when people who do have to work are trying to get their last few minutes in. I mean, bro, do ya have to play ya boom boxes all the time? Look, how many Alhambra water bottles you guys got with no machine for them? Saving change, E? You don't own it. It's some company's property and just like the streets, it's the governments, man. You don't own them."

I laughed about the jugs and gave it to him for that. "Well, it's ours until somebody moves us out."

"And that's okay. Things are always something to someone who has nothing, but when you've got something, then you find out what you really need."

I looked at him and smiled. "You know what? I'll understand that better, bye-in-bye. Man, when y'all was in England did y'all eat tea and crumpets?"

"A lot of tea, no crumpets. And the food doesn't have much seasoning either."

"But you blessed that you could go."

"Yeah, they love us too."

"So what about your dad?"

"Like I said, he works for the government so he's always on the go. I talk to him a lot over the phone and we see him about four months out of the year. What he does for the government, I don't know." Digga stopped. "Wow, I'm finally admitting it. I don't know?"

"Why is that so important now, you saying I don't know?"

"Cause I always pretended to know who he was. So I always waited to see what the other kids would say about their dads, then I'd make my dad bigger that theirs. But Emmanuel, I don't know?"

"Is that good or bad?"

"I don't know."

"Man, I'll take your problem any day and put a ghetto twist on it for the wild."

"Well bro, you've heard the saying, what you don't know won't hurt you?"

"Yeah."

"It may not hurt you, it may kill you."

"Word up."

"What?"

"That means thank you for the information. Wasn't you

listening in school?"

We laughed and made some peanut butter and banana sandwiches. Just before lights out we saw Grandmaster ending his workout.

"Hey, you see Grandmaster over there?" asked Digga.

"Yeah," I answered

"I bumped into him playing around yesterday and he told me to be careful or he'd cook me in hot grease."

"What did you do?"

"I left him alone, dude. I write checks, I'm not a fool."

A yell came for the rotunda: "GENTLEMEN! PHONES OFF! LIGHT OUT! FIVE MINUTES!"

The night crooners were at the back of the tier performing their nightly show under the spotlight of the moon through the missing cell glass:

"Heaven help us all...

Heaven help us all...

O' lord hear our call, when we call."

Then the lead singer wearing cardboard glasses hit this verse that caught me in the chest:

"Heaven help the boy who won't reach twenty-one,

Heaven help the man who gave that boy a gun,

Heaven help the people with their backs against the wall,

Lord, heaven help us all...yeah, yeah..."

The guy was crying and the crowd clapped in time very low. The harmony-parched hearts of the many veterans of incarceration standing around, who knew that they didn't have much time to waste because they were standing right next to their futures.

The old "G's" looked at us, the little or next "g's." Their eyes said, "Enough of the G's, we need some N.G.J.M's. Never Gangsters, Just Men. A new line of fathers who were responsible, not robbing, stealing, fighting, shooting at each other, or anyone else. The new line of men whose story was 'I didn't have to live life asleep, just to go to jail to wake up.'

Then out of the darkness, one voice softly soloed:

"Lean...ing, lean...ing, safe and secure from all alarm."

Their harmony grasped rays from the moon and joined as an all call of mercy for these young boys behind bars.

"Lean...ing, lean...ing...leaning on the ever, las...ting, arm..." ending with everyone's personal touch.

The old deputy shadow stood at the entrance to the gate, hands on his hips, not saying a word. It wasn't till the last note faded away did he hit the power switch. The noise from the boiler rocked us to sleep and covered the youngsters quietly whimpering for their mommas through the night.

I got up in the morning and Digga was gone. Rooster, who worked cleaning the front office and always overheard something that wasn't inmate business, said a deputy said that his charges just "disappeared." I thought, Paid, and gone away. I didn't even get the chance to say goodbye either. Found out that some money talks loud in silence.

November 3rd, same day we got that new President, Bill Clinton, I got released. He beat daddy Bush and this rich cat who was talking straight head because he was using all his own money, H. Ross Perot. Dude said it more than a few times, too.

"I can say what I want to say. I'm using my money." And he said what he wanted to say.

I was out! Man, I felt like the president. Michelle threw me a small, controlled, not-acting-a-fool and don't-invite-no-fools party. She got this new friend in her life named John. Now you know a momma and her son being each other's for so long, he challenged every change in her life because he don't want to share her. John was mid-height, stocky, quiet, but you could feel he didn't have an ounce of fear in him. So I thought it wise not to just challenge him for no reason. And actually, he never gave me a reason to. John was not trying to be one of those midnight silos, in at dark, out before light. He was seriously up here for his, which just happened to be my momma.

We had a good time talking loud, dancing, and eating

everything in sight. That jailhouse food was nasty, but I put on some solid weight. Carla, the Mexican girl from my old high school, brought Sandy. Oh, my God! She was still beautiful, thick, but still wasn't letting nobody ride that booty. I got the chance to really start knowing her. She had a good job working in an accounting firm and was seriously different from some other sisters. Straight, God-fearing, homebody-taking-care-of-her-daughter-on-the-way-to-church-every-Sunday-morning girl. She wasn't just a normal church girl either. Some of them were wilder than the ones who didn't go, you know the kind at church in a thin sundress, no stockings, some high-heeled pumps, and got to let everybody know she got a thong on! Come on, man?

She was also serious about her future and just what I thought I needed at this stage in my life. Again I started shooting a little play at her, but she came right out. "If you want to get to know me, you got to come to church with me."

So guess what? I went to church with her, Grandma, and Michelle. Now, you know I still had a lot of that jail in me when I got out, and I forgot about what Mr. Hortan taught us in class about us with the maze experiment too. So when I went to church, I looked crazy so nobody would say anything to me.

But remember that preacher? Well, I got the chance to meet him face to face. I knew he had never laid eyes on me, but it was like he could preach straight through me. Everything he said, cut. It was a big church and he even couldn't see me, but he saw me through that Bible. The words he said haunted me like a ghost. Every time I'd do something foolish, I heard his words on the back of my neck, digging through my flesh like a cheap chain.

The people at the church, man, just as bold. I guess they was crazy too, crazy for Jesus. Man, they hugged me so much when they found out I was Mrs. Harris' grandson.

They had me sweat'n with my loud Market Street suit on. Grandma was just as proud of me standing there looking stupid. One brother they called Elder Glass had these big old hands. He said something that just messed me up. He said, "God's got a work for you and you can't do anything to get away from it. Try to run like I did, and see what will happen."

Man, it was like everywhere I went, I was marked. I was going out one night, all dressed up in that loud suit again, and a knock came on the door. The Men of Breakthrough from the church were just coming by to check on me, at least ten of them. Every man was clean.

The smell of Hi-Karate and Aqua Velva rose as clear as the blue sky, marching through my nostrils, which made the brain come to attention. It completely filled the room and you felt their presence like a deep root cleaning.

One brother said, "Young man, we didn't come here to change your plans. We just came by to see how you're doing and pray for you."

I was thinking, cool. Just pray, and leave because I'm on my way to the party! All I had on my mind was dancing to some jams, get me a freak, get high, come home, get some, and get out! Period!

Man, those brothers praying affected me. I could feel this presence that was deep. Some of the brothers were laid down on the floor. Oh, it done got crazy up in here. Elder Glass laid his hands on Michelle, and she went O-U-T!

I wanted to go over and touch her, but I couldn't move. I held it together not to mess up my white shirt and thangs. Then the brothers quietly left. Michelle was still out on the floor. I just kneeled down and looked at her. She wasn't dead, but wherever she was, she was in some solid peace. I was quiet not to mess up her "out" because I sho' didn't want nobody messing up my high. A few minutes later she came through. I helped her to her room.

In the bedroom, she just started crying and lifting her hands. After all this I was still determined to go to the party. I thought she would try to stop me, but she turned and said,

"Have a nice time."

I tried to shake it off while walking down the block. I almost had myself together by the time I reached the garage party. I got in and found the wildest babe who was ready to get loose on the dance floor. With that one bulb as everybody's spotlight, it was perfectly dark enough for us not to clearly see who or what we were dancing with. Mr. DJ was popping the songs back to back! *"One Nation Under A Groove, I Just Want To Be What You Want Me to Be"* by Cameo.

Then the DJ hit the slammer by Chic, "La Freak, *Freak Out!"*

We all hollered.

It was the song that the sisters would throw their boobs and butts in a blender and you touched as much and as fast as you could. I was on her up and down. The place was hot. It was so packed the back door couldn't open. I popped my coat off and threw it over my shoulder and pointed at baby like a cowboy about to lasso his bull. That turned the crowd up a notch.

She threw her non-Right-Guard-wearing arms up in the air, and funk went flying E-V-E-R-Y-W-H-E-R-E! Shot straight up my nose, burning my nose hairs with the same velocity of the ignorant mistake of putting too much horseradish on your roast beef sandwich.

One of my boys who was dancing next to me must have smelt it too because his eye bucked out as he pointed at me and said, "She hot dog, she hot!" I just let it go because that's what you get when *you're* up to no good anyway. As she turned around and bent over, I proceeded to stomp in my 'monster strut' like Gaiter in *Jungle Fever* right up to mount the booty, but guess what? A few tears started coming out the corner of my eyes, on the dance floor! I played it off like something was in my eyes.

The music slowed and everyone tightened up with whomever they had near. Heatwave's *"Always and Forever"* blasted through the component set speakers that were pushed to their max. She laid her grease scary curls on my neck, which was a straight visual for me down her blouse. She knew I was looking all the time.

I was straight shoot'n game at her. Then she started talking, too fast, mouth open too wide, and gave up just too much information. Oh, Lord, have mercy. She said she had been in the Army, but was discharged for 'a character and behavior disorder.' I was slowly trying to back up. By the look in her mouth I thought, she must have bit a hand grenade. Her teeth were scattered two by fours all over her mouth. I was scared that if she closed her mouth, she'd do some serious damage to her tongue. I was looking over my dark glasses and watched one of her eyes that would buck out, then all of a sudden starting jumping. I thought it had kangaroo in it.

Well, one thing led to another, and even though I said that I had wanted to commit myself to Sandy, I never said that I was committed to her commitments or convictions. I took baby back to the house and was determined to get her between the sheets, and she acted like she didn't have no problem going either. Although in my mind I knew this was wrong, maybe the act would make it right. Right?

Got home and went in my room. Here was where I found out that for some, clothes is camouflage. When she dropped them jeans and popped off that thong, everythang went loose! Oh man, where's soap and water? Did ya dush? Have you ever used some vinegar and that hot water bottle hanging on a coat hanger in the bathroom, something? But I wasn't the most consistent bather, and my private area was having its upheaval too. I'm starting to feel a little bad, so I thought about anything, trying to convince myself this was worth it. I pretended we smelled like roses, but it was what it was.

I said, "It's gonna be a funky night tonight."

"Sho you right, baby," she slung back at me. She snatched her bra off and slung it somewhere. My lip dropped. Her back and chest bore the gouged imprints that said somebody had pulled the emergency cord on a train, just after it ran over her. One nipple had a cut under it as if it was smiling.

"Girl...how yo chest get like that?" I said.

"You know how we do it. When you fight'n family, you don't use no guns. We from down south, we fights with a straight razor and I cut her up, too."

"Her who?"

"My sista."

"You mean, you won, and you came out looking like that?"

"Yeah."

"Wow...hum." I was trying to find a trap door anywhere to fall through.

Why did she have this Tyrannosaurus Rex walk? She said her shoes were too tight and she fell during basic training down ten feet on some forest timber. The imprints could be seen where she landed, hips first.

We got on the bed and as I was pulling off my pants I knocked over the tape player and it came on. Yep, that preacher! I had been listening to a sermon he preached called: "Deep in a Hell Hole! It's Hotter than You Think?" Man, I hurried up and turned that thing off.

Baby said, "What was that?

"Oh, nothing. Just a word to the wise, but who wise, girl?"

When I rolled over, I hit the headboard and knocked the Bible right on the top of her head, bapp! I threw it across the room and tried to get busy, but man, it wasn't right at all. She was leading me, and all I could do was look over at that Bible that was on the floor near the fan blowing the pages back and forth.

I was so messed up, I just went limp and stopped. Now that's bad for a brother to admit, but I was just that messed up.

She pushed me off her, blowing like a Brahma bull. "What's the matter with 'chu, boo!"

"Nothing, just go home," I answered, still staring at the Bible.

"Oh, don't worry, sex-joke. I got me a soda out of you. But you know what? You can give some, and get some, unstrapped! You'll feel me again." She grabbed my T-shirt and wiped between her legs like an old soldier, then threw it at me. I jumped out the way. She put her clothes half on and Tyrannosaurus herself right out the door.

I picked up that shirt with a stick and took it outside to the garbage can. Now, I may have left a few women victimized by my love-making tactics, but this was the first one I had to accept. Plus, she left three things with me.

First, her bra, which was dirty and nasty. I was too stupid and kicked it under the bed. When my room got hot, the aroma would lift and hover over as if it owned all four walls of the house. I couldn't figure out why I kept smelling that woman? When Sandy would come over, she would only sit in the living room which was cool with me, but I knew my rope with this was getting short. Michelle pulled me to the side before I left the kitchen and busted me out cold, but at least it wasn't in front of Sandy.

"Whose funky clothes is in your bedroom, Emmanuel?"

I hit her with the stupid swollen lip, weak-eyed Mack face. "Wha-what Momma?"

"I know when you get to poking your lips out with that slop on the end, you up to something, or lying. Which one?"

"Naw, Momma. I'm cool."

"Okay, mister stanky cool. Somebody stank."

Second, her funky odor was on me. I couldn't shake it, and Sandy picked it up. (You know women can do that?) I would get close to her, and all of a sudden she'd pull away, looking at me strange. You know me, I'd try the old Mack smile again, but she would say, "Okay, boy. I'm not the one." I knew it was coming, but I didn't know when it would get there.

I went over Sandy's house late, high, and uninvited. Her

father met me at the door standing in his socks and drawers looking like a semi-retired Sumo wrestler. I got a clear intuition this was not the time to even ask for an invitation in, but he did let me speak to her on the porch. I didn't push my luck but I asked for a ride home, which she did. But when we were almost near the exit to my house, she blasted me.

"Emmanuel, who do you think you are, just showing up at my house without calling, and high on top of that?"

"Why you trip'n? Just get a brotha home. I sprayed on some cologne and ate some tic-tacs before I came. Y'all need to stop trip'n."

"My mother said the last time you came by without calling, you didn't even brush your teeth. She could smell your breath through yo neck!"

I giggled and rocked my head, spinning the last residue of weed in the back of my mind. "Okay, I'm going to let you have that one." I turned the radio up loud and started singing, "Ain't gone hurt no body, to get on down," and danced in my seat.

She slammed the off button. Her voice changed. "Emmanuel, who have you been with?"

"What you talk'n 'bout, girl? I just asked you to give me a ride home. You know you mess'n up my high."

The car came to a screeching halt. "You know what, Emmanuel, get out!"

"What?"

"Get out now, Emmanuel!"

"Girl, do you know where we at! We on the freeway!"

"I don't care, get out now!" she screamed, pushing me in the face like a man.

"Get out here? I can get ran over by a car?"

She pushed me in the face again. "How are you going to tell me you want to be serious with me and sleep with another girl?"

"Wait. Who told you I've been with another girl. I don't know anything about that." I decided to use some reverse psychology on her to see how far she would go. "But hey, you said you want to be with me too, but you don't show it? What if somebody else does?"

"Just because I won't sleep with you doesn't mean I don't care for you. You are getting closer to my heart every day and you know that. But I've learned to love me enough not to give myself away anymore, and only wind up with me at the end. If sex is all you wanted from me, you don't know what love is. Get out, Emmanuel!"

So I got out on the freeway right at the Army St. exit with cars flying by!

Sandy yelled, "Don't step out in the middle of traffic! That will mess up your high!" and sped off.

So I walked down the off ramp, constantly looking over my shoulder for any drivers swerving because somebody may be as high as me.

And third, she gave me a disease. My wee-wee shriveled up and burned so bad when I peed, I couldn't even touch it. I leaned over the toilet on my tippie-toes, gritted my teeth, and breathed in small puffs till the last drop came out. I knew I had to run down to a clinic and get some meds. I couldn't go to where Grandma and Michelle worked, so I went across town to General Hospital. And lo and behold, guess who worked there– one of the members of the church. I didn't know her, but she knew me. She hugged me just like we were at church too. Cool stupid me, I was so embarrassed. She told me about confidentiality, but I always thought church folks talked too much and told everything. So before I thought the news would get out, which it didn't, I finally came clean with everybody. I called Michelle and told her what I did. She told Grandma, and Grandma said, "You'd better clear this up with Sandy today! Not tomorrow, today!"

Then I called Sandy. When she heard the truth from me, she was silent. Scary silent. The silence reverberated through the phone line, down my ear socket, and stuck an arrow in my throat. She was hurt, and I mean hurt bad. I begged her to let me come by and talk. After a while she said yes, but I had to be clean, clear headed, willing to shut up and listen. For her, I was all ears.

When I got to her house, her father and his dog, a well-groomed old Doberman Pincher, met me at the door. This was scary. He was one of the old-school fathers who worked hard because his hands were always dirty, like up-under-the-skin dirty. When we went in the living room to talk, he sat in a chair right in plain view. Even though he wasn't facing me, the stiffness in his back and neck and his rocking slowing back and forth was his way of sending out old school 'Morse code.' If I misread the message, a lot could get tore-up in this living room, mainly me.

"Sit. Down, Colander," he said to the dog.

The dog lay in comfortable but ready position with ears pointed up like radars.

This had my undivided attention. I guess they both wanted to make sure that none of the fool in me popped out, and believe you-me, I poured concrete on the top of that Jack-in-the-Box tonight.

Sandy led me into a painful place in her life. Every step was barefoot, sensitive to the touch, as if walking on a glass ceiling over a sleeping child being rescued from an abuser. They were doors that had been shut from the residue of memories that were trying to be left behind. She had been under the scalpel of an unskilled surgeon, whom she immaturely trusted.

She shared that before we got together, her daughter's father was unfaithful to her, which was why she would not stay with him. She tried over and over to make them a family, but he said that she wasn't fun now, she was a responsibility. One day she and her daughter were at the bus stop. He drove past them with another female in the car. Her daughter was little and didn't know any different and said, "Daddy, daddy, my daddy car." Her daughter was so happy and she was so sad.

She confronted him about the situation. He totally bypassed the woman and the car issue. It came down to answering about being a father. She couldn't run from the truth.

"I wasn't ready to be a father. You made me a father," he said.

"I made you a father? I thought we both were in this?"

"I didn't ask you for no baby. Did I?"

"No. Well…?"

"Well what? We was having fun, girl, we was having sex. You know I walk up on you and put my hands round yo hips and start kissing and squeezing, I didn't change that, you changed that. You brought this baby into this, not me." Then he got real funky with her. "Y'all always want a baby, thinking y'all can control us. Do you know what it is to be made a daddy before you ready?"

"Is that what you think? That I got pregnant to own you? I got pregnant loving you."

"Woo-hoo! Loving me, girl, you in it too much. I'm scared of you."

Said she really had to look at the situation for what it was. They were both to blame, but she was the one with the child. She even noticed how he was embarrassed to be seen with her. He was always somewhere else when they needed to get something for the baby, when he couldn't stay from on top of her before. It was something she would not run away from, and would not let another young punk put her in that situation again.

My eyes never left hers.

She was determined not to be a welfare baby-momma either. Said when she had to receive AFDC, she would hold her check for two days, not to be seen hustling to get it cashed. She had some friends who were holding project-seminar potlucks on how to 'work the welfare.' More babies, more money. She said, "That will not be me."

She also was very protective of her daughter too. The few

times we went out, she didn't do it at the inconvenience of the baby, and was not trying to get me to play baby daddy either. Her daughter was well cared for and she would tear a patch out of someone for messing with that little girl.

She mentioned her daughter came home from daycare one day telling of the caregiver's son giving them "A Santa Claus," and how one little boy was crying. Because her little girl could talk well, she told her to tell her what a Santa Claus was. She picked up her doll and showed her. She said, "He pick him up by his head off the ground, and mommy, he was crying." Sandy knew what that was, and it was *on* like popcorn. The next day she was up there and tore into the baby sitter and her son. Though Sandy worked in corporate America, she could go straight ghetto on you if necessary.

Now, adding my foolish stunt with military monster baby, I might get my discharge papers. But for some reason she wasn't ready to give up on me. With her hand cupping mine, she had let me inside her heart. Her eyes painfully wet with the disappointing dew of a brighter day, as she remained in confidence of a promise greater than me in her tears.

She also got some brothers and my stupid butt didn't even consider that danger in the unfolding process. One known as "Mighty" and his name was that for a reason. Everything he did was 'mighty.' If the brother was talking, it was 'mighty.' The brother drove one of them old big cars and you could hear it coming a mile away, it was 'mighty.' If you saw the brother eating a taco with extra, extra hot sauce, he did it 'mighty.' If he had to put them 'thangs' on somebody, oh, it was 'mighty!' And the brother had some mental-health issues beyond his control, and guess what? They were 'mighty.'

News got out that somebody heard he had called in to the health-clinic radio talk show for some advice on 'how not to kill this fool that had just hurt his little sister.' You know I was sweating like a cat in Phoenix, at 12 noon, with no shade! Michelle even said she saw him at church down in the deliverance line crying out really fast, "Please help me, Jesus! Please help me, Jesus! Don't let me kill this boy! Don't let me kill this boy!"

Everybody but the bold was giving this brotha fifteen and a half feet on this one. They said it took some time and some gallons of oil to get that brotha delivered. I was praying that it worked. One time I saw him standing in the park with no shirt on, flexing his muscles with his eyes closed, arguing with a Christmas tree. Somebody took a picture and put it in the local magazine. I wasn't sure if this was a joke or not. It was entitled, "Is This Yours? Come Get Him! The Children Are Afraid To Play In The Park!"

She looked me in my eyes. "God said that I should prepare myself by being a virtuous woman and I know the right man will find me. I didn't go looking for you, Emmanuel, you came after me. And if you are not the right man for me and if you're going to do me wrong, get out of my life. So at least you won't be in the way of the right man who comes for me." She leaned forward and caressed my face, kissing me on the lips. Two pools of relief were released from her eyes, running to the bottom of her chin.

"And just think. I was about to let you into my heart. And you know what? I love you, but I don't need you." She paused. "I'm going to do us a favor. I'm going to let you have some time off to think about us."

"What you mean by some time off?" I answered, but I kept my voice down because Pops immediately stopped rocking. I saw the dog's ear twitch.

"Exactly that. You don't need to see me for a while. You need to see you right now."

I was trying to stay cool. "So does that means this is the end of us, we breaking up?"

"No. It's the beginning, depending on what you choose. Maybe? I'll see you later?"

"If God wills again, huh, church girl?"

"You know it. And don't be hawking me, Emmanuel. I heard about you brothers not having enough sense to let a sister alone when they say no."

"Huh?"

"Oh lord, deaf and dumb now. Don't play with me, Emmanuel, you heard me."

She picked up her purse and walked out of the room.

I sat there numb for a minute. Now I was face to face with those words again, causing me to make a choice. I looked over my shoulder. Her father was still there and the dog too. The deep bend in her dad's cheek and the pucker in his lips confirmed the conversation really had come to an end, and there was no pursuit to be made up in here. I got up and headed for the door.

He met me there and opened it. "Good night, young man."

"Good night, sir."

I got in my car and started driving. *Anywhere*. I turned on the radio, The Quiet Storm on Love 94. I was on Sloat at 19th Ave and saw Sigmund Stern Grove, the place where every kid in San Francisco went on a field trip.

Announcer: "Enjoying your evening with the Quiet-Storm on Love 94. Hey, this is Dave Cordell and the night will be cold and wet with showers coming in from the east, so you should be with the one you love tonight. It's going to be a cold one. And for those who need a reminder of who you have, we have The New Birth with '*Wildflower*' on Love 94."

The sound hit those nailed-down speakers with throat-clearing conviction. The emotions of that powerful trumpet intro waved in the air like a charge to war. My bottom lip quivered and eyes were as heavy with water as a pregnant mother carrying groceries with her sleepy two-year-old in her arms. I drove with my gangster lean as my face fell apart on my way to Ocean Beach. Many a baby was conceived in the back seat of cars out there.

The brother hit the verse, "She's faced the hardest time

162

you've have imaged, many times her eyes hold back the tears, lord, lord."

My face muscles couldn't hold it together any longer. The pressure broke behind my eyeballs and tears scattered like glass. My mouth was wide open, looking like I had mad cow disease and slobber ran with the frequency of a popped water faucet. I got out of the car with the music still blasting and started dancing my invisible heartache.

"She's a sweet and tender flower, growing wild."

I hollered, "Ahaaaaaa!" and started choreographing my moves through the sand like the Dramatics.

Before I knew it, I was standing in the water in my new Stacey Adams from Flagg Brothers, and I don't care. Average White Band turned the corner and ran up out of the station, *"If I Ever Lose This Heaven."* Oh God, I didn't know the verse but I knew the chorus. The stars shifted and formed a glow of Sandy. Even in the darkness, her tenderness and kindness had been my sunshine. How could I lose her? The breeze caught under my arms and lifted my jacket in a Marylyn Monroe moment.

I danced with the winds as I stomped and kicked up sand for special effects. I was loud, but everyone was so busy in the back seat getting they groove on, I didn't even attract no attention. It was just me and that friend that would faithfully meet every visitor and rock us to sleep, Mr. Midnight.

As I got back to my car, half-wet, sweaty, and shoes full of sand, Bobby Womack's *"If You Think You're Lonely Now"* rose up and sat in the seat right next to me. I leaned against the car door and thought, man, this cat is trying to drive it in! Wait until tonight? Tonight was here. I was really lonely now. This must have been the DJ's night to talk to me directly. "My last song before I go and turn the night over to Lady T. Night to bring in your morning is to those who need a miracle. Here's The New Birth again with *'Dream Merchant'* on Love 94." I dried my eyes and opened the door to empty the sand from my shoes. I listened to the song as I lit my half a joint.

"Hey, hey, Mister, Dream Merchant? Bring her back to me, make my dream come true." Even though it didn't have anything to do with God, I wished he heard the song. I sang it to him. Maybe he would help in this nightmare I made. Drunk with pain, I rolled down the Great Highway. I stopped down by the store to get a beer because I needed a quick buzz. Guess who I ran into? Sunshine and Sweet T. Those brothers were as sweet as pie, still in them platforms and skirts, thighs big as football players, but would cut your behind up with a straight razor if you messed with them. Hey, they were gay, but they weren't punks when it came down to it.

There was another fella we called "Switch" because he could work them hips like nobody's business. He had fallen out with his family years ago because of his lifestyle, but when he got sick, his brother Kenny took good care of him. He stopped dressing in drag and everything. We would see Ken coming from work with food and a white bag of medicine. Michelle and Ken were good friends. They would talk when he would come to the clinic for his brother. Every now and then, you'd see them walking together. Later as Switch got worse, I would see Ken holding him up as they walked and talked. Switch would be laughing, then slowed to catch his breath. Ken was a patient brother. He would wait on Switch as long as it took then helped him up the stairs. Then we didn't see Switch no more. Ken told us he had passed away. Grandma and Michelle went to the service. She said that most of his family didn't even show up and those who did, sat in the back. But there was Ken. He sat in front, alone.

He would always say, "He's my brother. I don't care what none of y'all say. That's still my baby brother." We had to respect the brother for that. Not turning your back when it's really needed was not the norm for my generation. I learned that no matter what happens, family must be forever.

Then I found myself over by the church. Since Grandma

164

said those church folks started praying for God to move on that block, a drug dealer wouldn't be found nowhere near there. Pushers would say they heard God calling them, and they'd be running.

Lights were on. Hum, it was family night there. So I went in and sat in the back with some old dark pee-funk glasses on the edge of my nose. Weed was still the calm for my nerves then. The little children were sitting up in the choir stand. The service was about over because the pastor was up. Not dressed in a suit, not preaching, but just talking to the people. He had on a white shirt and some dark pants. Man, he didn't look so intimidating after all.

Then he said something about a heavy spirit and how the Lord was going to use the children to break through this feeling that was so heavy. I didn't know what the news was in the church, but I could feel it and needed some lifting myself. I nodded like, "Okay, let the children sing."

So the children stood up and they had a little big-headed drummer. The sister with the nice butt was on the piano. They started singing this song called "Give Thanks."

Now I didn't know what happened in words, but it was like those kids took us right to heaven's doors. I bent over in my seat, putting my head between my knees. That song was singing into my soul. All the people were crying and those children were sincere. I looked up and dried my tears and started looking for the exit. My heart was beating so hard I'd thought it was going to burst. My mind went to the weed. This some strong chronic? When I left the main church area and reached for the door, an older dark-skinned usher was standing there.

She looked me in the eyes and said, "God loves you, son."

I broke right into her arms. She just held me as I cried. I heard her saying, "Lord, save him, protect him, Lord," over and over. She lifted my face. "Baby, you got a home?"

I answered, "I live with my momma."

"Naw baby, I mean an eternal home."

I paused.

She took me by the hand over to a seat as she spoke softly. "I'm not going to force you. You think about what I just said, I'll be back."

I sat there with all kinds of things going through my head. I dried my face and got myself together.

"Nope, I ain't ready for this stuff yet! Let me get out of here while I can."

So I dashed toward the door and ran right into that usher again. She just looked at me. I looked straight at the door and pushed it open real hard. I know it probably hit her when it swung back because she was standing so close. I started walking fast, walking anywhere. I forgot where my car was for a moment.

I started talking to myself out loud. "Mack, what you trip'n on. You don't need nobody! You the man! You don't need no God, no Jesus, no church folks! You make your own heaven! Your own hell! Where we going, Mack, huh? Just say it and we there."

I finally got to my car with a thimble full of gas left in it. The more I listened I started to identify this voice speaking. It was Little Mack, declaring his right to be who he was and where he was. I thought it was the wolves again, but this sounded too much like me. He was thriving, struggling for space, yet deceptive.

Then, like in one of those movies of a person with many personalities, another voice cried out. It was Emmanuel. The part of me that knew he was endangered and needed help. The essence of me knowing the vital importance of his very existence depended on his willingness to live.

"I've got to do something, but what? Man, I can't do this by myself. Lord please, help me?"

I was jerking back and forth as my car ran out of gas. Before these boys got into an argument in the street, I got out and ran toward my house before somebody else could see me. Michelle was up looking at a gospel video tape. I hurried past her and went straight into my room. And of all nights, she had that thing up full blast! My ears were burning. Mack's mind wanting to yell, "Turn it off!" But Emmanuel's heart was pumping, "Play, tape, play!" The trustees for my life had taken center stage. The fight engrained in my psyche had manifested. The bull and the matador had blown out of a dusty arena. Both of them were me. And even though one had to submit to the other, they knew they couldn't live without each other. I was being torn in two like a raggedly T-shirt. The air ran out of the room.

"Momma! Help me!" I screamed, pulling at my clothes.

Michelle ran to my room with the authority of a chief surgeon. "Emmanuel, what's wrong?"

"Momma, you got to help me get these boys in line!" I said almost out of breath.

Michelle took a deep breath. "All right, if you really want me to help you, let me help."

"Didn't I just scream for you, woman! I mean Momma. I ain't playing this time, help me Momma, please!"

And my God, she went over in the corner of the room and started praying. My chest and ribs turned into an accordion, my lips swelled and trembled like a baby rattle. I started bending over and screaming. Michelle wouldn't even look up, she kept on praying. The more she prayed, the worse the situation got. I was on the floor vomiting and convulsing. It felt like disgruntled construction workers were running up and down some steel stairs inside my soul with axes breaking up my organs at will. Every now and then, they'd stick a piece of dynamite in a hole of the walls of my abdomen, light it, and run.

Boom!

My inside would cry, "Ohhhhh!"

Boom!

"Ohhhh!"

I was lying on the floor like a baby all balled up in a knot. I could hear her asking God for power, power over the enemy that was trying to destroy her child. I sensed some hot feet near my head just standing there, but I was too scared to open my eyes. She turned to me while I was on the floor and shouted, "Devil, take your hands off my boy!"

I tilted my head up to see who she was talking to. What in the world was this woman doing! Girl, you done gone berserk?

I guess Little Mack and Emmanuel inside were wondering too, they were like "huh?" I thought we were the only ones lying on the floor? Michelle knew what was going on with me spiritually. I started to feel a tear going on inside. It got so intense that I couldn't say a word. All I could do was groan. All the events from my birth up until the jail were just a preview of the featured film. I was being warned by other events of what would soon be *the inner war*. If I didn't win here, wasn't no need to go on.

As Michelle ended her prayer, I bellowed out, "Hoah!" and went limp. The room got quiet, still. Michelle was across the room on her knees. I looked through my blurry crusty eyes. I didn't have enough strength to push myself up. Snot was all over the place. My room was a wreck. I still to this day don't know where my other shoe went.

Michelle helped me up on my bed and I just lay there in all my clothes, one shoe, snot and all. She put some covers on me and tried to explain what had happened to me. All I could do was lie there and let the tears roll down my face. I found out how a baby felt when it came out of the womb. Man, glad to be out, yet almost died trying.

Two days passed before I got out of the bed again. Didn't eat or drink anything. That room smelled like funk to the fifteenth power! When Michelle got home from work, she told me something that caused me to make a decision. "If you ever get into that soul-sick place again, it will be seven times worse trying to get out the next time. Boy, God's got a purpose and plan for you, and you can't play with it anymore."

I turned over toward Michelle. "What is it then?" My throat was so sore I could barely speak.

Michelle stood up and walked toward the door. Then she paused. "I guess you've got to ask Him, don't you?"

I frowned. "Where do I start, Momma?"

She smiled and answered, "Just start with you and an open heart. You'll find out how."

So I started on what I could first improve on my own. I cut that wild jerry curl out of my head that had me looking like the Candyman with a mop on his head, got some decent clothes, and got back in school. And you wouldn't believe who my summer-school teacher was, Mr. Hortan. I never thought I'd see this man again.

The first thing he did was put his arms around me. "I heard about you going to jail, Emmanuel. I warned you about the maze."

"You know what, Mr. Hortan? After all you taught us, maybe I missed it? I mean, someone like me? How can I help the maze if I'm still in the maze?"

Mr. Hortan face froze. "I see something happening inside you, son. It can only be identified in someone's eyes who had the same look. You're getting a change of heart and it shows. And you're not looking so mean."

"Yeah, mean mugging all the time takes a lot of effort. Maybe I can use that energy somewhere else."

"Sit down, let's talk."

"Okay."

We sat down and Mr. Hortan reached in his pocket, took out his wallet, and pulled out a little brown piece of folded paper. As he smiled at me, he put his hands up to his lip. "What I have here is something that can change your life. If I give you a secret to deal with your maze, you must make me a promise."

I looked at him sideways. "What is it? I don't promise

nobody noth'n."

"I'm going to ask you the same question again, Emmanuel. If I give you a secret to dealing with your maze, you must make me a promise."

"Okay, I hear you. Yes, I will. What is it?"

"That you'll share it with the person you hate the most."

I backed up from him. "What! You got to be losing your mind!"

His eyes blew out like two cue balls in reverse. "You know me, sir. I will not tolerate disrespect by a young person."

"Okay. Mr. Hortan, I'm awake now. I'll do it."

From then on, Mr. Hortan took me as someone I had never been, a son. I was always Grandma's baby, Michelle's boy, and Mack's little Mac-Pac, but this was the first time I was a son. Evolving me from a boyish nature to a man, starting very simple.

On that piece of paper were principles that would change my life forever.

Mr. Hortan asked me to meet him downtown at Powell Street.

The first thing was being on time.

My cheek twisted like a pretzel. "How can I help my community when I'm worried about what time I get there? I get there when I get there? If that ain't good enough, they just have to wait for me." I bit a hot dog with mustard running off the side of my mouth.

Mr. Hortan handed me a napkin. "First things first, and wipe the mustard off the side of your mouth," he said, slightly pulling up his pants at the knee. "Okay, suppose you're a doctor, and you are late to surgery, or you forget to wash your hands?"

I poked my head up like a gofer coming out of a hole.

"One, your patient may die or get an infection. Two, they'll sue or like in some cases the family in the hood wants to get revenge. Three, it might be me on the table."

My eyebrows shot up and I stopped chewing for a moment. "Yeah, you right, on time, on time, got to be on time."

"Timing and being on time is crucial to every endeavor. Your time is yours when you've paid for it, but it's someone else's time when they are paying for it. Time costs. If you're late to your first child's birth, you will never get that back again. If you're late for an important interview, that will be the lasting impression of you. If you're late to your wife's mother's birthday party, you're done. Time is precious, yet not forgiving. On time, Emmanuel, you hear me? It's time to grow up."

The time thing had become real and too close for comfort. Grandma was out of her high-blood pressure medicine and had had a root canal. Both of her medications were at the local Walgreens. Michelle had told me to pick them up, and guess who was late. I watched her suffer all night.

"I'm sorry, Grandma. I tried to get there, but I got hung up," I whispered.

She was in too much pain to talk, so Michelle claimed to be her mouthpiece.

"Emmanuel, I heard all those excuses, but it don't take away Momma's pain." Michelle answered.

Grandma lay there, breathing hard and moaning.

"I wasn't out playing around, Momma. I was really trying to get there."

"So what held you up then, boy?"

"Um, I had a run to make."

"Did you make it?"

"Naw."

"So your grandmother has to suffer because you didn't make it, right?

I went over to my Grandma and kissed her on her forehead. It was hot and cold to the touch. "Grandma, I promise. You will have your medicine first thing in the morning."

She opened her eyes and whispered, "Thank you, baby."

I took a towel and wiped the blood off the side of her mouth. I walked toward the front door.

"Where are you going?" said Michelle.

"Back to Walgreens."

"But they don't open until morning?"

"Then I'll be there till morning. I'm not putting my grandma through this again. I'll be there till they open."

So I got in my car, drove to Walgreens and parked there in front all night. Slept right in the car till the doors opened and I ran in to get Grandma's medicine. Michelle gave them to her. I sat there with my eyes locked on her until she got comfortable. That time I learned about time. It can heal and hurt. This made me late for school.

Every time I was late to class, I had to write on the board. And if I made a mistake, good God, I had to write it ten more times. I was much older and bigger than his other students, but Mr. Hortan taught me with his eye contact not to react or to intimidate when challenged.

I learned how to respond by letting others know that I was aware of my error, yet able to correct it without going off. He would purposely invite me somewhere and knew if I didn't organize my time, I would be late. That's how I learned to plan.

One day Mr. Hortan invited Michelle, Grandma, and me to visit his house. When we drove up, I saw him looking out the window. Like I always do 'cause it's about me, I got out and started walking toward the door. Michelle got out on her side and helped Grandma, who was getting out too slow for me. When I reach the front door, Mr. Hortan snatched it open. I had a grip on the handle and it caught my elbow almost snatching it out of joint.

"Excuse me, sir! How many ladies are with you today?" His face was all bent out of shape, breath hotter than July right in my face. I looked behind me thinking, dude, did one crawl out of the trunk or something?

"Well, I don't know who you see! There's Grandma and Momma. Two! *Dos*! That Spanish if you didn't take the class."

Mr. Hortan took the floor and I knew I was going to get it. "Ah, excuse me," he said, catching everyone's attention. "Let's return to the car to instruct Mr. Emmanuel Harris how to treat female passengers exiting vehicles."

He made us all get back in the car. Grandma and Michelle were just a laughing and I had my lips poked out.

Mr. Hortan stood outside the car. "Now, the first thing you do, Mr. Harris, is put your lip back in before you run over it." We all bust out laughing. "Mr. Harris, please step out of the car and lock your door."

So I got out and slammed the door.

Grandma shouted out, "Oh, lord. I think Mr. Hortan should have Mister Emmanuel start all over again. I don't know 'bout chu', but that's just me, honey."

"No! No! I'll do it right!" I opened the door quickly and closed it quietly.

"Go around the rear of the car and open the rear door first. Extend your hand out and help your mother out first. She is a lady, isn't she?"

"Yes, sir." I did as he said.

"Now close the door and open the front passage door." I open the door and extended my hand to help Grandma out.

"My, my, my," said Grandma. "Now ain't this somethin?"

"Now, close her door and walk with them, not in front of them, but escorting them."

As we all walked to the front door I said, "How is this going to change our community? Closing and opening door like *massa* kids? Long as folks' arms is working, they can open they own doors. That's how I see it."

He stopped with his back toward me. He turned quickly. "When we value our women, our queens, the women who bear our children, then the world may start to respect them and us.

We must make their path safe, and opening the door for them frees them from *massa* kitchen. You're still eating their food, right?"

I shut up.

When he opened the front door, I saw him kind of peeking over his shoulder watching to see who would walk in first. I took a step, but caught myself.

"Ladies always first."

Grandma's mouth still was hanging open. "My, my, my."

We went in the house and all Grandma could say was, "My, my, my!" All through the house. Almost acting like she ain't been nowhere before. (But you know I will never let that come up my throat.)

Mrs. Hortan took them all through the house and you could hear Grandma first, close and loud, "My, my, my!" Then you could hear her far away, "My, my, my," like a broken record. Then we all went into the dining room for dinner.

When we almost reached the table, I stopped. "Mr. Hortan, before I get stuck on stupid? How should I care for the ladies?"

He smiled. "Pull out their chairs and ask them to be seated."

I nodded. "Okay...I think I can do that without messing up." So I pulled out the chair for them. Wow, all that silverware!

"Mr. Hortan, which fork is for what? At home we just get one out the drawer and go for it."

Mr. Hortan reached over and touched me on the shoulder. "Emmanuel, you can eat with your hands if you want to. Remember, you're at home."

The waiter and waitress brought the food with a big silver cover on it. They set one in front of each one of us. Now, you know me and my crazy imagination from watching the old horror flicks said, "What's this, a head!" Everyone cracked up.

I checked out Mr. Hortan's manners while he ate. "Mr. Hortan, it's like you being a gentleman ain't no put on. I mean

174

it's really you."

He looked over at me while cutting his meat with a knife and fork, putting a piece of meat into his mouth. He waited till he had finish chewing. "Emmanuel, there is no easy way to be a gentleman, and it's really hard to become a real gentleman. But a real man is always a gentleman. For one thing, you've got to be tired of being treated like a boy and being a boy. It's the first instinct of becoming a man."

He took his napkin off his lap and wiped his mouth. "When we've finish dinner, let's all go into the den because I've got something to share with Emmanuel and I desire all of you to be there."

As soon as everyone was finished, I rushed over to help Grandma get up. And she said her favorite three words, "My, my, my." As we all sat down the maid brought in tea for everyone. Mr. Hortan requested the ladies be served first.

Grandma still singing her tune, "My, my, my."

Mr. Hortan asked if anyone wanted a milkshake. This was the first time Grandma broke her record of the my-my's. "Naw baby, that give me gas."

We all talked about different things and I was impressed with the wealth of information Grandma knew about her history. Mr. Hortan was attentive as Grandma poured out, and keyed in some things that just baffled me. Mrs. Hortan asked if she could write down some of Grandma's information to put in some kind of project she was working on.

Grandma said, "Go head baby. It's all free."

Mr. Hortan looked at his wife. "Honey, a change in plan. Take the ladies in the parlor. I believe it's best to speak to this young man alone."

Mrs. Hortan stood up. "Yes, honey. Ladies, shall we go?"

I ran over to help them up. As Grandma was going down the hall, all I could hear was, "My, my, my," echoing.

Mr. Hortan looked me in the eyes. His were as magnifying glasses, piercing right into my soul. "Emmanuel, what I'm about to share with you is not all the elements in changing society overnight. But if our children and our children's children can benefit like you and I can from our ancestors' efforts, then our little stint in this world must be better, not perfect. I need you to really take this seriously. Many men never decided to grow up, and it stalls the next man behind him."

Then he reached in his back pocket and pulled out his wallet. He took out that little piece of paper again. It was still old and wrinkled up.

Clowning, I tried to put a serious look on my face and deepen my voice. "How old is that? Saved it from the last time you went to Fish & Chips?"

He was looking at the paper with his head down. Then his voice cracked like he was about to cry. "Oh, the principles are eternal, but this paper is about thirty years old, older than you."

He looked at me and his eyes were full of water. "My father couldn't give me a house and land, but he gave me something better. It's the way to get houses and land and better yet, keep it."

This was serious so I put away all the clowning. "What, a financial plan, a combination to the safe, what man, tell me?"

"No." He shook the paper in his hand. "A value plan of life."

I was speechless.

"Let's get started." He handed me a pen and a piece of paper the size of one he had. "Write it down, just the principles. Don't worry; you'll never forget the definitions because you'll have to live them out."

I put the pen to the paper and started the class that would change my life forever.

"One," Mr. Hortan said, "how to treat women.

"Two, know how to work hard.

"Three, education and using proper English.

"Four, how to use your influence.

"Five, take responsibility for your actions.

"Six, how not to fear, yet deal with authority.

"And seven, learn how to be thankful."

It took me awhile to finish writing, but Mr. Hortan was very patient.

"Now, put the paper down and listen to what is being said. And please don't make the mistake of thinking you know what I'm about to say, just be quiet and listen."

He sat forward with his hands clasped together as if to pray, looking me straight in the eyes. I was scared to move.

"Emmanuel, you must learn that women, not just our women, but *especially* our women must be treated with the utmost respect. Historically, they were belly warmers for the slave master. They did not have to just care for their children, but also the ones they had by the masters and his white children as well." He saw the expression on my face of anger. "Son, I want you to get more than angry. I want you to get aware."

I started nodding, calming down. He had my undivided attention now.

"And now in this day, they suffer from the abuse of us. Most of our young media-pimped rappers, who are now your role models, refer to our woman as female dogs. That's the true definition of 'bitch' if you really want to know. Our young girls don't even have enough sense to listen to what they are being called. These were once queens of our motherland. We must restore them to their rightful place, as the jewels of our heart. Respecting, nurturing, loving and encouraging them, not just pumping on them and using them for ego-recycling bins. Then some of us won't even walk the street with them for their safety after he's been licking her from head to toe! And remember, dogs make puppies."

I frowned a little with his bluntness, but brother was telling the truth. I was as guilty as anyone.

"Our women first, then all women. Many of our women get most of their self worth, their self-esteem from their man.

177

Whatever flaw she has, we made her that way. So you must place her back in the high place in your heart, which is the place of honor. Got it?"

"Got it."

"Second, learn to work hard at whatever job you have. But yet have a vision of where you would like to be. I hate to say this truth but too many young black men have poor work habits."

I cut in on him. "Yeah, I mean yes, you're right."

"Yeah, I know I'm right! No one will keep someone who cannot at least get there on time and accomplish an assigned task. Get up and get there! Properly dressed, wash properly, and do what you are told. If you ever decide that you want to lead and be the boss, how you follow will be the test. If you're a poor follower, you'll be a poor leader and that's the kind of following you'll get, poor. Get this down in your system–work hard! Have you ever heard your grandmother say, you pay the cost to be the boss?"

"Yes, and she's the boss."

"Yes, because she's paid the cost. When you finally understand, young man, that you will get nothing for free in this life but trouble, you will begin to use your energy so you can be compensated well for your hard work. It says something about the real you."

"Work hard. I've got to work hard," I answered right on his heels. "Say, Mr. Hortan, if I'm out working hard and the next man just over there goofing off, what am I suppose to do about him?"

"Don't worry about him. What he's not doing is not your problem. When the man next to you is working hard, he's your competition. That's your next supervisor, so don't be mad with him, out work him!"

"Man, Mr. Hortan, I ain't...I haven't heard it said like that before. Man, that's deep."

"Good, Emmanuel. Third, education and proper English."

"What! So I got to talk uppity too now, right!" I said almost pissed off.

"No, being able to speak proper English should be as common as tying your shoes." He looked down at my feet and I stretched my face to peek down too. And wouldn't you know it, I had one shoe untied.

He looked at me and smiled. "You see what I mean?"

I burst out laughing, "Yeah, you got me."

His eyes pierced my soul. "Emmanuel, your education is not the total sum of your ability to achieve, but it takes the limits off what you can achieve. I never want to hear you say that you cannot do what someone else did because another person knows more than you. Just say 'when I learn what you know, then I'll do what you do.' Then learn what he knows and do what he does better than him.

Education takes time and discipline. When you learn, you must be able to properly articulate what to say. See, when you speak business language, the business world has to respect you. And if you have education to back up your English, you're dangerous, explosive, and in demand. Right now, your education is shot."

That shot heat right into my ears.

"But you cannot come in saying 'dis, dat, and ain't.' I'm not putting down some of our ways of communication, but if you're going to play in the real world and make a difference, you must be able to be understood. This only comes through education and speaking proper English, which is our language. I want you to be able to make the world listen to you."

That struck a chord in my mind that made me almost bite my lip. "People understand what I'm saying? They answer back, don't they?"

"Yes, but most of the people you communicate with on a daily basis with do not speak proper English either. You all have made up some new language just for yourselves, but you're not a world within the world. And you have to live in a world that if you are going to do well, understand, they don't talk like dat!"

"Wow. Did you have to say it like that?"

"Yeah, so you can see what 'dat' sound like; from a man who does not have to accept that."

"Mr. Hortan, that don't even sound right? You talking like that. Guess you're not going to make this easy on me, uh?"

"Only if the world had made it easy on me, and it didn't. So what do you think they will do with you, young man?

"Eat me alive?"

"Down to the bottom of your feet. Only if you don't understand."

"I got you, Mr. Hortan. Like Grandma said, you can't fight with the truth."

"Absolutely. Fourth, using your influence, and Emmanuel, you have influence."

I kind of smiled with my chipped front tooth looking like a hyena and poked my chest out a little, but Mr. Hortan had a remedy to deflate all that pride.

"Maybe it's on the negative side now, but still it is a powerful influence. What I mean literally is, in the drug world, people live and die by the power of influence. But enough on the negative, it's about your influence to persuade for the positive. The same power you once commanded to destroy must be used to now repair and rebuild. There are people you know who did things you wanted them to do because of influence. Now, let's take that same power, on the same people, and make a change."

He pushed his finger into my chest.

"Just like you made that sister sometime ago do something wild for some drugs, make her do something now to help her get off that stuff. One thing I know you inherited from your father is the gift of gab. Go talk to her about a program, talk to her about taking care of her children, talk to her and let her know that tomorrow can be more than a high day? It can be a better day. Just like you said, you used to 'talk the drawers off them,' now talk them into 'keeping them on' because they are worth more."

I sat there silent. My forehead felt as if it had been removed and the hollowness of the night whisper blew my thoughts away. Mr. Hortan didn't disturb me. I was being lowered in an elevator of my words and fast tongue, pulling my jaw as if I were a bass being drawn from the water because of my greed to feed.

I pulled myself from the invisible. "People responsible for themselves. All I did was put the product out there, I didn't make them buy. If they buy it, it's on them. I ain't responsible for that."

"Yes, they are responsible. No, you're wrong, you are responsible."

"No, I'm not."

"Yes, you are."

"So, we gonna go back and forth till one of us give in or what?"

"No, son. You'll see in time. I don't have to be right, right will speak for itself."

"Yeah, we'll just see," I cut him short. "On to the next one. See what right say for itself when it's time."

Mr. Hortan went forward without skipping a beat. "Fifth, with influence comes responsibility for your actions."

I stopped him because I didn't know how to end an argument. "You mean, Mr. Hortan, just like that. No more on that point."

"Do you mean why didn't I continue to argue that point?"

"Yeah, you not mad or nothing. Like you just moving on?"

"Yes, Emmanuel. My time is important and I am responsible for giving you these principles, not arguing with you. As I stated before, with influence comes responsibility for what you've done. Someone must be responsible and take responsibility for what is happening to our community. We, including myself, are a part of the problem even if just standing by and not doing anything. Now, we must be a part of the solution." Mr. Hortan paused to catch his breath.

"Now hear me, and hear me well. If no one takes responsibility for our problems, then we are put in the hands of others who don't really care but to program us to death. We don't need another program for someone else to use us to make more money for him or herself. What we need is to be responsible, to see it used to help the ones who really need it, and not just there to get their non-profit funded."

He snatched off his glasses and pointed them in my face. His voice went loud and furious. "Emmanuel, *you* are responsible for a lot of hurt in your neighborhood. You must now change hands and bring healing to the place you once brought hurt."

That stopped me cold in my tracks. For a moment I was spellbound, face to face with myself. I had never been confronted with my past and its effects. Usually I could point to someone else and say it was them, but today, there was no other face but me. I had to look at me.

"I don't like what I see. I don't want to see my pain," I said.

"Why, son?"

"'Cause my pain hurts. So because I hurt, they hurt or get hurt."

"You are still hurting now, Emmanuel?"

I could barely lift my head. "My daddy in jail and when I went to see him, he hurt me. My momma mad at him so whether she knows it or not, she mad at me. That hurts. I put my grandma through all kinds of craziness till she hurt, and that really hurts. I hurt so bad sometime, and can't even cry." Mr. Hortan paused as I landed back on earth.

"Emmanuel, the only way you can stop hurting is that you must be healed."

"And how do I do that?" The tears started to fall down my

face.

"You've admitted you're hurt. The healing has started."

I felt warmth in the middle of my chest. Every time I took a breath, a twine of tension unwrapped itself from my shoulders. The vice grip of disappointment and anger slowly loosened from the base of my neck.

"What's number six?" I said

Mr. Hortan answered, "Six, dealing with and not fearing authority."

"You mean the police." Now you know I had a problem with them from jump street. Just in that instant my chest went cold, my shoulder became the baby cow in the cowboy's lasso, and I put my steel shoulder pads back on.

"Yes, the police. Never again run from the police."

I froze. My chin went numb as if hit with a Louisville Slugger. I tried to process this reverse of reverses. This was killing the cat-and-mouse game in me.

"Be a man and stand up. Look them in the eye, especially when you haven't done anything! Never give them a reason to do you any harm. When do you get off probation?"

"Two years."

"Then you've got two years of walking the straight and narrow. Don't be a fool and play into the judicial system's hands. Get out of the system because you can't help having your hands cuffed to it. Authority is needed and where there is no authority, everything and anybody is right. And we all can't be right."

"But the police so...cold. That don't play fair; dirty cops jack'n brothers and take'n they dope then selling it back to us for double. Now you want me to just stand there and let them take my sh–"

"Don't curse at me, boy!"

"Come on, Mr. Hortan, and I do apologize for almost cursing at you. But you have got to be kidding. I don't like no police, and now I got to stand there and look at someone who don't like me? What if they wanna do something to me? I ain't going to stand there and let them, I'm gone."

"And they will shoot you in the back like a dog and you can be the next funeral celebration, so your boys can rent tuxedos? Think about it, Emmanuel. Never run again from law enforcement if you've done nothing wrong."

Those words crippled my game. It was fun trying to be one up on the police, and now I was being challenged to move from being in the hunt, which was so comfortable, to the place of humility. I dropped my head and replayed a conversation with Mr. Hortan three months ago when we saw three brothers I know walking, one with a golf club.

"Think he's going to play golf?" Mr. Hortan said.

I snapped back. "Maybe?"

"Emmanuel, he's going northbound. The nearest golf course is southbound, a hundred mile in the other direction."

"Guess he's still about to tee-off, hum?"

"Do you think he'll have to deal with the law, you know, after his game?"

I was stuck. But some light was beginning to shine through. "I can't worry about them. I'll just have to see how I do when I get to that bridge, Mr. Hortan. You've been there and know better, so all I can do is trust you on this one." I landed from that conversation and lifted my head. I turned toward Mr. Hortan.

He smiled. "Seventh and lastly, you must learn to be thankful. You can do a lot and receive more, but if you're not thankful, you kill it...and you die."

My eyes got big. "What do you mean, you kill it and die?" A light bulb with a big question mark went off.

"You'll never lack anything when you're thankful for what you have. It doesn't happen often, but have you ever noticed people with a lot, messing themselves up when they can't get more?"

"Yeah, I saw something like that on the news."

"Well, that comes from not being thankful for what they have. Man! Pig's feet, pigtails, hog-head cheese, chitterlings, and grits were the leftovers from the slave master. That is what they gave to our people. Now, these things are expensive in the supermarket. Son, all the other six principals are empty without this one. And not just being thankful, but thanking God. I can't speak for anyone except us, and I'm not trying to speak for all of us. God brought us out of our Egypt, through slavery even before we got to America, through civil rights. God is the only one who can bring us out of this bondage."

He stopped and looked up. A tear came out of the corner of his eye. Then he began to moan something. It was "Amazing Grace." After he finished humming he looked at a picture on the wall. There hung an old ship with a white sailor. "Do you know where that song came from?"

"No. I just know my grandma sings it."

He pointed to that picture. "That song came from a white slave-ship captain who was on a ship and heard the slaves moaning and put word to their tune. A storm had been ravaging them, causing the slaves to moan in sickness and agony. The captain had an epiphany, and not only did he write the song, but turned the ship around and was a slave runner no more."

Then Mr.Hortan walked to the window and spoke, looking up toward heaven. *Amazing Grace, how sweet the sound, that saved a wretch like me. I once was lost but now I'm found, t'was blind but now I see. Through many dangerous, toils and snares, I have already come, t'was grace that brought me safe thus far, and grace shall lead me on.'*

That slave master felt something in that hymn from those slaves. I don't even think he himself was aware of those words that would keep our people till we were to see God Himself. Be thankful, and you'll always have the tools you need to do life's job."

I just sat there staring at the floor. His words went through my head like clothes in a tumbling dryer warming up.

"Okay, Mr. Hortan, nothing else but to do it now."

He put his hand on my knee. "Don't look for miracles overnight, but look for miracles. And this isn't the place for boys. Get off your mother's breast, and throw that dirty baby blanket of excuses away. James Brown said it best, 'This is a Man's World'" "Yeah, ain't that the truth." The weight of reality held my gaze fixed to the floor.

Chapter 9 'n a half
Those Letters! That Letter!

'96 was a bad year for us brothers in the Hip-Hop Mecca. Hammer had to sell our first big pretty house in the Fremont Hills. The boy from Milli Vanilli done lost his mind and got hit in the head trying to steal a car. The owner came out and caught him. "Vapp!" right upside the head. I guess after their cover was blown, he may have been thinking what else could happen? And Lord, somebody assassinated the next President of the United States, Tupac. Man, we were down for a while over that one.

A lot of corner medicinal mara-ju-wana and forty-ounces were sold at a discount to help the many depressed up-coming artists. As budded as we were, our hearts ached bad as we sent out love up in puffs of smoke to Las Vegas. Then went and ate the Arab corner store man out of house and home with the munchies. Now I knew how Grandma felt when JFK was shot. But it wasn't all bad; Michael Jordan and the Bulls were still unstoppable.

I couldn't figure out what kept setting Michelle off though. She finally had a good man in her life who was crazy about her. He and I got along well, but every time she would come from picking up the mail, something would happen. Just straight to her room and close the door. I'd hear her mumbling something, and then she'd come out of the room blasting at anything and anybody. Only problem, she would never tell me what it was.

"Why does he keep talking to me that way? Don't he have anyone else in his life that he can torment? You, where my sardines! How many push-ups he can do, can John do dat? You can't send noth'n right? This man makes me sick!" she'd yell.

"Momma, what are you talking about? What sardines?

187

What man are you talking about?" I asked, puzzled.

"Don't worry about it, Emmanuel. This don't concern you."

"Well, you going off and nobody know why? That don't concern me? We are the ones who have to face whatever don't concern us and we have to live with it? I don't think it's fair for you to put us through something we didn't do or don't know nothing about."

"Get out of here, boy. I'll talk to you about it later. I need to call John."

I tried to throw a little humor in. "Call John? This don't concern us, but you calling John. He got something to do with you losing your mind every other week you go to the mail box. He suing you for something? You done went crazy and slash the tires on his bus? Ha, Ha!"

"Ha, ha, very funny, boy. I just need to talk to him."

"Look, make your call and finish cooking this chicken because I'm hungry."

"Boy, you old enough to finish your own chicken?"

"Yeah, and I'll burn your kitchen down too."

She went in the other room and called him. I was turning the chicken over and stretching my nosey neck toward the door at the same time. I heard her yelling at John about the letter. Whatever he said on the other side jerked the angry from the atmosphere and calmed her down.

"Yeah, John...I hear you...Yes, I know you love me, but he keeps saying all kinds of crazy things about me and you...Okay, I'll say it. I'm special to you and you alone, but John...Okay, I will stop reading them, ...I promise...When are you coming?...Don't you need to go home first...Okay, okay, I'll be ready...Thank you, baby...Say what?...God loves Michelle...John loves Michelle...Michelle loves Michelle...Bye. She would get off the phone with this big grin and head toward the bedroom. Dude, if that's all it takes, I'll call John for you.

I had to find out what was setting her off. It was something in those letters, but I wasn't sure. I decided that when she and John left, I was going to find them and see what they said. This tension was like a midnight mosquito around my ear and it had to be put to rest.

I called Grandma and asked her why my momma was tripping.

"Hey, Grandma."

"Hey, Mister Man. How's my friend and what's going on?"

"What's up with these letters and Michelle? She be going nuts and it don't make sense."

"Oh, it make sense, baby. It's still ya father, son."

"Mack? I thought they were over a long time ago?

"Son, it takes a long time to get some people out of your system, and Mack and Michelle ain't sick enough of each other to take the medicine to leave each other alone. That's all."

"You mean they still be mess'n around too?"

"What you mean mess'n around?"

"You know, Grandma, sleeping together?"

"No, I think they stopped that a long time ago, but they still dreaming of the past they didn't have and mad at themselves."

"Grandma, I'm going to stay out of that."

"Yeah, I had to learn the hard way. I ran into that brick wall of trying to tell hardheaded people to leave each other alone and got my feeling hurt a many a day. But when I learned, I learned."

"That makes sense, old lady. Okay, Grandma, I'll talk to you soon."

"Bye baby."

John's position was that he not going to be a part of the Mack madness. And even as much as he cared for my mother, he was not going to be a part of the Michelle, Emmanuel madness either. One day Michelle and I got into an argument in the kitchen, and he walked in.

I lashed out! "What you in here for, Mr. John? This conversation here don't involve you, so you need to leave."

He didn't move. His face was settled, not a muscle twinged. His eyes locked with mine. I was use to a good mean mug session with many, so I was there with him, fella. He stood there not intimidated by any of the psychological pressures being released in my funk.

"Why you staring at me, dude?"

"John, go ahead, honey. Could you just step out please?" Michelle said.

John still didn't move.

I picked up a knife. "Oh, you can't hear. Bus too loud! Dude, get out!"

John's eyelids narrowed, his brown pulps fixed. His voice low and clear, but as powerful as a wrecking ball. "What are you going to do with that?"

Before I could answer, he had snatched the knife out of my hand and slammed it on the counter, Blam! Michelle jumped back and covered her ears.

He went totally old school on me. "One, if you pick something up, you'd better be prepared to use it. Two, don't you ever pick up something and direct it towards me again."

I stood there because there was something calmly scarier in his voice. Michelle didn't move either.

"Call me when you're done, Michelle. I'll be at home."

"John, don't leave, we'll be done in a minute."

John didn't stop and Michelle went out after him.

"John, I said we'll be done in a minute."

He turned toward her, still calm. "And I said, call me when you get done. I'll be at home."

"Why do you have to be like that, John?"

"Michelle, I'm not like that. That's why I'll be at home when you call."

"What? I don't get it?"

"You will. Finish what you have to finish, and again just like I said, I'll be home when you call."

Michelle walked up to him and he embraced her. "Okay."

He kissed her forehead and walked away. He was the type of guy who was not going to get caught up in anything that did not concern him. People at the church at times would be in disagreement and would ask John about his take. He would say, "That doesn't concern me. Read your Bible, figure it out. The answer's still in there if you haven't torn it out," and walk away.

A few nights later I decided to confront my mom about the letters. I walked over to her room, but the door was closed with the light on. I thought she was in there reading those letters again, but I could hear two voices. Hers and John's.

"Michelle, I want to take our relationship all the way but we have to straighten something out right now," John said. Michelle started to jump in a cut him off, but he stopped her.

"Baby, let me finish this time. I need you to hear me."

"I'm sorry, go ahead," Michelle said.

"Michelle, I love you and I want to marry you. You have been the best woman I've had in a long time. After my divorce, I said I would never get married again, but I'm willing to do it again if it's you. But we have got to get these letters and Mack stuff straight and over with now."

"John, he keeps writing things that hurt me and he talks bad about my son and Momma."

"Then why do you keep reading them?"

"I don't know?"

"I know."

"What is it then?"

"You're still in love and hate the man who hurt you."

"What? You are tripping, John. I don't love Mack."

"Yes, you do. You said he was your first, and he is the father of your son. When a woman lets a man inside of her, many a time it may not mean anything to us, but it means something to that woman because he leaves something inside of you. Not his semen, but you've let him near your heart, and to have his baby too. Michelle, you're in love with him and hate him in the same breath."

"And you want to marry a girl in love-hate with somebody else, uh?"

"No. I don't. I want to marry a woman who has loved or lusted in the past, whatever you want to call it, but who is not in a love-hate war with her past. You're bringing your past into your future. I know you wished you and he could have made it and been a family with your son the same way I wished me and my daughter's mother could have made it. But we didn't. I love my daughter's mother because she is my daughter's momma, but I am in love with you."

Michelle joked, "Don't ever talk about you love some other woman."

John laughed.

I pulled a folding chair in the hallway and sat down just far enough to dash in the bathroom if the door opened.

"I'm not intimidated about you having loved Mack, but I can't share my life with a woman who lives in her past, especially a woman that is referred to as 'you' and is cussed out by someone every time he writes her saying 'where my sardines!' That is not my life, nor my madness. You can't draw me into that."

"And what about Emmanuel?" Michelle asked.

I kind of sat up in my seat and put my ears on full volume for this. If he had said something crazy, I was going to buss-up in there and go off.

"What about Emmanuel?" he answered.

"I need to know where my son plays in this."

"You really want to know?"

"Yeah."

Now I was rocking back and forth real fast. It's enough for my dad to be talking about me crazy, but another man in my mother's life on me? Won't happen!

"Your son is your son. I will not try and play his father, but everything a part of you will be a part of me. He's not looking for me to be a daddy to him, but I believe he would love to see someone really love his mother. I think he and I will do just fine, just leave that to me. I know he loves his mother and I love his mother. We are in love with the same girl."

I sat back in the chair and released the steam coming up the back of my neck.

Michelle grabbed some tissue and blew her nose. "You're the first guy that wanted to be a part of my son's life, besides his teacher. Anytime I would be dating before and had trouble with him, the guy would say, 'Let me let you go, you need to handle your problem, or Call me when you've taken care of your Mack Pack. Can't you find a baby sitter?' Anything to get me away from my son. But Emmanuel is and has been my life, and I'm glad someone has found me, and wants him too."

"If we are going to be family, Michelle, that means all of us must be a family."

Then I could hear them kissing.

"Ooow…let me get out of here before I throw up." Even though my momma was only thirty-five, they were like senior citizens sneaking in the broom closet to me. I went in the living room. Something was sticking out of Michelle's purse. It was a letter. I leaned back to see if either one of them was coming out of the room. I grabbed the letter and went out to my car and there it was; his name and prison number, return address, and the key to my mom's frustration.

I took the paper out and locked my gaze like sewing needles to the lettering. I could feel threats in his vulgarity, and a rope to hang her in every misleading sentence. He still thrived off intimidation and control, even from behind concrete walls.

Girl, U know what! Why is U still messing up on my commissary? All I do is ask U to send me my box of stuff, U can't get dat write. Glad I got some mo ho's sending me stuff beside u. Where my sardines! And sending that off brand mayo, U better be happy I'm locked up cause I make you eat that mess. Why my boy don't keep in touch with me. U and yo momma got him like a lit house sissy and he gonna get took out if he don't know how to handle his self on the streets. Man I ain't got time for this, just send me my stuff and some money for canteen. Monday is visiting. U could at least come see a brotha. Ya babies daddy if noth'n else. U no I got love for ya.

Still Mack-issh

I couldn't read any more. My stomach loafed with slime till it stretched to my groin. My panting chest pressed pain against my lungs until I thought I would pass out. My momma had been getting hustled in black on white. It was her pain and her high in the same breath. His words were her downers that blew her self-esteem, and his consistency was her uppers. The jailhouse pimp was crawling up her spine and fighting to hold on to her. I threw the pages across the seat. The sheets caught a breeze, yet quietly sat down and one folded in the form of a mouth. The open floor vent blew on it motioning a conversation in process. My mind didn't even have the time to fight against the unbelievable. I just jumped in the conversation.

"What! You papers. You ain't no man."

It answered back, "Awe, you must not under estimate the power of the pen, Emmanuel?"

"The power of the pen? How are you even talking to me, paper?"

"I can say whatever I want to say, Emmanuel. The gutter darkness sketched from your daddy's hand rubbing against an incarcerated pen bring us to life, reaching right inside your mother's soul, and she responds to the brightness coming from me, Mr. Paper. As much as your father enjoys sending us, and your mother hates to see us coming, they love the construction of our destructive behavior in the back of their minds."

I reached out to grab the sheet, but it stops me.

"No, no. I'm not the problem. I'm the message, the masseur, and the move.

All I do is lay in the corner with all my brothers in single file. We're silent, we're poised. We wait for his, your father's mind–watch this, 'to wake up.' We never say a word. Then when he thinks, he brings our soul mate R.D. Pen over, and from the ruptured imagination of his anger he drafts the rope in ink that he mailed to your mother's heart. We're more like mating boa constrictors in the Everglades, the more you think about it. You know, all curled up together in love"

I flashed.

"You're a piece of paper. The pen is ink. And you say you are controlling my parent lives? You mean to say after all these years of fussing and feuding, you can still keep it going? I can grab you right now and take this cigarette light and burn your butt up."

The sheet shot hard. "I control ya momma."

I reached over and grabbed the paper crumbling it up. "Here now fool! Who control who! That's right, you tore up now!"

I heard another voice from the back seat.

"No, I'm not. I'm right here."

It was another sheet, but the same thing.

"Nope, too many trees on the planet to stop me. And with recycling, too? You just can't get rid of me that fast."

I turned around. My eyes opened and stretched, my bottom lip hit the floorboard. I started to reach for it, but stopped. I stared at it as its movement resembles the effects of the breaths of an asthma attack.

"Why are you breathing like you sick?"

The sheet yawned. "'Cause I'm wearing y'all out, and every other sheet-tied soul out, too. Have you ever seen the heart of someone when they see me? If I bring good news, it races like a toddler on its first adventure in the park. It's exciting, fresh, everything is new. And I see the same heart when it gets me like ones sent to your mother's, or how y'all say it, ya momma's. The push of plasma flows like lava, bursting blood vessel and sending the central never system into sure panic. I love it."

"You mean, you get off by bringing this kind of madness to people lives?"

"No, I don't bring it. I just carry it on my sleeve. It's Mr. Ink that roles right into their minds." The corner of it bent up in a smile. "Hey, Emmanuel, have you ever wondered why your mother's attitude changes with you when she gets me?"

I stopped. I did notice that whenever she had read the letters, she didn't want to see me for a while.

"Guess since you so smart, you must know. Why?"

"Have you ever thought about it?"

"Man, if you know, say it!"

"Hey, I'm just doing what I do, man. Don't hate the mail man for delivering the mail. Don't hate masseur for rubbing the rough areas. You're the one going through yo momma's purse! I was just sitting there minding my own business waiting to take her for another emotional high, till 'old sticky hands' came over, namely you, mister." The paper paused and took a breath. "When she reads, the letters jump off the page and ingrained themselves right into her pores. When she sees you, it reminds her of the pain he caused."

"What you talk'n about Mr. Paper? Oh, lord, I was calling this thing by name. "My momma loves me. My momma would die for me. You 'bout to get burnt up now!"

"Before I go just think, Emmanuel, just think? Yes, she loves you. But you're a living reminder of him. The him that invited her to put herself through hell. Yeah, they had some good time pump'n and sweat'n, until that pump had a bump. Then everything changed and she wasn't fun anymore. You stopped her fun, and the ride of responsibility for your father, was too much cargo for him. You're right she loves you, but she has not let go of the *him* in *you*. And she hates him in you, and she loves it."

"You lying. I'm going to ask her." Again my mind flashed that I was talking to a piece of paper. I picked up a lighter. "Aaa, you ever seen a hot number?"

"What's a hot number, boy?" answered Mr. Paper

"You."

I grabbed the sheet and set it afire. At first it screamed, then I could hear softly,

"Ha, ha, ha, ha, ha!" Then louder and louder.

I got out and went to Michelle's bedroom door. It was closed.

"Hey, Momma, you there?"

"Yes, Emmanuel, what's up?"

"I didn't mean to disturb you and John in the middle of y'all mix but I need to talk to you."

The door swung open. "Come in" said Michelle.

I was a little shocked thinking that John was in, but he had left.

"I thought I was going to have to get some WD40. Y'all bed was squeaking so loud."

"We were not having sex, boy"

"That's where it looked like it was going last time I peeked in. You need to close your door."

"You need to stop peeking. Boy, what do you want?"

"I was talking to this...never mind. What's happening between you and my father with those letters?"

"None of your business."

"It is my business when I get treated like an un-emptied porta-potty when you get finish getting high off them."

"What are you talking about?"

"Momma, you really don't care to see me for awhile after you've read a letter from my dad."

She paused, and looked toward the mirror. "One of the things your father used to do when we were in school was to

197

send me little notes between classes. He said he was a poet and he 'know' it. But he could write and make me smile and laugh just at the right time. Sometimes he knew I was having a bad day or going to a rough class. He'd have a little saying for just the right moment. His words meant a lot to me. And when my father died, even though he didn't know him because we had just got together, he came to the funeral and read a poem about fathers. Wow! Like he really knew something about being a father? His words have always got to me, even when they hurt."

"So John is talking about he wants to marry you. You've taken this madness out on me, you gonna take it out on him, too?"

"That's the problem? Well, it's not a problem to him because he won't. He's been through this before and as much as he loves me, he doesn't love my issues enough to jump in the bathtub with them and me. He's not one of those crazy men that can't live without you. He can love you enough to leave you."

"Yeah, I know y'all love each other and all that, and he's cool to me what little I know of him, but I have overheard some of you alls' bedroom chatter and he will leave before getting pulled in that alligator pit. You and my dad scatch'n like two wildcats that can't live with or without each other. How you get pulled into that, Momma?"

"Young, stupid, I don't know? You just get in how you get in for most women, but for a few of us, we stay in way too long. By the time the hammer has hit you hard enough in the head for the eleventh time, it can almost be too late and you don't really know how to get out."

"Like really leaving my daddy alone?"

"Yeah. Like really leaving that fool alone."

"Now don't talk to bad about the brotha, 'cause you was wit' him in yo day, lady."

"Yeah, and I was a fool, too. The part now is getting him

out of my system."

"Oh, that deep?"

"Kind of like getting Mack down was easy, so I sure can't get him out of my butt over night. Really, and it's on me, this has been way too long. The reason I didn't want you to see the letters is that I didn't want your relationship with your father to get worse. I never taught you to hate your father."

"But you never taught me how to love him either?"

Michelle paused. Rarely was that mouth not going, but she was stuck. She stared into my eyes. No anger, no rage. "You're right. I haven't taught you to love him because I was hurt by him, and loved him at the same time. You were my piece of him I knew he couldn't have, and you're the piece of me that I wanted him to have. I didn't want to be with him, but I could have some of him in you. Then when I couldn't fight back at him, I guess in some way, I swung at you."

"You didn't ever whip me momma 'less I needed it. What you mean you swung at me?"

"In the back of my mind, I didn't think it was fair for me to be stuck at home with a baby, and him still running the streets. Every time I had to go somewhere, I couldn't just get up and leave. I have to pack for me and my baby. Yes, your father did spend time with you, but it was when he wanted to. When you were sick at night, school, Mack was doing his thing, and I and your grandmother were there. Then he'd show up for an event or graduation with a bunch of balloons and junk. Boy, you would go running and just leave me and ya poor grandmamma."

I laughed, but just briefly. A picture flashed of me running to my daddy. I saw my joy cause her pain, again.

"But you are his son. Until I learned better that he loved to shine all the time, I would be angry at you for being so excited over him. But I loved to see you being daddy's little man."

"Okay, Momma, so what are you going to do, because John ain't playing this mess?"

"I've got to give Mack up. But sometime, Emmanuel, it hurts so good."

"I think you need some mental help, girl? Want me to get you a forty?"

"No boy, I know what to do. I ain't crazy, and I don't want to lose John."

"Yeah, he got Michelle-itis seriously. And I'm still going to get y'all some WD-40 for y'all bed."

We burst out laughing.

"Go get the letters, Momma."

"What?"

"Go get the letters, every one of them."

"And do what?"

"Give them to me."

"What?"

"Give them to me, Momma."

"And what are you going to do with them?"

"The same thing you should have a long time ago."

"Which is?"

"If you've got to ask, you ain't really ready to end this."

Michelle got up and went to the closet. She pulled out a box big enough for a small refrigerator. My mouth flew open.

"How long have you been getting letters from this fool?"

"A long time."

"I see! Man, we could heat up the whole house with all this! These are going in the fire place."

"What are you going to do with these, Emmanuel?"

"Like I said, if you have to ask, you ain't ready yet. You go'ne keep this fool in your life or what? And miss a man that really loves you? Come on, Momma, you've got to choose one of the other? Give me the letters."

Michelle pushed the box toward me and stood there.

"Now, Momma, do something."

"What?"

"Turn around and walk away."

"Boy, stop being silly."

"I saw this on TV, Momma. This man told these women in the same stuff as you to turn around and walk away from their past. So they did it. And he said never look back. Those sisters walked right out of the studio. Don't know where they went, but they left whatever that had them messed up behind, so turn around and walk away."

"All right, mister psychologist."

As Michelle started walking away, she stammered and grabbed her forehead.

"Keep going" I yelled.

I really didn't know how bad these sheets of scribbled carnage had dug into her soul. It was if she were an addict walking away from her dealing, a prostitute breaking ties with her pimp. The withdrawal was serious.

Before she reached the door, I said, "Are these all of them?

She yelled, "Yes! I mean, no! Get my purse."

As I went and got her purse, she leaned over and pulled two shoe boxes from up under the bed. And I thought I was the only one that had the Converse box keep-alls. She pushed them towards me. "Take these, but don't read them."

"Why?"

"One box is Mack's nasty love letters; the others are letters to you."

I got pissed-confused. "Momma, how could you be with John and still reading that stuff from Mack?"

"You know what? You really find out how sick you are when you start playing hide and seek from yourself."

"So he kept you hooked by keeping you hot. A letter crack-head."

"Excuse me?"

"I don't mean to disrespect you, Momma, but he played the tune you want to hear. It must have meant something because you kept them under the bed. What was that about?"

"Do you wonder why so many sisters read them romance

novels?

"No, why?"

"'Cause y'all really don't get it! Fellas will give you sex out the box, but who knows how to romance. To chase you into your fantasy and catch up and take you away because the man is in love with you. Not in love with what's between your legs, but love you. Sometimes our satisfaction is dreaming of what we may never get. So we read the novels and run through the pages with the wind blowing through our long white-girl hair."

"Momma, are you about to go into detail, because this is making me sick."

She laughed. "No man, but you need to know what's going on inside a woman, 'cause a lot of you are missing the mark."

"So Mack was your fantasy, I see."

"Yeah, for a minute. At least I could run butt naked and not be found until I was ready."

"Oh God, Momma. Too much information!"

"Boy, grow up. You the one talking about you helping me? Your mother is not old nor tore up. And I want to know what it means too?"

"What means?"

"For me to be a love story book for somebody."

"And Mack was that?"

"No, but just him hunting from the pages was exciting. Made me feel like I was something worth fighting for."

"Lord, have mercy."

"You sound like yo grandmamma, boy."

"Yeah, I know. Woo…I know what she means now."

"What?"

"As soon as you try to run game, game gets run on you."

"Why you say that?"

"'Cause you probably wrote my dad back and had him thinking he was coming back home to the hottest thing in town knowing you wasn't going to give him no more booty. He sparked your fire and John got all the benefits. Like I said, game running game, but personally, I don't think it's right or fair to John."

"Why? He's the one getting me?"

"But he don't know he's getting a woman hot on another man's ink, and under her bed are piles of letters like bumble bees from another man's nets. Yeah, the honey is sweet, but he ain't making the hive wild. When you danced with him in the dark, he's another man. You always trying to get me to do a sista right, do a brotha right."

I had an idea. "Momma, let's do something we haven't did in awhile?"

"What?"

"Let's use the fireplace. I know the last time we used it I forget to open up the vent and almost burned the house down, but I think we will enjoy this inferno. And we've got plenty of stuff to burn tonight and it ain't weed either. "

"Okay. I'm going to the bathroom. I'll be back."

While Michelle went out, I decided to read one of Mack's letters to me. I found one about two years ago and decided to see what he was trying to say to me then. Michelle warned me not the read it.

"Hey man, yo mother said you doing good in school. Go bye and see yo other grandmamma too. Yo momma's momma ain't the only grandmamma you got. Tell her I need some more money on my books and have my brother get my clothes at the property room. All the brothers here know about you going to make the Mack name live on like the kings name did. Michelle said some old teacher trying to teach you how to be white too. Don't listen to that mess! You a hustler and you gonna always be a hustler. Might be a few things you can use in the game, but don't forget where you come from with me. I'm ya daddy and I'll put you in yo place. Keep them other little punks in line too. If you can keep them in line now, you won't have no trouble keep'n control of the streets when you old. And if you get into a fight and somebody kick yo butt I swear I'll come home and beat yo butt. Don't lose no fights with my name on it and make me look bad. See even from here, I still got control. All I got to do is make one phone call, and somebody can be busted in the head. You know, Mack style. I know you heard about Ray-ray in the hospital, he had it coming too. That's the kind of power yo father got. When I get out, I'm gonna to take you to Great America and shopping. I'm gonna dress you up just like yo daddy. Ask yo momma did she get my letter. She gone always be my top one and tell Breva to bring that baby to see me. Be good boy. Hustlers forever.

Mack"

I just sat there with my lip rolled in the mouth. It was years ago, but the feeling was now. It was like looking at the blueprints of disaster. If my father had his way, I was being primed to be him, madness all over again. The corner of the page was bent and I knew it had something to say.

"Go ahead; say what you've got to say."

"Don't you want to be like me?"

"Be like you? You mean paper?"

"No, silly. What I said. I'm a little old and unloved, but you can still be what you see."

"If you're talking about what my dad wrote, no."

"Well, if you change your mind, just save me somewhere where no one can find me but you. All that other paper, they deserve to be burned. They weren't doing anything but talk'n head anyway, but you and I can be friends, Mack...oh, I mean Emmanuel."

The corner collapsed and went silent. It would be the first to bathe in the flames. So we made some microwave kettle corn and had our own goodbye indoor smoke-out. Using the fireplace to burn the memoir, we slowly threw in the letters. The flames weaved and turned colors as every page hit them. The embers jumped, danced, and screamed as they twirled in the wind tunnel current that carried them in a reverse Santa Claus direction. The chimney's large throat sucked them up and blew them in a puff pillow in the north wind. You could hear them bellow all the way as they hugged the cold darkness.

"Hey, Momma, I've got one more."

"Which one is that, Emmanuel?"

"A letter from me to me."

"What are you going to tell yourself?"

I grabbed a piece of paper and as it unfolded, I felt it grin at me. "Go head, E-man, say something good, like your daddy, know you should!" shouted the paper. Then I heard it whisper something to my insides: "Say something eternal so the depths of your soul can hear it. Fool, you don't know the power of words?"

It thought I didn't catch that.

"Check this out, Momma.

Dear Emmanuel, did you hear what your father has said about you? Of how he wants you to end up like him? Well take note, little letters on the paper, my daddy won't decide what's going to happen to me. I love him, but I won't be like him. I'm going to be what my grandma told me I was–a good man who came from a great man. I got my name from a great man named Emmanuel. He told my grandmother that if he never saw me, to tell me that God had something great in me. So no matter what I've done, or the mistakes I've made, my granddaddy told my grandmamma that I was going to make it. I know right now I don't know what it is, and too stupid to look for it, but it's for me, because my granddaddy said so. So whatever words you thought you had for me, mister paper, go burn it!"

I grabbed a lighter and lit a tip of the letter. As I turned it from tip to tip before throwing it into the flames, a despairing smiling face with tears appeared to gasp for air.

I blew the ashes, and took a hand full of popcorn.

"You good, Momma?"

"Yes, I'm good."

"We good then."

Chapter 10
Mutual Combat/Mutual Respect

Well, you may guess like all other stories, there comes an end. But this is truly where it all really begins. Until there is true change, there is no progress. I listened to the radio news as I drove to work this morning and it really made me wonder how much things have and haven't changed. On the good side, we've gone from 8 tracks to cassette players, yelling across the streets to cell phones, LPs to CDs, Beta to DVDs, walkmans to I-Pods, and now we got the I-Phone. I can't afford another upgraded anything.

The kids laugh at me because my numbers have fallen off my cell phone, which they call, "Dad's GPS Get-tro."

The hauntings of history still breathe afresh in the present. Hank Aaron received death threats in 1974 when he was about to break Babes Ruth's home run record, and as if some sacred idols must never be destroyed, even now in 2007 as Barry Bonds closes in on his record, he needs extra security precautions at every professional baseball park. Wow, everyday you're waking up to America. You may find new heightened inventions really benefiting only the wealthy posted on the internet, or the stripping of heath care leaving the elderly as sheep without a shepherd, or a car pulling upside another and sprinkling it full of lead. Hatred is still hatred.

Driving by a home with an American flag in 1960 meant something different in 1970, which meant something different in 1980. In 2007, with an active Iraq war, it could mean patriot, being loyal, fighting for freedom. Yet, if you see one as you've driven off the road in unknown territory asking for directions, it may summon 'a fighter,' racist, extremist. Same flag, just depends upon who's holding the pole.

After many years of trial an error, ignorance and stupidity,

206

I began to see the effects of what I had done to my maze, my community, my life, and the effort it would take to repair what I had destroyed. I know in my limited lifetime the problem will not go away, but my goal is whatever I didn't live to see, maybe my children would benefit from it. I found a motto set by an old hero before me saying, "Maybe we couldn't, but ours next can."

I'm thirty-five years old now, married with three children. I got the privilege to make the lovely and so beautiful woman, Lady Sandy, my wife. It was hard work to get her, so I protect my investment.

Sandy's baby Brittany, our eldest daughter, is eighteen, Emmanuel Charles the III, is thirteen, and this sixteen-month-old gangbuster we call "MJ, Miss Michelle Christina, Jr." We named after her grandmother. This one is taking me awhile to grasp because she's always walking and talking. I'm baffled trying to understand what she is saying, and then everyone looks at me. "Daddy, she's talking to you?" To her everyone she meets is, "Hey, pooh-pooh, me potty?" I've never seen a toddler with so much boldness.

I just laugh at myself, me, so old with a baby? That's what I get trying to play 'king of the mountain.' As much as Sandy kept many keys to her heart hidden from me back in the day, especially the one for some sexual healing, when we got married, she threw that key away. I know I'm 'whipped' on her, always got a brother begging for more and in the back of my mind scared to ask knowing, I might not be able to handle it. She told me, "if you want it, you can have it, but you've got to keep everything that comes with it." So I got a baby.

When MJ is restless at night, Sandy will just come with her wrapped up tight in a blanket like the PG&E went out, and drop her in my lap. "Here, Man Mountain Mack, this is yours." All I can do is laugh and start rocking her. Sandy's taught me that sex is not love, but love can deeply involve sex without being perverted. And after fourteen years of marriage, she can

207

still break something new on me and we're back on our honeymoon.

One night I came home late from work and heard soft music coming from our bedroom. I thought she had a hard time putting MJ to sleep and was playing some music to help her go to sleep. But the more I listened from the other side of the door; this wasn't no "putting-a-baby-to-sleep music." I came in the room. There were low lights, mild cheddar cheese and grapes, some sparkling apple cider on ice, and Sandy laying on her belly across the bed with only a silk top; one toe on one side of the bed, and the other touching the other side of the bed. I had to catch myself. Rather than just running and jumping on her like a wild nut, I went in and took a quick shower. When I got to the bed she whispered, "Thank you, honey, I've been waiting for you."

Now in church the choir sings songs with verses concerning your walk with God saying, "Ninety-nine and a half won't do," and "Don't let him catch you with your work undone." I would be pointing at the kids, making their eye's bug-out, suggesting they'd better have their homework done 'cause ninety-nine for Sandy 'might not do.' But, oh lord, don't let her catch them with their homework undone! But this night, I could imagine the children pointing at me. I had to take care of business because ninety-nine and a half with Sandy on this midnight special would be my work undone. Had to make one hundred for my girl that night.

My wife and my mother get along well. I've learned a few things about being spoiled, especially being a man. When you get married first, then have to grow up, your mother can't just come in, take over, and rescue you. I used to call Michelle when Sandy and I would have our differences. Immediately like I loved it, she would defend her spoiled boy and tell me how to deal with 'that girl.' But Grandma had warned her to stay out of our challenges and let us work them out. One day Momma decided to call Sandy and get her straight, but it turned the other way around.

Michelle shot out a few hot words, then Sandy stopped her cold, but calm.

"Mrs. Harris...Mrs. Harris, stop please. I know you love your boy. But he's my husband now and not a boy that should always run to his momma every time he can't have his way."

I could hear Michelle trying to cut in again, but Sandy held her ground.

"No, I'm sorry, Mrs. Harris, but you need to let me finish what I have to say... thank you. I'm not sure and really don't care about any of Emmanuel's prior relationships and why he may have called you to rescue him, but this is not the one. With no disrespect to you, but this house at 2701 Louisburg Street, I run this here. He was used to getting his way, but he has a wife and family now. Just like you will not let someone come in and run your household, trust, nobody will run mines."

It was sincere and sensitive, cold and hot. I was trying not to be seen down the hall and knew I had it coming once she was finished. They talked for a while, and then I heard Sandy laughing.

"I'll get him for you. Ah, Emmanuel? Your mother wants to talk to you?"

You would have thought I belonged in Fisherman's Wharf Wax Museum. The gulp in my throat was so loud that I almost couldn't hear anything.

I answered, "Huh, baby?" all sweet and everything.

"Come on. Don't play stupid, and don't go deaf. Here's your mother."

"You two alright?"

"We were always all right. She wants to talk to you now."

I took the phone. Hand shaking ninety-miles per minute because I knew I had overstepped my boundary. Sandy stood right there with her arms crossed as if she would knock me out at any moment.

The tone in my voice went high. "Hey-hey, Momma."

She shot, "Don't hey-hey, boy. You know what?"

"What?"

"You can't be calling me when you two get into it anymore."

"Why?"

"Because my daughter-in-law asked me not to, and your grandmother told me to stay out of y'all stuff."

Now, you know I had to slip-slide a little. "But Momma, you know you the only Momma that understands her son."

"No, I'm the only momma that let you remain spoiled."

"Spoiled. Who's spoiled?"

"You. Rotten."

"I am."

"Yeah, and your grandmother admits she helped."

"Wow. I just thought y'all care about me a lot."

"Yeah, too much. You know Sandy made a good point."

"What was that?"

"She said Pastor spoke about spoiled kids who grow up to be spoiled adults and how the parents are the blame because they marry them off, not even telling the person getting their spoiled brat. Now somebody else has to deal with it. Told some of the members they ought to give them back to the ones that made them that way. Said the church was hollering. "

"Uww, that was cold."

"Yeah, but it was right."

"So you out, huh?"

"Yes. I love my daughter-in-law for sticking up for her family even if she has to stand against her family. Does she call her mother and father when y'all get into it?"

"No. She's not really an arguer. She kind of gets to the point and leaves it there. If I'm right, she'll admit it. If I'm wrong, well, it tells on itself. No matter what and no matter how bad it gets, she never tries to hurt me in it. And if I pull at her even when it didn't go good, she turns and puts her arm around me. Momma, I'm still learning."

"Good, son, and today, I am too. Bye."

"Bye."

I put the phone down and scurried around Sandy, who had one eyebrow up and her lips poked out. I kissed them.

"Well, what do you have to say for yourself, Mr. Emmanuel? Are you going to keep people out of our stuff?"

"Last time. Everybody's out. It's me and you. You know what?"

"What, Emmanuel?"

"Remember that night I went and stayed on the couch?"

"Yes."

"I'll never forget what you told me and how you felt."

"Which was what?"

"Of how you felt that I left you naked and unprotected. I mean, I was just on the couch, but it was deeper than that. And I'll never forget how you punch me in the chest and said don't ever do that again. I think I'm starting to understand that we are one, and if my one is not with me, then I'm not me."

"Yes, we are one. Rather five with all yo kids."

We laughed and held each other. I could feel her heart, along with all her other fine physical pieces in my grasp. She never holds back her love for me. She makes me feel her.

She's a great mother to her children, but she will bust them out. Yesterday, Sandy found a text message on Emmanuel's phone from a fifteen-year-old girl who wanted to "go with him." She blew up! I did all I could to stay out of the way. All I could hear was her telling him as he pleaded with her was, "Go get your father!"

I yelled out, "I'm trying to put MJ to sleep?"

"Excuse me? She can sleep later. Get in here!"

When we came from the back, the light hit MJ's face and she started to whine. Sandy took her from me.

"Put that pacifier in your mouth and be quite," Sandy said.

MJ put that pacific in her mouth, lay her head on her mother's shoulder, and shut up. I stood back and enjoyed watching my son's song and dance trying to explain this text message. The boy was hee-hawing and slip-sliding like a hockey puck, but his mother was not buying any of it, and slapping him back into play at his every move.

"You are thirteen years old, mister man, and you sho can't handle a fifteen-year-old hot momma."

Emmanuel answered, "Momma, it's not like that?"

"Then what is it like? Oh wait, let me read it!" With lighting speed and one stroke, she snatched the phone from his hand.

He backed up and bumped up into a chair hard. His head and neck double-clutched like a rubber band. I thought he broke something.

Grandma always warned Michelle about trying to be buddy-buddy with me when I was young. She'd tell her, "Don't you play with that boy. 'Cause if you play with a puppy, he'll lick you in the mouth."

Sandy wasn't giving Emmanuel the chance to even pucker his lips up.

"Yo boo, got something n the pot, and it's hot, only my man got. R-U-him? Let me know, we can go, this week, take a peek, at the twins on the upper flow [Boo's-Tee]."

The boy was speechless. I was tickled pink. His older sister was crack'n up.

Then Sandy threw a curve ball. "Boy, have you ever seen some titties?"

His eyes were as wide as a fish bowl. He turned and locked eyes with me.

I hunched my shoulder and threw my hands up. "I ain't never seen none. I can't help you brother," and winked at him.

He smiled, but he wasn't out of the woods yet.

I took MJ from Sandy's arms and went to put her in the bed. I felt sorry for the brother, but I had my turn and it was his turn to go through it.

My brother-in-law, Mighty, is doing fine. He has church in

his house and his wife, whom he met in recovery, sings about four to five solos during service. Sandy warned him to stop playing with that woman or marry her. He just smiled, popped his fingers, and sang, *"Secret Lovers, That's What We Are."* He kept on making and breaking promises until she snapped and showed up to his job at six o'clock in the morning wearing a white Satin & Lace Torolette, thong, Sheer Caress stocking with straps, and flowers. Scared that brother to death. He hurried up and married that girl.

He preaches to the kids and plays the piano. The only thing that concerns us is that he gives the children real wine for communion, but other than that, it's good enough for me. Some may say it's wrong, too far-fetched, but if you knew how far they've come, we will take this as the cherry on the cake. He works security at midnight for one of the local supermarkets near the Castro. The manager said it's been great having him there. People don't give him no trouble and the guys love him.

One day he forgot his hat so I took it to him. One man tapped me on the shoulder as I was leaving and asked how I knew Mighty. I told him our relationship and he said, "We love Mighty. He's a man of compassion, a man of strength." Then he whispered, "Every now and then he pulls up his sleeve and flexes his arm muscle for us, and we all scream, Mighty, Mighty, Mighty!"

I smiled and left that alone. I said, "I've seen him use the big arms before. They can make you scream in more ways than one. Thank you for appreciating my brother-in-law. He's been through a lot and he loves everybody. I'll let him know." Mighty better be careful before he winds-up in a calendar centerfold somewhere.

He still fades in and out with memory loss at times. That's when we know he hasn't taken his meds. Once Sandy had to catch the bus home and saw Mighty sitting on the back seat, hair straight up in the air as if he stuck his tongue in a light socket, with a newspaper in his mouth. Another day I went grocery shopping at his job. He walked me to my car laughing and talking, said hi to the kids, and walked away. Before I could put all the groceries in the car, he came back.

"Excuse me, sir, what's your name?"

"It's me, Mighty, Emmanuel, your brother-in-law? We just talked a minute ago."

"Oh, have a nice day sir." And walked away professionally. You got to love him.

I found out that the Macks, the Daces, and the addicted don't go away. They just change names and addresses. And more so, thank God, the grandmothers don't go away either. They are a little younger these days, and not by choice for most, but they do pray for their grandbabies.

Today in my desire to help redirect some other young lives, I continue to talk to them when many don't listen. It's frustrating. I learned for every one you save from destruction, there's one hundred or more who are willing to take their place. It's the system of breed and bleed. Eliminating the evil may not be the solution or even possible, but exposure to better things brings a new part of life, a choice.

I love my daddy. I love Mack Anthony James. I take the children by to see him as much as possible. I've learned to love him, and work with who he is. He hasn't changed, just too old to do as much and run from the police. He lives with his cousin, who the government pays to house a few fellows trying to get themselves together. They go to classes, AA meetings, and stay busy as much as their health will allow. But they're old, and in their free time sit out in front playing cards and smoking cigarettes.

Many of the youngsters still look up to them and like to hear the old stories. A few of the young ones want them to teach them how to win in the game. But Mack knows better now. I overheard him talking to two young brothers and he's still brutally honest.

"Y'all don't be no fools like us. Yeah, I'm Mack, still pack the best mack, a matter a fact I still got my rack."

He'd cut a rhyme to the boys to lift them off the ground, but then drop them back to earth.

"But I'm old, no gold, prison taught me how to fold, gray headed, with a curl, being done by, the last girl, who can find Luster Curl, and ain't got noth'n to show in this world."

Then he would shoot straight with them. "You see us standing around, talking loud. I bum a cigarette off him, he bum a cigarette off me, he got a piece of candy and three of us want a piece, but look at us? We ain't going nowhere. Most of my kids' mommas won't even let me see my kids. We too old to do anymore harm to ourselves, and don't need to mess nobody else life up. Yeah, we legends; but the only thing out live the legend is the lies they tell about you. Don't be no fools like us young men, don't be no fools." Then he'd sit down and turn his head. Curl activator all over the back of his shirt.

His grandchildren love him, except MJ. I think he talks too loud for her and she won't let him touch her. He's always boxing with Emmanuel. "Pip-pow-pow, keeps ya hands up, boy." Emmanuel's really shocked how fast his grandfather's hands are. Mack teaches him how to protect himself if he has to. But Emmanuel is really quite mild mannered and Mack doesn't push him as he did with me. But every time I bring them by, he's like clock work. He's got a bag of penny candy for everybody. As hard as that is to find today, Mack always had a way of getting what he wants for his babies.

"Come on, girl, Grandpa ain't gone hurt 'chu," says Mack to MJ.

"Daddy, you know you talk so loud you scare her," I answered.

"That's all right. Don't force her, she still my girl."

MJ walks up slowly, grabs the bag, then turns and runs. But before she can get away, Dad will have patted her on her behind. She runs to me and grabs me around the leg.

He'd yell, "Got cha'!" and she laughs loud.

215

My dad has other children too. I've been able to keep in contact with some of them, but they have little to do with him. He still calls us his Mack-Pack. Before I leave, I kiss him on the forehead every time. He doesn't even look up, just winks at the kids and taps me on the leg. That's his way of kissing me back. I had to grow up to understand that.

Everyday I'm learning to live by the principles Mr. Hortan gave me.

Through his teaching in how to respect our women, I got a real queen, and my queen makes me a true king. Sandy never lets me do her like I have done other women. She was never desperate, never looked desperate, and never allowed me to put her in the place where she owed me anything. Trying to win her family, I had to break down and do some old-fashioned courting.

I called Mr. Hortan so many times, trying to find out what hoop they would try to get me to hop through next. But he would always assure me that they were not playing games, but seeing if I would pay the price to be added to their family.

He told me, "These people are not looking to add someone that would constantly bring harm and shame to their family, and they are not going to give you a free-access pass in. You will have to earn their respect, and you will have to bring something good that will add to it."

I started with respecting her parents and their home, calling before coming, and going through her entire family, including uncles, aunts, and cousins with the full once-over to see if I was any good for the taking. I had to have some things already in place before I asked her father for her hand in marriage.

I open the door for my queen, and share the same respect for other women. Many times when I have my son with me, I teach him to open the door, or give up your seat on the BART train. Many times some of the women will not even say thank you, just walk through or sit down. But I've matured in knowing I do it not for the applause or self-gratification. It is because I am a self-respecting gentleman, and I'm teaching Emmanuel to be a gentleman. When it happens, I say this right in earshot of the woman who needs to hear it.

"And if they don't say thank you, you are still a gentlemen, right son?"

"Right dad," Emmanuel answers.

The woman responds, "Oh, I'm sorry. Thank you."

I've learned that without the woman, there is no real man. My mother and my grandmother have royal blood in their veins. Momma has John, and we all cater to Grandma's every need. They are the ones who gave so much for me that I can't do enough for them. They just crack up when they see me getting on Emmanuel about his manners. Grandma reminds me that I once was a child too, and to give him space to make mistakes. But I love everything about them.

Sometimes, I sit up in bed and watch Sandy sleep. She may have had a rough day at work. She still comes home and takes good care of her children. I'm just baffled by her strength. Works, picks up MJ, cooks, helps Emmanuel with his homework, slaps Brittney upside the head for not following through on her responsibilities, then talks to her and dries her tears. Everybody's down for the night, then here I come, and she never refuses me. Man, she is some kind of woman, and all mine.

Through working hard and Mr. Hortan's name, I'm a counselor at the youth correction center. As bad a kid as I was, here I am, loving to be around these bad kids. But I have also found myself looking in the mirror, through the eyes of some of these babies, seeing the same tears. Most of the cries moan out to somehow say, "Why am I like this?" just as I did. The hours are long, ten hours a day and mandatory overtime. Many times when I'm off work, they call me in because of some major disturbances. They must have faith in me to bring some calm and order to the situation. Most of the kids here are children of the children in the neighborhood. I can see their parents' resemblance in their smiles, though few and far between. Some of my old running-partners' children are here. I've asked a few of them where their fathers are, and only a few know.

When it seems like I am making no progress with some of them, I take a walk and take out my piece of paper. I peer into years of someone who didn't give up on me in every fold. I catch my breath, and go back in. I found out that many of the young girls would act out just for me to come over and talk to them. They would say how their mothers and aunts would talk about me and how bad I was years ago. But I always remind them that that was then; this is now, and how they should not be trying to keep old history of acting like bad girls just to be known as being like their mothers. Hair wild, haven't bathed in a few days, then they cry because they miss being home. I sit there as long as needed until they are doing better. Many ask me why I care, and my reminder to them is that somebody cared for me, and there's a grandmother somewhere worried about them. Their faces grow somber and their eyes find reality when I speak about someone out there who cares and is waiting for them.

About a month ago, a young lady refused to leave the facility until I came to see her. I was actually on vacation and had two days before I returned to work, but the staff said she wouldn't leave till she saw me. Mya was wild as a coyote when she came in, but had made great improvements since being here.

"Hey, Mr. Harris, I have a letter for you."

"You stayed here for two days just to give me a letter?"

"Yep, just wanted to make sure you got it. Stuff be coming up missing around here and nobody was going to steal or throw this away."

"So, do you want me to read it or do you want to read it?"

"I'll do it. Dear Mr. Harris, Thank you for coming over

218

and talking to us girls. I really appreciated it and starting to look at my life a lot different. The night we were fighting and you came in throwing chairs freaked us out. We was like, man, he flipped! We thought you needed some medication or something, but you were just showing us ourselves. You made us sit in a circle and had the other counselors leave, and then you talked to us like we were your daughters. Telling us what boys really think about us when we do anything just to please them. Thank you for letting me in your life. My father yells at us. I know he loves us, but that's all he knows, so we run away. My mother is scared that she will lose me, but I promised her I will not run away again. Please help me and my family.

Love your spicy knot-head, Mya"

"Thank you, Mya. I've got your back, and I've got some help coming for your family."

Thank you, Mr. Harris. Well, back to the neighborhood."

"It's what you make of it, lady. Be a lady."

"I will. Bye."

I watched her walk out and without her consent, have to go back into the wild orchard that ran her here. But I did know one thing, she was looking for more, and that was a great start to change, even if no one ever picks her from the tree.

Through education and proper English, I have an AA degree in Children's Studies and Urban development. I can also negotiate funding for programs in my maze. I committed myself to bringing something into the children's lives in the maze other than chaos. That meant that for many, they would be spending more time out of the home with me and my staff.

I had to have a place where they could come and be fed, do their homework, exercise, and get a grip of a better future before they returned into their everyday hopeless present. My maze hasn't changed much, but there are sprigs budding out of the charred ashes. Most of the characters of the demise haven't changed game, just roles.

Early on, when I'd come to the meeting to make a

presentation, some of the board members for the funding would look real strange at me. I believe they remembered me from my past and that's when I found out why Mr. Hortan hung so strongly on the use of proper English. I would hit them with straight business professionalism and my planning would be flawless. At first they would thank me, but no calls would come for funding. One time during a presentation, the committees' faces were emotionless and eyes as faded glass in Disneyland. Sorry, I went straight 'ghetto' on them.

"See, that's why folks come in and goes off in you all's meeting because all y'all do is sit there and pretend like you want to help. I'm trying to do something beforehand and give these children something to hold on to. But do y'all really care? Or maybe it's better when they run up in y'all house with guns, then y'all really ready to talk about money for the bad kids then?"

That didn't go well at all in my favor. One board member was kind enough to at least address my concerns after he landed from wherever his mind was.

He said, "Mr. Harris, we can see that you are very passionate about your program, but your actions may not help you fulfill them. I advise you to first calm down, and then if possible return tomorrow with your presentation, minus the anger. I know your outburst was because you want see it happen for the children, but we have got to trust that your endeavor will not fold when the going gets tough, like you've just demonstrated. We will see you again at one o'clock tomorrow."

Mr. Hortan gave me the third degree over that, and advised when I returned to first apologize, and then go back to the principles I had learn. There I go, having to bite the bullet again. I did apologies this time and I got the funding needed to help our babies. Now with a strong track record, we have been approached and asked how much do we need? But this wasn't an overnight success. Trial and error, greedy associates I had to fire, and working through the uncommitted that had to be weeded out, finally giving me a group of committed souls who were willing to risk all to save some.

I can kick myself in the behind for not taking my education seriously when I was younger. Many of the courses were easy and English 101 was exciting. I would come to class ready and so proud of myself that I was able to read an entire book and liked it. You go, boy! Sandy would help me prepare for tests. This was a little embarrassing because she'd set us all in the dining room in classroom style. Me, the baby, Emmanuel, and Brittney all enrolled by force. Emmanuel would be giggling the whole time as I'd stumble over some words, but hey, what can I say. Sandy reads and has MJ repeat after her. Late at night she and I lie in the bed and listen to MJ in her crib still trying to say the words. I plan to teach English to the young middle-school boys one day before I leave this earth.

With influence, I hit the places where I had the baddest name because it was there that needed the most change. Your past can be an alliance or an enemy, and first impressions can be a lasting image. It took a while for many who knew me before to believe that I had metamorphosed from the cornered cocooned Little Mack into a man named Emmanuel, who cared about this place, that didn't care about itself. In small gatherings either on the corner, a park gym, a church social hall, or even in my living room, I share with those in the community how I take personal responsibility of destroying what they presently live in. Most of my life people would listen to me, whether for good or not so good, but it's not about me anymore. It's about us now.

One day two groups of young men were about to get into it at the bus stop. Sandy had the car; I was tired, and really didn't want to get involved, but I got off the bus. As soon as my foot hit the pavement, everything stopped. To most people, I am just introducing them to the 'Emmanuel' me, but everybody here knows Little Mack. And to these youngsters, I'm still the baddest thing they've ever seen. I walked right in the middle of the crowd of about ten of them.

"What's the matter, little brotha's?"

"Man, these suckers up the block always starting something," one young man said.

"Dude, y'all tripping. We were just trying to catch the bus and y'all rolled up on us," said another from the other side.

I stared at them, one at a time. "You all know that don't nothing go down without a big baller calling it. So what are you fella's going to do? Beat each other down, shoot each other? What? Tell me? I don't see no big balls hanging?"

The boys were quiet.

I pointed to one young man. "You're Tank's son, right?"

"Yeah."

"What started all this?"

He hunched his shoulders. "I don't know?"

"Really? But you in for the kill, right?"

"Yeah, I'm down with my boys."

"At least know why you're down. I mean, if you have to go down. Wouldn't it be good to know why?"

Everyone was silent. Another bus was a block away.

"You know, I wouldn't want you to go overseas to fight a war when you don't know why. So don't fight a war at home when you don't know why. Go home, and if you find a real reason to beef, then ask ya momma for a steak! But stop getting caught up in somebody else's mess, not knowing why?"

I got on the bus and four of the young men got on with me. The others just stood there mouthing to each other. I sat in the front and they went to the back, noisy, but at least with no holes in one of them today. A chill went up my spine at what I was–a victim and participant of the past.

I knew where they were because I had given validity to the hype that now could blow them into lifeless respect. What more could I have done for those boys? I came to a temporary conclusion; trying to hold a big rally to stop the violence was not the solution, but taking time to defuse your own community-planted mortars from the past will be my day-by-day challenge.

In taking responsibility, I work wholeheartedly, giving of myself to personally see that people are not needlessly hurt in my neighborhood. Though mind you, I have to still take a hand in a few necessary butt whippings with the aide a few of other brothers on the ones who were determined not to listen. We once had been the cause, so now we seek to turn the vision for our community around. We take our problems personally because what affects one, infects all. We were seeing the offspring of our planting, so the challenge was uprooting the bad sprouts.

I met with some of the major neighborhood players and 'told them' to give me some money to take the kids camping. They laughed, but pulled some stacks out of those safes for me too. I met with a longtime dealer-addict named Billy, who is known as Candyman. I gave him a choice.

"Man, it's only a matter of time. You've done business like this long enough here. I need you to move," I said.

"Hey Mack, you know I ain't hurting nobody, man. Why you come up in here like that?"

"Because I can, and you know me. I need you to help me help these people."

He burst out laughing. "So how I'm suppose to help, Mack? Tell Candyman how he 'pose to help!"

"I didn't ask you to stop selling the candy; just take the store somewhere else."

"You know, Little Mack, with that kind of talk, you could make some real enemies," he muttered under his breath.

Then the 'Mack' in me jumped out. I stepped up on him hard. "Who wants to be known as my enemy, huh, Candyman? Who wants their name dropped in the ear of my father as one who wants to do something to Mack's boy?"

He got real quiet. His hand quivered as he lit a joint. "Mack, you serious?

I stood there.

His eyes exploded. "You are serious. Mack, you one of the main ones who gave this game over here power! You and yo daddy along with us other hustlers been slang'n and slap'n for the longest, and now you want to walk up in here like you the long lost hope and–"

I pinned him to a wall by the throat. The joint was still gripped with the strength of a vice grip.

"Mack!" he attempted to heave out.

"And what! Candyman! Yeah, we did it when we did, but we messed up a lot of people for life with our slang'n and bang'n. But if we are going to at least give their kids a chance, something got to change. And you know me, Canny! We ran like gazelles and who could stop us? But, I ran into a brick wall a little while ago called life, and when I learned I needed to be giving it rather than taking it, I made a choice. Billy, it's over for the dope game in this house. Take the mess somewhere where they don't care, because I care."

His gaze stayed glued to me with the pressure I had on his throat. I pried the joint out from between his fingers and took a drag. "Hum. What is this, chronic?"

I slowly released him.

Catching his breath, he slowly took the joint from my hand, and hit it with the force of a Hoover vacuum cleaner. "Naw, Perquevo Gold, the fine Columbian; you know like Steely Dan sang, man." He massaged his throat to clear his voice. He took another hit. "Man, let me calm my nerves. Got me smokin' my own weed, and Mack, you calm down with that hands-on stuff. It ain't necessary with us who know you."

"Cool, Candy."

He sat down. "You know, Mack, ever since my momma went back South and gave me this house, I've been doing my thang. This been a dope house so long and so much craziness done come from here, I heard the mailman paid the property taxes the last five years because he knew my momma and we wouldn't lose the house. So you want me to just up and leave it, huh?"

"No," I answered. "This is your mother's property. Just do right by something. So many times, the police done ran up in here you can't even count and crack-heads running everywhere. Is that what your mother worked for all her life; to see her son take his inheritance and smoke it away? Look at you. You're addicted to your own candy. You got weed lips, all black and crusty. If you can't do right by the hood, man, do right by your mother."

Candyman turned and looked at himself in a broken mirror. He rubbed white stuff off the edge of his lips. I walked away.

A few weeks later, the house was up for sale. His mother bought it back in the '70s for about twenty-three thousand dollars, and it sold for six hundred and fifty thousand dollars. The IRS is sick if they think that fool's going to pay a dime in capital gains taxes. A big win for him, no matter what he does with it, and peace for one street in the neighborhood.

I've learned how to deal with authority, too. This was the most challenging of all. Yes, with all of Mr. Hortan's warnings, I still went to jail two other times for some weak stuff. Every time, he'd come by and visit me with that little piece of paper pinned to his jacket, and put it up to the glass. He'd shout, "Emmanuel, repeat it! Again! Again!" We wouldn't have any other conversations. We just had that piece of paper; repeating it over and over again. Then he'd leave me sitting there, and I'd get up looking stupid. Man, that was so embarrassing. Both times I got arrested, I probably could have been cited and released for little stuff – expired tags, drunk in public, but I reacted and went 51/50, instead of responding in a manner that could have easily quelled the situation.

Back then Sandy wouldn't have anything to do with me

when I was in jail either.

I'd be on the other end just hoping I could hear her voice.

"Collect call from county jail from Emmanuel. Will you accept the charges?

"Emmanuel, who?" said Sandy. (Click)

My heart would drop like a pancake. All I could do was walk over, take a seat, and wait. I never stayed long on either occasion, but every moment away from her helped me understand that I had to be on "time's" side. She would not do no time with me, so I will not do time without her.

Now, many of the cops in my neighborhood stop in the center to talk about old times of how I used to out run them, they'd later catch me, and my grandma would beat my butt in the station. I asked, "Why didn't you guys stop her?" They told me for one, I needed it, and two, they were scared she'd beat them. The respect they had for her made me feel good. I don't fear the police anymore. I don't necessarily trust many of them, but most are doing what they are entrusted to do, protect and serve.

I learned they are not all the enemy. The worst enemies are internal. The deceptive thoughts I felt that kept me for a while not trusting me, so I could trust no one else. Sometimes, I see lights flashing and hear the sirens and wonder, what are they saying? When I was young, they meant get on the run. It's time for the gamers to see who could get away from the police; up the street, over a fence, through a back yard, and cut up new pathways. The new cops would want to see who could handle their black and white around the corners and cut us off at the pass. Then try to run with us and all that equipment on? It was cat and mouse at its rarest form, but I finally got tired of being the decoy to train the Greyhounds.

I learned that every time I ran, I'd never get that time back. As I stopped running from the law, I learned to not run from my personal responsibilities. If a bill is late and the phone rings with some nasty collector, Sandy doesn't face that, I do. One night late, a call came in.

"Who is it?" I asked Brittney. "It's somebody who wants to speak to mom."

"Give me the phone." Brittney handed me the phone. "Hello?"

"Can I speak to Sandy Harris?"

"No. This is her husband, Mr. Harris. What is this concerning?"

"We just need to talk to Sandy."

I looked at the caller ID. It was the phone company. "If this is the phone company, my name is on that account, too. You can talk to me."

"Please hold, sir, and let me check."

The phone was silent for a moment.

"Yes sir, we see your name is also on the account. We are calling about a payment that is due at this time."

"Wait. For one, it is too late for you to be inquiring about a payment. Two, we did send the payment out. However, it may be late and that is my fault. My wife always gives me the bill to mail out and I did mail them out late. Three, don't ever ask for my wife when it comes to a payment, ask for me. Is this conversation being recorded?

"Yes, it is."

"So, you did hear me that you will not ask for my wife, you will ask for me, right?"

"Yes sir, but may I ask why this is necessary?"

"Because there was a company that called and insulted my wife and when I found out that they were local, I paid them a visit. I said that just to say that will never happen again, and also want to make sure whoever is on the other side of this line knows that if they ever get to talk crazy, the other crazy person on this side of the phone will come through the line at them. Is that clear?"

"Yes, sir. Have we been okay with you?"

"Yes, and it will be better not to call my house this late in the evening anymore," and I hung up the phone.

Brittney burst out laughing. "My daddy. He so hard on everybody about Mommy."

Brittney asked why I was so protective of her mother. I told her that her mother was the very first precious piece in my life and I don't let anyone hurt her. Brittney smirked, because she knew I would get on her about their relationship. I would remind her every now and then, when she thought she wanted to stand up to Sandy.

"Hey girl, your mother is the only queen in this house. Any other rebels trying to take her place must find a new palace to live with her own king to pay for it."

"You don't have to remind me, Dad. I know whose house this is," answered Brittney, rolling her eyes.

"Make sure you find a man to do the same thing for you."

"You're always looking out for us so much, Daddy, just chill," and she walked off with her little musty self.

I hope my life will provoke her to not settle for just anybody who's got some gold in his mouth, but someone who will add richness to her life. My grandmother said if I could raise this first one, the others wouldn't be too much of a problem.

When I talk to Grandma about being tired and needing a break, she would hit me with some more old school wisdom such as, "Get some rest, boy, you ain't too young to go crazy," or "If you don't want to get old, you'd better die young." Those sayings kind of slap you back into reality.

Most of all, I know how to be thankful. That preacher from the tape is now my pastor. He's made me realize the area in my life that was the most important, but I had made a wreck of it first. It was spiritual life. I dedicated my life to working with kids. I knew God could do something with something I couldn't do anything with. It didn't happen to me when I was in church. I've seen a lot of people running down the isle, crying and shouting when they gave their lives to Him. Then

I've seen some of the same ones back out there.

I saw that same usher one day in the supermarket. She walked over and hugged me. "How you doing, son?" Yet before I could get a word out she said, "Lord, touch him and keep him."

I froze, holding back the tears and grabbing anything I could off the shelf right there in that big supermarket. And it was the first time I didn't care about who saw me or how I looked. The power of God hit me.

She said, "Son, you got a home?"

I looked her in the eyes. "No, but I need one now!"

She led me in a simple prayer right between the canned tuna and the Mexican food aisle. Real quietly and with peace, I asked God to take over my life. At the end of that prayer, she kissed me and went right back shopping. That was about ten years ago.

Pastor teaches us practical things to live by, not religious fantasy. A lot of the 'used to be worst' guys in the neighborhood go there, searching for help. Thank God, this guy got something for them. Some stay, some stray, but at least they're searching.

Michelle married John on my second trip to jail. He never tried to be my father, but he would check me when I stepped out of line with Momma. Most of all, he loves her and I'm finally glad someone treats her like a queen. I've got a little sister...well, she is seventeen now and doing well. She's really lucky to have both parents at home. She loves her big brother and his bad kids.

When I first got married, I stayed frustrated a lot because it was hard to make ends meet. Every time my ends got close, someone would throw some hot grease and they would slide apart again.

Pastor shared about being thankful in everything, not for everything. As I started to apply the teaching to my life, as long as I had what I needed and not everything I wanted, I began to be thankful. Everything wasn't good for me anyway, and I knew I would have a house full of unthankful kids if I first didn't learn how to be thankful.

We go to church and people testify about being thankful and God supplying their needs. I could see Grandma rocking side-to-side real fast. The ushers would be moving in her direction because we all knew it was only a matter of time before she'd snatch off them glasses and almost loose that wig. Sandy just can't hold her peace on those rounds. After she cries over the other testimonies, she fans herself and shares about when our son had got Salmonella poisoning from some raw chicken near his bottle when he was a baby. The doctor told us she really couldn't do anything for him being so young, so we brought him to church for prayer and in seven days he was totally healed.

Grandma's big trombone voice needed no microphone to kick up an old hymn: "Glory, Glory, Hallelujah, Since I Laid My Burden Down." Everybody would join in tune like a feast was being set and white clothes were being washed. She'd stand up and point at some of the crying young mothers with small children by their sides going through tough times, saying, "Burdens Down, Lord, Burdens Down, Lord," encouraging and strengthening them with something coming out of her life in every word. The church would lose it then and dance about an hour. Piano man would be playing like he was enjoying himself, sweating and sliding all up and down those keys in those club jazz chords. Then he raised his hand and ended the song, yelling, "Thank ya! Hallelujah!" He'd be holding a B flat minor chord, then switching back and forth between the forths and fifths, electrifying the crowd to yell with him. One usher and his mother came over and fanned him, got him some water, and then he'd tip out with the famous Baptist one finger up.

I sat there and rejoiced in my own way, swaying my head to the music, wiping the sweat off my face, and holding MJ who would be asleep with that heavy head on my arm. I shed a few tears on the inside now and then.

After Sandy danced a while, Momma would come over and fan her. She'd pass out and that's when that hairpiece would fall out, too. Then Emmanuel would start clowning by putting it on his head.

I see Mr. Hortan every now and then, retired but still active. Has a bunch of kids in his big custom RV, turning up the hill going toward his home. I could see one guy in the back window grooving to the music. Later on that week, I was pulling up to the gas station and there was Mr. Hortan. He hugged me.

"Mr. Harris, where are your principles?"

I looked at him and smiled. "I got them, and I still remembered the promise I made to you. I fulfilled it, too."

Putting his hand on his chin, he asked, "Oh, whom did you share it with?"

"Joe-Nathan Young," I answered, looking him straight in the eyes, which was something I could not do for a long time.

"Joe Young, Jr.! Your arch enemy!" His eyebrows stuck straight up in the air.

"I couldn't find anyone I used to hate as much as him."

"Wa, Wa, Wait a minute! You said, you use to hate? What does that mean?" He was grinning.

"Since I've learned better, and Joe-Nathan had a lot of the same characteristics that I did, who better? Plus, I've learned about hatred and I don't want that seed in me or my children."

We walked into his RV, which again was filled with his students. He asked me to get in so he could introduce me.

"Ladies and gentlemen, this is Emmanuel Harris. Some of you may have heard of him as 'Little Mack'."

One of the young guys whispered to another, "Yeah, he got a lot of weight in the hood. Boy ain't no joke."

Mr. Hortan got in and closed his door. "So tell us about your sharing with Joe-Joe...or Joe-Nathan as you refer to him."

I paused for a moment to collect my thoughts. "Well,

everyone, I learned his name in the hospital after the big fight we had in jail a long time ago. When he went to prison, he got his knee busted on the yard playing football. He walks with a brace now. When he got out of prison, he went back to slinging drugs until his grandmother took sick. His grandmother and my grandmother where the best of friends. I heard on her deathbed, she asked him for one thing. She asked him to make sure that when he raised his children, not to put them through the hell he and his daddy took her through. He went on a big guilt trip, blaming himself for his grandmother illness. The night she died, she wanted to see him, but he couldn't be found. He was out there doing his thing and as usual by the time he got the message, it was too late.

When he got to the hospital, all the family was there. His daddy was still in prison. He got to hollering and screaming to the point his grandfather had to knock him out to keep the police from taking him. His grandfather is a retired fire fighter and still strong. He was one of those first and last lumberjacks who you would not want to be caught playing hide and seek with his axe. My grandmother was working that night and saw it all. She asked me and mother to go to the service with her.

"It was a good service until Joe-Joe and his dad came in. Then for those two it went to 'this is a black funeral; this is how we do it'."

Some of the kids understood and snickered.

"It was something, crying, slobbering, noses running all over everything and anybody who got too close. Someone would come up to take a picture from the right or left of Mrs. Young, and it was as if those fools were posing to see who had the most snot and slob, mind you, coming out of their mouths. Joe-Joe laid on his daddy like he was three years old, and Joe Young's greasy prison skunk curls were down to his shoulders. This show was only for the patient at heart.

"Mr. Young Sr., let it go for a while. After the message, the correctional officers escorted Joe Young up to the coffin to see her again. It was pitiful to see Joe Young shackled down and in red jail clothes. His father told the officer not to take the shackles off, didn't need him trying to do anything crazy. Then Joe-Joe ran with his coat half off, one shoe on, and threw himself like a rag doll down beside his daddy.

"'Mommaaa! Mommaaa! I'm sorry, Momma, I'm sorry!'"

"Then young people, Joe-Joe literally fell out, plop!"

The children's mouths were almost hanging to the floor.

"And as for his dad, have you guys ever been to the zoo and seen a monkey throw a fit, leaping and pounding its fist in rage?"

One young lady answered, "Yeah, last week with Mr. Hortan. Monkey was going off!"

I said, "Well, Joe Young was one of the monkey's uncles that day. His powerful legs and knees lifted him from the ground and hit his chest with such intensity that the walls shook. He slammed his cuff palm into his forehead. Fool Joe-Joe woke up and blew it when he reached in his pocket, took out a bankroll, and put it in the coffin saying, 'See Momma, I'm paying you back. Tell God, I paid you back!'

"That did it. Mr. Young grabbed him and his daddy, putting them both out. He told them, 'Don't cry now, boys, don't cry now!' He drug those knuckleheads by the back of the neck like two little bad puppies. The correctional officers following close behind, but not interfering."

The young people were listening and breathing so hard it looked as if it were snowing inside.

"'Take this one back to prison, now!' Mr. Young Sr. said, looking at the correctional officers. Joe Young was sniveling like a little boy and said, 'Ah, Daddy, don't do me like that'. Mr. Young grabbed him by the chest.

'Don't do who like that! You did you like that!'

"Mr. Young looked over at the officers. 'Take this one back to 'hiss house.' Isn't that what you all call it, son?'

"Joe Young dropped his head like a little mannish boy.

"'Yes, sir,' the officers answered and took him away.

"Then, Mr. Young turned to Joe-Joe. I was sitting in the last aisle watching. He looked at Joe-Joe and spoke real slow. 'Joe-Nathan Young the third. Your grandmother is gone and there is nothing you or I can do about it. She knew the Lord and is with him now, but you and I are still here. You must make a choice now, son, before it's too late and guess what? It's half over already. Don't come back in the service. You've said your good-byes.'

"Then he walked back in. I knew Joe-Joe wouldn't go against his grandfather, so I went out to the lobby where he was. I looked down the corridor and he was still snorting, sniffling, and shaking his head. So I walked down the hall slowly and sat down across from him. I sat there being judgmental for a moment, lifting myself above his behavior, but the words of my grandmother whispered to my memory, 'There go I, if not for the grace of God'. Both of them going fifty-one fifty, and as many a time I pushed my grandmother to the edge of fifty plus. My mother used to call her for everything.

"'Momma, Emmanuel's not home!

"'Momma, let me tell you what this boy did!

"'Emmanuel did this! Emmanuel did that!

"'Momma, you need to talk to Emmanuel.'"

"The only real differences between him and me at that time were our positions across the hall. There were other services going on at that funeral home. One was very quiet, and the other was hell.

"Down the hall a mother was going crazy, a young sister. I got up and looked in the room. There was a small coffin, and a guy standing outside the door where we were. I asked him what happened. He shook his head and said the mother was the cause of it. Her daughter got killed because somebody was after the mother. Now she was all over the floor. Then he said, 'Hey man, just check out the crowd for the little girl.' The people were hurt and a lot other children in uniforms were crying. I thought they must have been classmates of hers because I could see her dressed like them. There were balloons, pictures, and big cards around the pink coffin.

"But no one cared about the mother. With all that emotion, only the morticians were trying to care for her. Then they helped her to her seat. When I saw her face, it was 'Giga-momma.' I remembered her because I used to sell to her years ago. She sat by herself on the front seat, kind of looking around as if to see if people were watching her. Then the people started coming around to see the little girl, who had a cap on her head. They just stood there briefly then walked straight past the mother. The people left, and then it was just Joe-Joe and me. I told him I was sorry about his grandmother. He didn't say anything, just sat there.

"'Why you here, Mack? You here to do something to me?' said Joe-Joe

'No, but I did make a promise to give you something,' I answered.

"'A promise, Mack? When you start making promises? Oh, you got religion now? What Mack got for me?'

"Calm down, dude. Don't you want to know why?"

"'You trip'n, Mack. Okay, tell me why. My grandmamma gone, Daddy always locked up. I ain't got noth'n to lose.'

"I told him the conditions of what I was to share with him. 'For one, you needed it just as much or more than I did, and for two, I've hated you the most.'

He stood up slowly with his eyes all tight and blood shot from crying. 'So we even, I hate you too. So give it to me, Mack.'

"I told him he'd need to sit down and I got my piece of paper out of my wallet. He sat there quietly as I shared with him what you shared with me. I told him if we ever make it to be fathers and our kids are going to live something different, we had to do something now.

235

"He was pissed. 'What am I suppose to do about that! That ain't my problem?'

"At the same time, the mother of the dead girl came out. She was pregnant and turned to Joe and asked him to help her get a hit. She talked about how she could hear her baby crying on the inside. He turned and looked at me.

"'Let that be the reason,' I said.

"He looked at her. 'I ain't gonna help you kill another baby!'

She just looked at him. 'Oh well, I give the next hustler ma money. Joe-Joe, you get'n soft,' and walked away, lighting a cigarette. The mortician came out and closed the door. Since we knew the mother and how she lived, we asked how she paid for the funeral. He told us that the woman didn't have any money and the coffin was a loaner. The child would be buried in a box and the city would cover the services.

"I looked Joe-Joe in the eyes. 'We may never walk together again, but at least somebody should be able to walk our streets without being a target. So we don't have to see another little girl in a box because of us again.'

"He didn't say anything, just sat there. I walked back into the service. That was about fifteen years ago. He now runs a public-educational center, helping ex-offenders get jobs and trying to send them to college." I looked over at Mr. Hortan. He had his hand over his mouth. He couldn't say a word.

One kid in the back said, "You mean, Mr. Joe-Nathan?"

I looked behind me. "Yes, that's him."

"He sent my brother to Alabama State two weeks ago. You mean he was like that?"

I turned and looked pointed toward Mr. Hortan. "Yeah, and so was I, but he was the key to change. Mr. Hortan, I must go. My family is waiting." I shook his hand and walked toward my car. "Ah, Emmanuel? Still have that paper?" Mr. Hortan yelled out.

I reached in my back pocket and took out my wallet. "Yes,

it's right here!"

"Don't forget to pass it on!" He smiled and drove off.

"I won't!"

I got in my car and turned on the radio to a local station. The announcer was excited about something. "Yo, check out the new debut rap single out by these new young brothers. They call it, 'Mutual Combat, Mutual Respect!'" So as I drove I let it play, story of two older men trying to kill a disease before it spread.

They hated each other, but needed each other, their lives had been proven,

To preserve creation, to save the next generation, they came to a conclusion:

Mutual Combat, Mutual Respect,

Mutually Fighting to save this Generation…

Mutual Combat, Mutual Respect,

Mutually Fighting to save the Nation…